"Carlson combines emotional depth with moments of humor and the characters' enduring faith in the face of loss. This is sure to tug on readers' heartstrings."

Publishers Weekly on *Welcome to the Honey B&B*

"In this equally hilarious and heartrending novel, Carlson draws on her own experience as a caregiver to provide a devastatingly real story of deep, quiet faith in the face of a family's worst fear."

Library Journal on *Welcome to the Honey B&B*

"A clean, wholesome, and fun read from start to finish, *Just for the Summer* by accomplished author and gifted storyteller Melody Carlson is especially and unreservedly recommended."

Midwest Book Review on *Just for the Summer*

"This read is the perfect book to cuddle up with during a stormy weekend."

Interviews & Reviews on *Second Time Around*

All Booked Up

Books by Melody Carlson

Courting Mr. Emerson

The Happy Camper

Looking for Leroy

Second Time Around

Just for the Summer

Welcome to the Honey B&B

All Booked Up

Follow Your Heart Series

Once Upon a Summertime

All Summer Long

Under a Summer Sky

Holiday Novellas

Christmas at Harrington's

The Christmas Shoppe

The Joy of Christmas

The Treasure of Christmas

The Christmas Pony

A Simple Christmas Wish

The Christmas Cat

The Christmas Joy Ride

The Christmas Angel Project

The Christmas Blessing

A Christmas by the Sea

Christmas in Winter Hill

The Christmas Swap

Christmas in the Alps

The Christmas Quilt

A Royal Christmas

The Christmas Tree Farm

Once Upon a Christmas Carol

All Booked Up

MELODY
CARLSON

a division of Baker Publishing Group
Grand Rapids, Michigan

Published by Revell
a division of Baker Publishing Group
Grand Rapids, Michigan
RevellBooks.com

Printed in the United States of America

Library of Congress Cataloging-in-Publication Data
Names: Carlson, Melody author
Title: All booked up / Melody Carlson.
Description: Grand Rapids, Michigan : Revell, a division of Baker Publishing Group, 2026.
Identifiers: LCCN 2025023325 | ISBN 9780800747251 paperback | ISBN 9780800747824 casebound | ISBN 9781493452651 ebook
Subjects: LCGFT: Fiction | Romance fiction | Christian fiction | Novels
Classification: LCC PS3553.A73257 A75 2026 | DDC 813/.54—dc23/eng/20250626
LC record available at https://lccn.loc.gov/2025023325

This book is a work of fiction. Names, characters, places, and incidents are the product of the author's imagination or are used fictitiously. Any resemblance to actual events, locales, or persons, living or dead, is coincidental.

Cover illustration by Nate Eidenberger
Cover design by Laura Klynstra

Baker Publishing Group publications use paper produced from sustainable forestry practices and postconsumer waste whenever possible.

26 27 28 29 30 31 32 7 6 5 4 3 2 1

Chapter 1

"Just burn them if you have to." Kenzie waved a hand toward one of the tall bookshelves filling all but one wall in the library room. The walnut shelves literally bulged with books collected over a lifetime. Several lifetimes, to be fair. "Just let them go, Mom. Be free of all these dusty, old books. Seriously, it's probably unhealthy to breathe the stale, musty air in here."

"I happen to like the smell of old books," Riva protested.

"But these books are like an anchor around your neck. This whole house is too much for you. Using the books as your excuse to stay is ridiculous."

"It's not an excuse." Riva looked up at the familiar shelves. The books were like friends. How do you get rid of friends? "What would I do with the books?" she asked, more to herself than to her impetuous daughter.

"Just imagine the huge bonfire you could have with them. You could invite the neighbors, roast hot dogs." Kenzie laughed like this was funny.

But Riva stared in horror. "B-burn books?" she stammered. "You can't be serious."

"Okay, I'll admit that's pretty drastic. But there must be some way to get rid of them." Kenzie walked along one of the floor-to-ceiling bookshelves that had been added to the library about ten years ago—designed to match the fine craftsmanship of the original shelves that had been built more than a century ago. Kenzie shook her head with an expression a detective might wear when investigating a crime scene.

Riva watched her daughter trail an accusing finger along the spines of books, as if the innocent titles were somehow responsible for her dilemma. At one time the legions of books had been neatly arranged by genre. But over the years, especially after Riva and Paul had retired, the shelves grew so crowded they'd resorted to stacking more recently acquired titles horizontally in an effort to utilize every inch. And paperbacks were double stacked.

Kenzie turned abruptly toward her mom. "How on earth did you manage to amass so many in the first place? I don't remember all the walls having shelves or being so packed in when I lived at home. Didn't you used to regularly donate boxes of old books to the library? What became of all that?"

"I suppose that's where it started. I donated your grandpa's old law books, ones I knew I'd never read. And that got me interested in volunteering for the Friends of the Library and helping with the annual book sales." She smiled sheepishly. "But I'd always come home with more books than I brought. Eventually I ran out of books I wanted to get rid of but kept bringing home books from the fundraiser." Riva shrugged. "And then there were garage sales. We found some marvelous first editions." She pulled out a Clancy hardback that Paul had been particularly proud of.

"And Dad probably didn't help much." Kenzie paused by the section that held her father's collections of westerns, war stories, historicals, biographies, and such. "Surely, you can let some of these go now . . . you know, since Dad's gone." She sighed. "He wouldn't want to see you trapped here by all these books. He'd want you to let go and move on."

"Let go . . . move on . . ." Riva frowned. By burning books? By liquidating his collection? Did Kenzie really think it was that simple? Like Paul's beloved Louis L'Amour titles, many he'd owned even before they met forty years ago. For some unexplainable reason it always brought her comfort to see the row of them up there. Like Paul was still in this room with her, leaned back in his worn leather chair, feet propped on the ottoman, reading glasses halfway down his handsome straight nose, happily lost in a new historical.

Riva removed a large book they'd purchased on a vacation in Mexico. She opened it, admiring the glossy photos of arts and crafts created in Oaxaca. "Oh my. I've never even looked inside this book before. It's beautiful." She held it up for Kenzie to see. "And you think I'd want to burn this?"

"Then give it away. Or have your own book sale. Just shake these things loose from you. Be free."

Riva set the book on top of her to-be-read stack, promising herself to look more closely at it later. "Oh, Kenzie, you are well aware of how most people don't want real books anymore. All my friends seem to have gotten rid of their collections. Either they don't have time to read or they only read electronic books or listen to audiobooks. Even the Friends of the Library have nearly given up on their yearly book sale. Maybe you should talk to them about book burning."

Riva forced an impish smile for her impetuous daughter. Naturally, it was easy to be impatient when you were thirty and just embarking on an exciting new career in an exciting new place. Everything was dispensable, and minimalism was the order of the day. And perhaps that made sense if you were on the move a lot. But it just didn't sit well with Riva. And now she wished she'd never complained about her oversized house and how difficult it would be to downsize, even blaming her resistance on the books of all things. She must sound like a foolish old woman to her hipster daughter. "Honey, I understand you wanting to encourage me to move on. I get it. I just don't think I'm ready yet."

"But the cost of keeping this big old house . . . it makes no sense, Mom. It's like these books are holding you hostage. Like this library has become your jail." Kenzie checked something on her phone as she continued her lecture. "I thought it would help with me coming here to clear out the last of my stuff. That having the upstairs bedrooms and attic cleared out would motivate you to get serious about moving. That's why I put in all this effort."

"And I appreciate that, honey. I never dreamed you would work so hard on it."

"I just wanted to make this easier for you. You're getting older, Mom. You need to take it easy." She patted Riva's shoulder in a way that suggested she was on her last leg.

"I'm only sixty-one. That's not so old. And I take good care of myself." Indignation rose up inside of her, making her stand up straighter . . . stronger. She could probably still beat her daughter at tennis.

"I know you're doing great now. But you aren't getting any younger. Why not get out of here while you have the strength and energy to move on your own. And, really, those new senior condos on the edge of town look pretty good. I heard they even transition into assisted living if you need it. Think about it—zero maintenance . . . all the free time you'd have. And the new friends you could make. We could get you into a nice two-bedroom, and I could still come visit you."

Riva felt her nose turning up. "I'd never want to live there. Honestly, it seems like an end of the line kind of place, where people go to die." She didn't care to admit she'd noticed old folks wandering or just sitting on the grounds of that new development. Some with walkers, some with wheelchairs, all moving slowly and aimlessly. And maybe she was delusional, but she just didn't feel that old. Not yet. "I do appreciate you clearing those upstairs rooms out so efficiently." It was her turn to pat Kenzie on the shoulder. "Setting a fine example for me on how easily you got rid of those things."

Kenzie laughed. "Well, what did we need any of that junk for?"

"Sentimental value?"

Kenzie held up her phone. "I took pics of anything that felt a little special. I'll have them right here if I need them."

"Right." Riva wasn't so sure, but it was too late to make a fuss.

Kenzie brightened. "You could do that with your books. Take pictures of all of them. Then let them go."

"Yes, that's an interesting idea." Riva knew she wouldn't do that as she looked up at the clock hanging above the library's French doors. "Good grief—it's nearly one! I should get you to the airport."

"No need. Samantha's picking me up. We're gonna grab a bite at the airport and catch up on old times." Kenzie's phone chimed. "In fact, that's her now. She's probably in the driveway." She hugged her mom goodbye, and just like that was gone.

Riva sank into Paul's old chair, then ran her hands over the well-worn armrests. Was Kenzie right? Was she allowing all these dusty old books to hold her hostage? Was this room really her prison? She looked up at the shelves and instead of feeling trapped, like her daughter had insinuated, she felt completely comfortable and at home, as if sitting among friends. Kenzie meant well and had certainly been helpful, but Riva had no more intention of getting rid of any of these old books than she did getting rid of her old friends.

She leaned back and closed her eyes. But what Kenzie didn't fully know was that Riva's finances were stretched thinner than ever these days. Thanks to no life insurance policies, annuities that got swallowed up in a bad economy, and a mortgage that Paul had taken out to do some much-needed repairs on their old Victorian house, her situation was approaching dire. So much so, she was considering finding employment. Or filing for early social security.

She knew she had to do something to keep from going under. Sure, the sensible plan would probably be to sell the oversized house and move into something more affordable—something with less maintenance. But what on earth would she do with all these books? Maybe Kenzie was right. Maybe they truly were holding her hostage. But if they were, she probably had some version of Stockholm syndrome by now, because she loved her literary captors anyway!

Chapter 2

Despite the gathering clouds, Riva decided to walk the six blocks to the public library. No, she was not going to get more books. That would be ridiculous. She had promised her good friend Laurel Wright that she would attend the grief support group that had started a few months ago. But seriously, Paul had been gone for more than a year. Did Riva really need a grief group now? Laurel seemed to think so.

Maybe Laurel was the one in need of a support group. She wasn't technically a widow. But she was a retired divorcée who seemed to be grieving her failed marriage. Or to be more accurate, she was grieving the loss of her lovely home after the settlement. Now Laurel lived in a dismal downtown apartment with an aging cat named Fred, and she spent most of her time solving crosswords and watching network TV. Poor Laurel probably had need for some support.

Riva blew out a sigh as she wrapped her scarf more snugly around her neck. Sure, it was mid-May, but the fickle Oregon weather hadn't received notification it was spring. She probably should've driven the short distance to the library, but the gloomy weather seemed to fit her mood as she trudged down the hill toward downtown. And perhaps her mood was just perfect for attending her first grief group meeting.

She paused in front of the big brick building, one hand on the door. Really, it wasn't too late to turn back. She didn't belong in a group like this. She was beyond the five stages of grief. Or to be more specific, she was in stage five now—acceptance. It had been more than a year. She was ready to move on.

"Riva darling, you came!" Laurel came trotting up to stand alongside her and slapped her on the back. "Good girl."

"Do you attend these meetings?" Riva studied her friend, wondering if the group had more appeal to Laurel than herself.

Laurel firmly shook her head. "No. But I'm friends with Margaret, the moderator. I told my friend Windy Brewer about this group, and she's been faithfully coming since it started up in January." She held up a white bag. "And I promised Windy I'd drop off cookies. Apparently, it was her turn to bring treats and she totally forgot."

"You hate cooking."

Laurel looked skyward where raindrops were starting to splat down, then she propped open the door and waited for Riva to pass. "Yes, but I do live above a bakery." She winked. "Pretty convenient."

"Right."

"Here." She shoved the cookie bag toward Riva. "You can take these to Windy. I have to go."

"Why don't you come to the group too?" Riva asked hopefully.

"No thanks. Tell Windy and Margaret hi. Have a good meeting." She held up a forefinger. "And call me when you get home. I want to hear how it goes."

"If you went with me, you'd already *know* how it goes."

"I'd rather hear it from you." Laurel made a sly smile. "Have fun, darling." And then she whooshed off. Probably to do a new crossword puzzle in front of one of her soap operas. Did they still make soaps? Riva didn't know. Unless she was deathly ill, she'd always preferred books to TV. She unpeeled her scarf and proceeded into the warm library, gazing around with satisfaction.

At least the grief group was meeting in a respectable location. Perhaps she'd simply hand off the bag of treats, excuse herself to peruse the new books section, and then quietly slip out the door and make a beeline for home before those dark clouds really started to open.

She tentatively approached the meeting room. A couple of women lingered at a table by the door. Maybe, like her, they were planning a fast break. She stared intently at the new titles rack and considered bolting, but before she could get away, the women were greeting her, forcing her to fill out a name tag and sign in to a guest book. And suddenly the taller woman whose name tag read Helene practically shoved her into the meeting room.

"That's Windy over there." Helene pointed to a short redhead arranging things on a refreshment table. Dressed in a long bohemian skirt, red cowboy boots, and a purple fringed scarf, the woman appeared to be a unique individual.

Riva cautiously approached the refreshment table, keeping a wary eye on the small group now taking their seats in a circle of chairs. She noticed it was mostly women, but there were a couple of men, all in a wide range of ages. "Are you Wendy?" she asked the woman, then glanced at her name tag and saw that the name was spelled Windy, like the weather. Interesting. Despite her rather youthful ensemble, the woman's face bore the traces of years of living and perhaps too much sun. But her smile came easy and looked genuine.

"Yes, I'm Windy Brewer." She looked at Riva's name tag, then stuck out her hand. "Hello, Riva Owen. Pleased to meet you."

Instead of shaking the offered hand, Riva clumsily pushed the bakery bag into it. Realizing her faux pas and regretting her bad manners, she forced a nervous smile. "Laurel asked me to give you these, uh, cookies."

"Bless that dear woman. You know Laurel, then?"

"She's a good friend. In fact, it was her idea for me to come today. I tried to talk her into coming with me."

"You and me both. If you ask me, Laurel needs this group more than I do." Windy opened the bag, then let out a happy squeal. "Lemon bars. My fave."

"Your name has an interesting spelling." Riva tipped her head to one side.

"Well, my parents named me September Wind." Windy grimaced, then smiled. "They were a bit . . . unconventional, to say the least." She artfully arranged the yellow bars on a flowery paper plate. "I was actually raised on a hippie commune in Northern California." She shrugged. "Used to embarrass me to admit that to anyone, but I've pretty much gotten over it since losing my husband. I've realized there are worse things."

Windy paused as a woman called out, announcing it was time to get seated and start their meeting. Windy quietly thanked Riva for bringing the bars. "Go ahead and get your seat." She fanned out some colorful napkins. "I'll just finish up here."

Feeling somewhat trapped, Riva made her way to the circle of folding chairs that were quickly filling. Was it too late to make a graceful escape? But the woman in front was smiling directly at her. "We're happy to see a new face today. Welcome." She squinted as if trying to read her name tag. "Can you share your name and what brings you here today?"

"Well, my name is Riva Owen, and I guess my feet brought me here." To her relief this stirred some nervous laughter. "I guess that's not what you meant," she apologized and sat. "I'm here because, well, my husband . . . he died." And suddenly the words began to pour out. "Paul was an attorney in town. Not really well known. But he was a good man who helped a lot of people. Anyway, Paul fought a brave two-year battle against lung cancer. Not that he was a smoker. He never smoked. But, well, he lost that battle more than a year ago, and I still really miss him. But I do believe I've moved past it. I've accepted that it is what it is. At least, I think I have. But a good friend kept urging me to try out your group here. Laurel's a friend of Margaret and

Windy too." She nodded as Windy took the last empty chair next to the woman in front. "But I don't think I need group therapy at this point. Maybe a year ago. I mean, like I said, I sort of feel like I've moved beyond . . ." She felt embarrassed now. Why had she rambled on like that? These people probably thought she was loose-lipped.

"We're glad you joined us anyway, Riva," the woman said. "Perhaps someone in this group needs *your* help. Or perhaps you still have some hidden issues that you're unaware of. That happens to a lot of us." The gray-haired woman smiled a bit sadly. "I'm Margaret, and I do know your friend Laurel. And I moderate our group sessions. Now we'll go around the circle like we usually do. This time I'll ask members to share their names and give a little update as to where they all are on this interesting life journey."

As they progressed around the room, Margaret didn't intervene much, other than to ask an occasional follow-up question from their previous meeting. The sharing steadily grew more spontaneous and appeared to be sincerely heartfelt.

Riva was amazed at how quickly she got pulled into the various stories being relayed. A couple of members got emotional, and a Kleenex box was passed about. When it came to a nervous-looking younger member named Blair, he sat silently for a long moment.

"How has your week been going?" Margaret asked gently.

Scowling, Blair pounded a fist into his palm again and again. "I'm stuck," he declared. "I can't stop being angry. I know it's a normal stage of grief. But I can't get out of it. I just get angrier and angrier."

For another long moment, no one spoke. Finally, the woman next to Riva asked a rather probing question about Blair's deceased brother.

After pondering it a moment, the frustrated young man began to share more openly, admitting to feeling a total loss of control in all areas of his life.

"Loss of control can cause feelings of anger," Margaret suggested. "And losing your brother like that probably feels like you lost control. You said he was your twin?"

Blair nodded, then pointed to an older man. "You mentioned survivor's guilt," he said. "That's *exactly* how I feel. I was the black sheep of the family. My twin brother was the golden boy, good and kind and successful. I should've been the one to die. Not Byron." Now he burst into loud sobs, which were followed with kind comments and motherly hugs and encouraging advice. More members were tearing up now, including Riva.

All in all, the intimacy of the meeting caught Riva off guard, but perhaps most surprising was the level of care and concern she witnessed among the odd mix of grievers. And when the meeting ended, she was almost sad to exit the library. Plus, it was raining cats and dogs outside. She decided to hang around a bit longer to peruse the new books section after all. Hopefully the rain would let up while she browsed.

Finally, not finding a title she cared to tote home, she decided it was time to face the weather. She was barely down the street when she heard someone honking and then hollering, "Hey, Riva!"

She turned to see an orange VW Bug with Windy's head poking out the window, her purple scarf flapping in the wind. "Need a ride?"

"I'd love one," Riva called back. She jogged over to the passenger's side. "Thank you so much."

"I just remembered you saying that your feet brought you to the library." Windy grinned as she put the car in gear. "So I figure you must live nearby. I'm guessing you'd be soaked before you got there."

"I'm nearly soaked now." Riva told her to turn left at the stop sign. "I live on Periwinkle Avenue."

"Swanky side of town, eh?"

"Swanky?" Riva chuckled. "It's the old section, that's for sure."

"The *expensive* old section. There are a lot of historical homes over there. Is yours on the register?"

"We didn't think it was a good idea at the time."

"Yeah, it can be a bit restrictive. But it's got some benefits too. If the fit is right."

"You seem to know a lot about it."

"My husband had a real estate business and I helped him in the office. Learned a lot from him . . . before he passed."

"I'm sorry for your loss." Riva remembered now that Windy had described her husband's death as traumatic and she'd admitted to still getting over some PTSD. "How long has it been?"

"Bill's been gone about seven years now, but I still miss him. Don't get me wrong, the man had his faults, especially when it came to business, but underneath it all, he was a good guy."

"Do you mind if I ask how he died?"

"No, that's okay. It was a car wreck. He got T-boned going through an intersection. A drunk driver ran a red light going about eighty miles an hour."

"Oh my." Riva sighed. "That does sound traumatic."

"Yes. I had nightmares for a year. Still do sometimes. But mostly I'm better. I just feel like I should participate with the grief group in support of Margaret."

"Is Margaret a good friend?"

"She counseled me the first couple of years after losing Bill." Windy put her car in a lower gear to climb the hill, revving her engine as she went up.

"Margaret seems like she'd be a good counselor."

"She was. And now she's a good friend." Windy stopped at the Periwinkle Avenue intersection.

"Go right," Riva said. "And you're a friend of Laurel's too?"

"Yes. We're not very close, but we live in the same building downtown. Although it won't be for long from what I hear."

"Is Laurel moving?"

"Not that I know of. But they raised the rent again and now I'm looking for something else." As Windy kept driving her little car up the hill, Riva hoped they wouldn't have to get out and push it.

"I thought Laurel said they just raised the rent last year."

"They did. They claim it's to cover increasing costs of maintenance, but then they never fix a thing. Have you ever seen the place? It's a real dump."

"Laurel says the same thing. I know she wants to move too."

"There's a deplorable shortage of affordable housing in Greenwood."

Riva pointed to her tall Victorian house. "That's mine there. Go ahead and pull into the driveway."

"Oh, I adore this house! This is really yours? I've always admired it. I used to drive by here, wishing it would go on the market and dreaming I could talk Bill into buying it." She laughed as she parked. "Not that we could've afforded it. Bill kept sinking all our funds into his business and a few other shaky investments, ones that eventually landed us in bankruptcy. Eventually, after he was gone, I lost the house I thought we owned free and clear."

"I'm sorry."

"It's okay. I keep hoping I'll get a great big insurance settlement for Bill's accident, but thanks to the courts and a zillion appeals from the insurance company, that probably won't happen until I'm a very old lady." Windy gazed up at Riva's house. "It's such a beautiful home. What a blessing for you to have it, Riva."

"Would you like to come in and see it?"

"Seriously?" Windy was already opening her car door. "You don't have to ask me twice."

Riva laughed then, running through the rain. She hurried ahead to unlock the front door and let Windy inside the foyer.

"Oh, it's perfect." Windy looked around as Riva removed her dripping coat. "I love these center cut oak floorboards. And this original molding and your beautifully carved staircase newel posts. It's even better than I imagined."

"Let me take your coat and I'll show you more."

Riva gave Windy the full tour, explaining her own dilemma. "Paul was a self-employed attorney, and our health insurance coverage was very minimal. The cost of his treatments and care and everything else really wiped out our savings. Even though this house was in my family, we put a mortgage on it years ago to afford all the improvements we needed. Electric, plumbing, and upgrades. But after Paul got sick, we were forced to get a second mortgage just to cover the medical bills. Now I can't really afford to stay on here." Riva paused in the library, and Windy literally gasped at the walls of books.

"Wow, this is amazing. I think you have more books here than the public library."

Riva smiled sadly. "Yes, books are my passion. And my problem."

Windy turned back to face her. "Problem?"

"If I were to sell my house, what in the world do I do with all these books? My daughter suggested a bonfire, and if I didn't love her so much, I might've thrown her out."

Windy laughed. "So you keep the house in order to keep the books? That's a new one."

"Pathetic, I know. But it's the truth. I guess I'll need to get a job. I've only worked in the law office. And despite my experience doing legal research, I don't really have the credentials. I'm hoping someone will be willing to give me a try." She frowned. "Although I realize my age could be disadvantageous."

"Your age? Well, that's just plain discrimination."

"Yet a fact of life all the same." Riva shrugged as she led Windy out of the library. "Want to see the second floor? My daughter cleared a lot out last week—mostly her stuff. I still have basic furnishings up there since Kenzie thinks I need to do some staging before listing."

"She's right. Staged houses bring higher prices and sell faster."

"Right . . ." Riva cringed at the thought of what she'd do if her home sold quickly.

"Anyway, I'd love to see upstairs."

Riva hadn't actually been up there since Kenzie had cleared it out. Mostly because she knew it would make her sad to see part of her life and her home vanishing right before her eyes. But when they got up there, Windy didn't seem to notice the bare walls or how they were in need of paint. She simply continued to gush over the spacious bedrooms, especially the ensuite in the back of the house, noting the quality of the roomy shared bathroom that had been remodeled in the 1990s, when Kenzie was born. "And the view of your yard from the ensuite is charming. Such a beautiful outdoor space. You must love being out there."

"I suppose I used to. But it was my late husband's domain. Paul loved being out there and keeping it all perfect. I've sort of let it go." How sad Paul would be to see how neglected it had become.

"I adore gardening. Whether it's produce or flowers, I love growing things. I used to have a wonderful yard. I think that was the hardest thing to say goodbye to when I lost my house. I keep potted plants now, but it's just not the same."

They were back in one of the front bedrooms now. Windy was looking out the window and gushing about the view from this side of the house. "I love how these rooms look out over the town. I'll bet it's pretty at night with lights on down there. Such fun." She turned, a wide smile on her face. "Your house is a treasure, Riva. Even better than I envisioned."

"Thanks, I've loved it all my life."

"All your life?"

"It was my grandparents' home. My dad inherited it when I was an infant, so I grew up here." She felt a lump in her throat. "It'll be very hard to leave."

"I can imagine." Windy looked at Riva with arched brows. "What if you could keep it?"

"I don't see how. Short of buying a lottery ticket and getting lucky." She turned to leave the room that she'd occupied as a child.

"You could take in boarders."

"Boarders? Like a B and B?" Riva paused in the hallway, then shook her head glumly. "That sounds like a whole lot of work. Changing sheets and towels and cleaning rooms and preparing breakfasts . . . not to mention booking and promoting and everything else that goes with it. I actually looked into all that last year but, after some research, I realized it wasn't for me." She headed for the stairs.

"No, I don't mean a B and B. I mean you could rent rooms by the month. Thanks to the lack of affordable housing, a lot of homeowners in Greenwood are doing it. You'd be surprised how quickly they get snapped up. Do you have any idea of how much a room goes for in this town?" Windy followed her down the stairs, describing some listings she'd recently viewed and how much landlords expected. "A lot of them are real dumps too. I can hardly believe they get that much. Makes me wish I'd hung onto my home and rented rooms there. But that ship has sailed."

Riva paused on the landing. "I wonder how much I could get?"

Windy tossed out a number she said was fair for a single room. "Multiply that by three for these rooms, although I'm sure you could get more for the ensuite."

"Really? That much?" Riva considered it. "That would cover my mortgage payment." She sighed. "But not my property taxes."

"You have that lovely spare room downstairs." Windy pointed up the stairs behind them. "And I'll bet there's a roomy attic up there. I noticed third-floor windows from my drive-by dreaming days."

"You're right. The third floor is large. Paul had it insulated and had drywall installed for a playroom when the kids were little. After they left, we talked about getting a pool table up there, but eventually we just used it for storage."

"Can I have a look at it?"

"Of course." Riva changed directions, heading back upstairs. She opened the door at the end of the second-floor hallway.

"These stairs are a little steep," she warned. But Windy was already scrambling up like a mountain goat.

"Oh, Riva, this is a glorious space. I would rent it from you in a heartbeat if you'd let me."

"Seriously? You *want* to live in my attic?" She pointed to the high windows in the gables. "Not a lot of light up here." She frowned at the teal paint on the walls. "And this dark wall color doesn't help. My daughter picked it out when she was a preteen." Riva looked down. "This old carpeting is pretty atrocious too."

"Those are easy changes. Fresh paint. Rip up the carpet. Add some cheery furnishings and additional lighting, and it'd be perfect."

Riva wrinkled her nose. She sure wouldn't want to live up here. "I don't even know what a spot like this would rent for."

Windy spat out a number slightly higher than what she quoted for the bedrooms below. "Anyway, that's what I'd pay for it. And I'd give you first and last, plus a cleaning deposit if you like, or you could let me invest that into improvements. You know, like paint and flooring."

"Really? You'd want to rent this for that much?"

"That's what I have set aside for my next move. It's what I was originally paying for where I am now, before the rate increase. And believe me, my apartment is pathetic. Of course, I'd want kitchen privileges since I don't think cooking up here would be such a great idea. I might like a hot pot for tea, though, and a tiny fridge for drinks . . . but I do love to cook. Not so much in my apartment though. My stove has just two burners that sometimes work, and the oven is useless so I don't really bother anymore. But I miss it." Windy turned her attention back on the attic room, strolling about, guessing on wall measurements and scrutinizing the whole space as if she planned to move in today.

"You really love to cook?" Riva studied the colorful woman she'd only met a few hours ago. "I don't mind making soup or something simple occasionally, but I don't particularly love it."

Windy's brows arched. "I'm surprised. I figured with that well-equipped kitchen and all that counter space, you'd be into cooking. It would be such a fun place to whip things up. And if I lived here, I'd love to cook for you as well."

Riva didn't know what to say. Windy seemed to be jumping to conclusions here. "Well, I used to enjoy cooking back when my kids were home. We remodeled the kitchen about twenty years ago, and putting meals together was fun for a spell. But then Kenzie headed off to college and Brent—that's my son—joined the Air Force, and I had to adjust to cooking for two instead of four."

"I know what you mean. I had to do the same thing. But after I got used to it and quit overbuying at the grocery store, I really enjoyed it."

"I sort of did too. Then Paul got sick and his appetite changed." Riva stood by the door, ready to call this house tour done. "I mostly made smoothies for him the last couple years . . . It wasn't much fun." To be honest, life wasn't much fun, but she didn't want to be a complete killjoy since Windy seemed so hopeful and optimistic, still obsessed with the horrible attic space.

Riva sighed and, overwhelmed by Windy's enthusiasm and tired of the stuffy attic smell, headed back to the second floor. "Look around as long as you like," she called over her shoulder, eager to get back downstairs and to her sanity.

All this talk about renting rooms to strangers and the possibility of letting this eccentric woman move into her attic, share her kitchen, and work in her backyard was discombobulating. What was Riva getting into? How could she put on the brakes? Good grief, she didn't even know this Windy person! What if she turned out to be a hoarder with twelve cats? Or what if she had a bunch of wild friends that she planned to invite over for noisy parties? Or worse, what if she were a criminal looking for a hideout to hole up in? Or what if she was involved in drugs? That'd be disastrous.

As Riva went into her kitchen, which really was pretty swanky with the stainless appliances and sleek countertops, she replayed how Windy had admitted to admiring and even "loving" this house for years. What if she was on a mission to get rid of Riva and attain the property for herself? Riva had recently watched a creepy Lifetime movie about that very thing. And it had been based on a true story! No, Riva decided, before this craziness went too far with Windy—if that was her real name—she would nip it in the bud!

Chapter 3

Riva felt her head spinning as she watched Windy's little orange bug back out of her driveway. From Kenzie's visit to the grief group to the strange hippie woman wanting to rent the attic, this had been a dizzying day! And really? Had she just told that woman she'd *think about it*? Seriously, what was there to think about? Riva's mind was made up. She didn't want to rent rooms—to anyone. Even if Windy was the finest French chef who'd cook all the meals and also a master gardener, Riva was *not* interested. She liked living alone . . . didn't she? She'd never felt truly lonely in her old house. The memories made it like living with family. But what if she lost her beloved home? What then? Riva's phone chimed, interrupting her scattered thoughts. She checked the screen to see it was Laurel. Maybe this was her fault. "Hello," she growled, answering the call.

"Are you okay?" Laurel asked.

"Yeah, just great." She knew her tone was sarcastic, but she couldn't seem to help it as she moved to the library. "It's been an, uh, an interesting day." She stared up at the book spines that normally brought her comfort but suddenly felt overwhelming. Like maybe her daughter was right. Maybe they were running her life, imprisoning her.

"So how did it go?" Laurel asked.

"What?" Riva sank into a chair.

"The grief group."

"Oh, that." She sighed. "It was okay, I guess."

"Then why do you sound so bummed?"

"It's your friend Windy."

"Windy?" Laurel sounded shocked. "What could Windy have possibly done to make you so grumpy? She's about the sweetest, kindest person I know. No offense, but she's even nicer than you."

"Thanks a lot."

"Sorry. So tell me, what did Windy do?"

"She wants to rent my attic."

"What?"

Riva explained the impromptu visit and house tour and Windy's suggestion to take in boarders. "And she wants to be the first."

There was a pause. "That's an absolutely brilliant idea."

"*Brilliant*?"

"Well, I know you've been worried about finances, Riva."

"Yeah, but—"

"Why not rent to Windy? She's a good person. Is she really serious about your attic?"

"She sounded serious. Which is suspicious. I mean, it's so ugly up there. Awful paint, horrible old carpet. But she's certain she can make it livable. She even offered to help with the yard and cooking."

"She loves plants, and she's a fabulous cook."

"Even so."

"I don't see why you're being so resistant, Riva. This could be the answer to your prayers—and to your financial woes."

"Right, just like winning the lottery."

"Well, sure, go buy yourself a ticket. What are the odds now? One in a bazillion trillion. Look, you've said more than once that you might have to let your house go. And what will you do then? Live in some awful apartment like Windy and me? Seriously, renting out your rooms is genius. And Windy knows real estate. She probably quoted you some very realistic rental rates. You'd be a fool not to consider this. What if house-sharing allowed you to stay in your home?"

Riva wasn't focusing too well. Instead, she was imagining herself living in a dingy little apartment like Laurel's. It wasn't a pretty picture. "So you would really recommend Windy as a renter? She doesn't have a dozen cats? What about smoking? Drinking or drugs? Is she a party girl?"

"No, no, and no. She's a solid citizen."

"Yeah, okay, and excuse me for sounding judgmental, but she looks, well, kind of . . . you know, kind of bohemian."

"She wasn't always like that. I knew Windy before her husband died, and she was totally different then. Believe me, she played a very traditional role. The perfect wife and mom. She worked part-time in her husband's agency. But Bill's death threw her into a tailspin. Her kids were already launched when she lost her home. That's when she returned to her roots."

"Her roots?"

"Her upbringing. In a hippie commune."

"Oh, yeah, she mentioned that to me."

"She started dressing differently, for starters. She said it made her feel happy and free. And she started taking art classes at the community center. She's a really good potter. Anyway, I'll vouch for her. Windy is a thoroughly good person. I'd absolutely recommend her as a renter. In fact, now I'm starting to get jealous. If you're going to rent to Windy, what about me?"

"You? You'd want to live in a room instead of a whole apartment?"

"If I could afford a really nice apartment or condo unit, of course I'd prefer that, but my options are pretty limited."

"You really think you'd be happy renting one of my bedrooms?" Riva felt skeptical.

"In your beautiful house? You bet I would."

"What about Fred?

"Fred's getting so old that he's an easy keeper. With a sunny window to sleep by, his favorite kitty food, and a clean litterbox, he's content."

"What about your furnishings?"

"I can store things. I really should just get rid of all of it."

Riva considered this. She and Laurel had always gotten along pretty well, but under the same roof? "I don't know, Laurel. I've gotten pretty independent since losing Paul."

"Don't forget that I've been on my own a lot longer than you, sweetie. I'm fiercely independent myself."

"I know, but what if sharing a house ruins our friendship?"

"Oh, I don't think that could happen. After all, we're mature women. It's your home, and I'd respect that. And we could figure out how to give each other space."

"I don't know . . ." Riva told her the rent Windy had suggested, including the more expensive ensuite. "You might not want to pay that much for just a room."

"Are you kidding? In fact, I want to put dibs on the ensuite. That's a beautiful room, Riva. I always admired it."

"Seriously?"

"As serious as a heart attack—just don't have one." Laurel laughed. "Okay, darling, I'm not going to pressure you further. Give it some thought. And pray about it too. Let God lead you in this. It's a big decision. After all, it's possible that you need to just sell and get out."

"But you honestly think it's a good idea to rent out rooms?"

"I think it makes perfect sense, but you need to feel at peace about it, sweetie."

"Right . . . yeah . . . I agree."

"Sleep on it. Pray on it. Let me know how you feel about it as soon as you decide. I've already given notice on my apartment and need to be out by June first. Did Windy tell you about our latest rent increase? I'm so fed up. Even if I can't find a new place, I'd rather camp at the houseless shelter than stay on here."

"Oh, Laurel, you wouldn't really do that."

"Hey, I'm a volunteer there. I'm certainly not too good to stay there. Although, come to think of it, they don't offer housing except in wintertime."

"Well, that's just one of the many things I love about you, Laurel. You've never been too full of yourself."

"So keep me on your short list for housemates. We'll be like the Golden Girls of the new millennium." She laughed.

Riva promised to pray and think about it. As they said goodbye, she tried to imagine Laurel sharing her home. It was true that she'd always admired her friend for her humble and straightforward can-do personality. She'd probably make a wonderful tenant. But was Riva really in the market for boarders?

Instead of stewing over what felt like too big of a decision, she took Laurel's advice and prayed, asking God for his direction and the peace that she knew would follow. And now, realizing she'd skipped lunch, she decided on an early dinner. Okay, it wasn't really a dinner per se. Probably nothing like what Windy would make if given the opportunity in this kitchen. But it was sustenance. So without really tasting the cold cereal drenched in skim milk, she perched on a kitchen stool and finished her pathetic meal in silence. Just like she often did at night. Was this really living? Probably not. But it was the best she could manage at the moment.

Distracted by her strange day, Riva hadn't paid any attention to the local news or weather like she usually did. So when rain started coming down in sheets, thunder boomed, and lightning struck the sky—not to mention the high winds that beat the side of the house—she started to get concerned. This was quite a storm! Was it on its way out or getting worse?

She was just turning on her TV to check the forecast when the electricity went out. Stumbling through her now pitch-black living room, she went to the front window to see . . . nothing. The entire town was wrapped in darkness. Hopefully it wouldn't be for long. She fumbled around, using furniture to guide her until she got to the hutch where she usually kept a few candles for the occasional candlelit dinners she used to make for her and Paul. She felt around in the drawers until she felt the waxy smoothness of two tapers. But . . . no matches.

Where did Paul stash flashlights? Probably on the laundry room shelves, which held a bit of everything. That was too far away in the darkness. Maybe there were matches in the kitchen. She bumbled along through the house, nearly tumbling over an ottoman and stubbing her toe on a dining room chair, until she was in the kitchen. She felt her way along the counters, searching several drawers, hoping to unearth the box of matches she felt certain were there in case of an emergency. Wasn't this an emergency? More than ever since losing Paul, she missed him! This was the kind of thing he would've laughed about and made light of, probably using his phone's flashlight. Did her phone even have one? Where *was* her phone? Hopefully in her bathroom where it had been charging.

Touching what felt like a matchbook in her junk drawer, she eagerly pulled it out and managed, after several tries, to properly strike a match. She lit both candles and then set out to find candleholders for them. Having light, albeit meager, made a big difference. She stopped in her bathroom to look for her phone, but it wasn't there like she'd hoped. It was probably nearly dead by now anyway.

She eventually got the candles in their holders and set them on the coffee table, then sat down on the sofa and considered her situation. They'd replaced the old oil furnace with a heat pump several years ago. And the fireplace that once graced this room had long since been closed up and was no longer functional. Not that it was particularly cold, although she was feeling chilled. And where was her phone?

She thought back to the last time she used it, remembering she'd been in the kitchen. Carrying a candlestick with her, she returned to find her phone on the kitchen island. Totally dead. Almost more than light and electricity, she was suddenly craving the sound of a human voice. She knew that Laurel would be very understanding and practical and was perhaps even trying to call her right now. Not that it mattered.

Outside, the storm raged on, and everything was still blanketed in darkness. Somewhere in town, sirens were wailing. Hopefully not for anything too serious. But it did make her wonder what she would do if she had an emergency right now. Run to the neighbors for help? A clap of thunder tailed by a lightning bolt lit up the kitchen and made her jump. She wondered what time it was . . . too early to go to bed and hope to wake up to a bright sunny morning? According to the kitchen wall clock, it wasn't even nine.

What would Paul do right now? Get more candles, locate a flashlight and spare batteries. But where exactly? In the laundry room, she pawed through the storage shelves until she found a promising carton. Just as she opened it, her candle fell to the floor. Worried about fire, she stomped it out and was in total darkness again.

Eager to escape the pitch-black laundry room, she felt her way out, following the faint glowing through the doorway, but soon she stumbled over the same chair she'd stubbed her toe on before. As it tipped over, she landed on top, hitting her shins and rib cage. And now she just sat down on the floor and cried.

"Why is this so hard?" she said aloud. "What am I doing wrong?" She continued to cry, rubbing her bruised shins and hoping her ribs weren't cracked.

She wasn't sure how long she sat there feeling sorry for herself, but the floor was getting harder by the minute. So she got up, grabbed the final candle, and slowly made her way to the master bedroom and to her bed. She set the candle down, then tumbled into bed fully dressed, pulled the comforter over herself, and continued to cry. Sure, she was having a pity party for one, but why not? No one was around to be bothered or hear her or care. And wasn't that what she wanted? She sat up in bed and considered this. Maybe that wasn't how she wanted things—maybe she was tired of being alone. Maybe it was time to rent rooms to other lonely women like herself. Windy and Laurel, for starters. She decided then and there that as soon as her phone could get charged, she would call both women and offer them a room each. And suddenly, despite the howling storm and claps of thunder, she felt an unexpected but very welcome peace.

Chapter 4

Sometime in the middle of the night, the electricity came back to life. When Riva woke up early the next morning, her alarm clock's digits were flashing. Outside, the sun was just rising into clear blue skies. Feeling hopeful for a better day, she opened the French doors in the master bedroom and peeked into the backyard. Her relief was mixed with dismay. The yard was littered with broken tree limbs and a few odd items that must've blown in last night. Still wearing her rumpled clothes from yesterday, she began to pick things up, making a pile of branches and debris near the gate.

Finally satisfied with the slight improvement, she brushed off her grimy hands on the back of her blue jeans and really gave her yard a good look. The state of her neglected garden beds was still dismal. Paul, bless his heart, would not approve. After his illness and treatments weakened him, Riva had discouraged him from even coming out here. It had been too depressing . . . for both of them. And even last year, after he passed, she could hardly drag herself out to mow the lawn or do the most basic chores. She remembered how, only yesterday, Windy had raved about the "beautiful" yard. Of course, she'd been looking at it from the second floor. Up close were weedy beds, overgrown berry bushes, broken planters, and crabgrass that was taking over the fence line.

Riva took a deep breath. Well, her yard might be a disaster area, but at least the clouds were gone and the air was clean and clear. And with her electricity back on, she could now charge her phone and brew a pot of coffee. As she went inside, she remembered last night's decision to take in boarders. Of course, that choice had been made in the thick of the storm. But in the light of day? Was that peace still with her now? Maybe so . . .

She gazed out the window above the sink as she ground coffee beans. From this vantage point, the yard looked better but still nothing like it used to look. At one time it had been so beautiful that Kenzie often claimed to want her wedding out there. Riva shook her head. Not that her career-driven daughter had any plans of getting married anytime soon. Although it would be fun to still have this house when the big event happened. If it happened. And what about when Brent came home on leave next winter?

Riva went to her phone, shot off a short text to Kenzie, asking how her flight went. Kenzie's reply was brief. It was a good flight and New York was great. So Riva decided to test the waters with her opinionated daughter. What did she think of her mom taking in female boarders? To Riva's surprise, Kenzie thought it was a great way for Riva to keep the family home. And then Kenzie had to go—busy day ahead. Nice that her daughter already had things to do, a life to live . . . more than Riva could claim these days.

But if all her rooms were rented, where would her kids stay when they came to visit? Of course, if she didn't rent rooms, she might not even have a house to visit. What a dilemma. She could save her downstairs guest room exclusively for her kids. That is, if they ever came home again . . . and if she really wanted to go through with this harebrained idea of taking in tenants.

The doorbell interrupted her conflicting thoughts. Who would be calling this early? She turned on the coffeemaker, then went to answer the door. To her surprise it was Laurel and Windy and a man with a head of bushy charcoal gray hair.

"Hello?" she said as she opened the door wider.

"We were worried about you," Laurel said.

"We called and called, but your phone didn't seem to be working," Windy added.

Riva slapped her forehead. "I'm just charging it now, but it was dead overnight and I lost power."

"We thought the storm might've gotten the best of you last night," Laurel said with a twinkle in her eyes. "Were you scared by it?"

"It was pretty wild," Riva admitted.

"Some of the lightning hits sounded very close." Windy squinted up at the tall roofline. "And with your tall house here on the hill. Well, you never know."

"We were walking over to Starbucks for coffee this morning and decided to check on you."

"Well, thank you for thinking of me." Riva openly stared at the man, wondering who he was, how he fit into this picture, and whether she should invite the three of them inside. Was this a social visit or just a wellness check?

"I'm sorry, Riva. This is Marcus Millican," Windy said suddenly. "My big brother. He offered to help get me started preparing for my move—if I ever find a place. He was meeting us for coffee so I just invited him to come over here with us."

Marcus stuck out his hand. "Nice to meet you, Riva. I've heard good things about you . . . and your beautiful home."

"Marcus." Windy elbowed him. "You weren't supposed to say that. Poor Riva will think I'm moving in on her before she's had a chance to decide." She smiled sheepishly. "I'm really not. I just need to start getting out of my apartment."

"Sorry, Riva. I realize you haven't made up your mind." Marcus winked at his sister. "But it sounds like a good plan to me. Plus, it'll keep Windy from camping out on my couch."

"I was actually just thinking over the whole thing . . . while I was making coffee. Do you guys want to come in for a cup? I rather absentmindedly made a full pot just now."

"Seems you were expecting us," Laurel teased. "And since we never made it to Starbucks, I would gladly take you up on the offer."

The others chimed in their agreement, and as they followed Riva through the house, back to her kitchen, Windy pointed out various historical highlights of the house's architecture to her brother. "As you can see, the woodwork looks fairly original," she told him. "And the only big upgrades were done in the kitchen and the baths, and it was very tastefully done."

"Refreshing that they didn't change everything like some homeowners," he said.

"And you should see the library," Laurel told him. "It's amazing."

"I'd love to," he said. "Wow, nice kitchen."

"Thanks." Riva set four coffee mugs on her marble countertop.

"And Riva said she doesn't even like to cook," Windy told Marcus.

"Well, I used to like it," Riva said. "Just not so much in the last few years."

"Try cooking in our apartments and you'll give up cooking altogether," Laurel said in a gloomy tone.

As Riva set out creamer and sugar, she wished she had something else to offer her impromptu guests. She used to make some pretty mean cinnamon rolls. But not in recent years. Windy continued to rave about how well the kitchen was designed.

"And it's so nice you kept it separate like it was originally," Marcus told Riva. "A lot of people are knocking down walls in these old homes to create great rooms, but it always feels like a compromise to the home's historical integrity to me."

Riva poured coffee as Windy gazed out the bay window into Riva's still unkempt backyard. "But really, why would anyone want more space than you have in here?" she asked. "It's roomy yet cozy. It's perfect."

"I've always liked it." Riva handed each of them a coffee. "We can take our coffee to the library." She was smiling, but as she led them to her library, she wondered if she was getting in too deep with Windy. It was one thing to have her home admired, but it seemed that Windy was growing increasingly more hopeful about actually living here. Was Riva really ready for that?

"What a room," Marcus gushed as he walked around, sipping his coffee and taking in the shelves of books. "This is fabulous. You know how many people have gotten rid of paper books, relying only on electronics?"

Riva nodded. "I think it's a shame. There's nothing like the feel of a real book in your hand." She looked at him. "Do you enjoy reading?"

"I sure do." He paused by what had been Paul's section. "And the collection you have here is fantastic."

Riva went around and pulled Paul's old office chair out from behind the big desk, then offered chairs to the others before sitting and taking her company in. What would it feel like to have people in her home like this on a regular basis? Was she really ready for it? For several minutes her guests just visited among themselves, commenting on and complimenting her home and talking about the lack of affordable housing in their area. She watched and listened with interest. She didn't disagree with them, but she still wasn't convinced she was ready to become a landlady. What would it actually entail on the business end? Extra bookkeeping and more income taxes and possibly more maintenance bills? Beyond that there would be more noise, more coming and going, cars parked in her driveway or out front . . . a lot to consider. Was she up for all that? Windy had already reassured her that, based on the lack of housing, the city was being lenient with existing tenant codes, but still . . . it was a lot to take on.

And yet there was something undeniably warm and friendly about having her three unexpected visitors this morning. Especially after the wild night of the storm. Besides, hadn't she made up her mind last night? And hadn't she felt a genuine sense of peace when she'd decided? She silently prayed again . . . and once again she felt a quiet comfort . . . along with the sense that God truly was directing her path . . . just like she'd asked. Maybe her next question was whether she had sufficient faith to follow.

Riva took a deep breath and dove in. "Windy," she began, "if you're still interested, I'm willing to rent you my attic room. But I totally understand if you've had second thoughts. I mean, that room really needs work. You might want to take a second look to see what you'd be getting into."

"Are you kidding?" Windy beamed. "I'm happy to do the work. I definitely want that room, Riva. I just didn't want to pressure you. I hope you didn't feel pressured."

"Not by you," Riva said.

"By me then?" Laurel asked with a furrowed brow.

"No." Riva smiled. "By God. He's been gently twisting my arm. And that storm last night really sealed the deal."

They all laughed and then Windy grabbed her brother's hand. "Come up and see my new room with me. You can help me get it ready."

"I knew there was a catch when baby sister offered to take me to coffee." He winked at Riva.

"Marcus is a very handy handyman." Windy tugged her brother up from his chair. "Come on, Mr. Handy Mandy, I want your opinion on a couple of things."

After they left, Laurel turned to Riva. "So, you're taking in your first boarder?" Her lower lip jutted out. "Does that leave me out in the cold?"

Riva nonchalantly sipped her coffee. "How about my upstairs ensuite?"

"Seriously?" Laurel's whole face lit up. "You mean it?"

"If you want that room, it's yours." Riva smiled, then further confessed how scared and lonely she'd felt last night. "It really did help me make up my mind."

"It was a disturbing storm."

"Strange how you feel more alone in times like that." She looked around the sunlit room. "But to be honest, in the light of day, I wasn't so sure. Until just now . . . when I took a moment to pray."

"And what you said about God was true? Was he really twisting your arm?"

"I've got a real peace about this so I'm convinced he has something to do with it." Riva could see the eagerness in Laurel's eyes. "Go on up to check out the ensuite. Who knows, that room might not measure up to your memory of it. You can still change your mind."

"I doubt I'd change my mind, but I do want to look." She stood.

"I think everything on the second floor could use new paint. The kids' rooms are pretty atrocious-looking from where posters and things were hung. But I'm thinking I should leave the color choices up to the tenants." She considered this. "Within reason and with owner approval, of course. I don't really want to see any chartreuse or magenta or fire engine red."

"Ugh, no worries. I'm pretty conservative. Off-white, probably. Or at the most, a pastel shade." She beamed at Riva. "This is exciting."

Riva simply nodded as Laurel made her exit, but as she gathered up the coffee mugs, she wondered about this move. Sure, it was exciting, but it was also unnerving. She'd just opened the doors of her quiet home. She knew it was right but hoped she wouldn't be sorry.

She was wiping down countertops when she heard Marcus call to her. "I'm in the kitchen," she yelled back.

"There you are." He joined her, leaning against the island. "Laurel wants to know if you have a tape measure she can borrow."

Riva opened her junk drawer, then dug around a bit until she found one. "There you go."

He pocketed it. "The two of them are already making plans to swap a few pieces of furniture, and Windy offered to share her storage unit with Laurel." He looked rather intently at her. "Your house is going to become lots busier, Riva. Are you sure you're up for that?"

"I'm not sure. It's a lot to wrap my head around, but I think it's the right choice. And if it allows me to stay in my home, well, then it'll be worth it."

"I noticed you have two other good-size rooms up there. Will you be letting those out too?"

She peered curiously at him. "Are you asking for yourself?"

"No." He laughed. "I'm happy in my condo for now."

"Oh, good. Because I only plan to rent to women." She closed the junk drawer.

"That's a wise plan. Do you have rental contracts?"

"Contracts?" She frowned. "Laurel is a friend . . . and Windy is your sister. Do you really think I need contracts?"

"I would if I were you. It's not that you don't trust them. It's just that it will simplify your life to have everyone on the same page."

"I'm sure that Paul, my late husband, would totally agree with you. He was an attorney and believed in dotting his i's and crossing his t's. So thanks for bringing it up." She refilled her coffee mug, then asked him if he wanted another cup.

"I wouldn't refuse a refill. Who knows how long the ladies will take upstairs."

She handed him a steaming mug, then led them back to the library. After they were settled, she asked Marcus about his childhood. "Windy told me about growing up in a commune. Was that your experience too?"

"Somewhat. I'm six years older than Windy so my family history is a bit different. I was in third grade when my parents joined the commune. I wasn't too thrilled to leave our neighborhood and my friends behind. Windy was a toddler so I doubt she remembers much about life before. My parents had been fringe involved with this group for a while, so I did know some of the families out there. Just the same, I never really fit in."

"Windy told me her given name was September Wind, but Marcus sounds pretty pedestrian to me."

"My parents named me August Storm." He grimaced. "They used to call me Storm. Windy sometimes still does, but I don't appreciate it. As soon as I was old enough, I changed it to Marcus." His dark eyes twinkled. "I had a childhood friend at the commune. River . . . don't recall his last name. Anyway, he was a couple years older than me, and he had this little black-and-white TV in his closet. His grandma snuck it to him for a birthday one year. Real contraband on the commune. But he and I used to get out of chores and hide in there and watch old reruns. *The Rifleman* was our favorite. We'd play Rifleman in the woods, using sticks as guns. He became Lucas and I was Marcus. So when I got out of that place, I decided to take the name permanently."

"How old were you when you left the commune?"

"Eighteen. I infuriated my parents by joining the Air Force."

"My son's in the Air Force." She told him a bit about Brent's military career and recent deployment to the Middle East. "He's always been a computer wiz, and the training he's gotten there will probably be good preparation for his next job." She pursed her lips.

"Are you worried about him?"

"Of course." She forced a smile. "But I try to use worry as a flag to remind me to pray for him. Better for both of us that way."

"That's wise." He shared how, after enlisting twice, he'd used his GI bill to get a teaching degree. "I thought serving in the military was tough, and then I taught middle school for more than twenty years. Let me tell you, that's really tough."

"Did you get combat pay?" she teased.

He grinned. "I should've. I retired last year. I'm still getting used to having all this free time on my hands."

"What did you teach?"

"Social studies."

"Sounds interesting."

"I suppose it was. More so early on. Kids have gotten a lot more complicated and less motivated. And computers are a convenient but invasive part of that. Mostly I enjoyed teaching history." He stood to peruse Paul's book section again. "That's why some of your titles here interested me. Someone loves US history."

"That was my husband's collection." She wondered what Paul would think of her new plan to take in boarders. He'd probably approve since it allowed her to stay in their home. That had worried him a lot before he passed. "Paul loved to read, but because of his legal work, he didn't always have time. Some of those books have never been opened. They were for his retirement . . . and then, well, he passed."

"How long has it been?" he asked gently.

"A year and a half."

"I'm sorry. I know that's hard." He removed a Clancy hardback from the shelf. "I lost my wife close to six years ago and I still miss her sometimes."

"Sometimes?"

His smile was sad as he opened the book. "It used to feel hard all the time, but I'd have to say it's down to just sometimes now. So, you see, it does get better . . . in time."

"Right." She wrapped her hands around her coffee mug. "That's encouraging."

"Do you have other children?" he asked. "Besides your Air Force son?"

"Yes. McKenzie is my firstborn, though she goes by Kenzie. She's two years older than Brent and just took a job in New York." She felt a twinge of maternal longing. "How about you? Any kids?"

"My wife had health issues so we never had any. I guess the school kids were enough for me." He held up the Clancy novel. "I can't believe I've never read this one before. I thought I'd read them all."

"Feel free to borrow it."

"Do you issue library cards to your patrons? And charge late fees?"

"No, I believe in the honor system." There was a noise upstairs, and she paused to listen. "Sounds like Laurel is calling for me. I better go see."

"Mind bringing her the tape measure while I finish my coffee?" He fished it from his pocket and held it out to her.

"Not at all." She took the item from his hand, then gestured toward the room. "Feel free to make yourself at home in here." Then, taking her coffee and the tape measure with her, she climbed the stairs. But as she went, her mind was preoccupied with Marcus. He seemed like a very nice man. And if she was interested in a relationship—which she was not—he might've been a good candidate. But Riva had decided years ago, right after Paul first got ill, she was a one-man woman. She would never marry again. Just the same, Marcus seemed like a good guy. And he was a handyman too!

Chapter 5

Riva discovered Laurel sitting on the bare mattress of the ensuite room with a thoughtful expression on her face. "So, what do you think?" Riva asked her, setting the measuring tape on the bed.

"I *like* it." Laurel stood, went over to the window, and pushed back the filmy curtains. "I like how the light comes through the trees up here. And there's a nice view of your yard too."

Riva looked from this vantage point. "My yard does look better from a distance. I'm afraid I let it go."

"Windy likes yard work," Laurel said.

"Feel free to replace those curtains." Riva felt the thin fabric. "They've been here for ages. They're probably about to fall apart."

"I think I'll try to gently wash them first. I like how the light filters through. My horrid little apartment has tiny windows that look across a grungy alley and directly at a solid brick wall. Very uninspiring." She turned around.

"Sounds pretty dismal." Riva sat on the edge of the bed, waiting.

"You can't imagine. So anyway, I'm making a plan now. I'd like to paint the room a very pale blue if that's okay with you. It sounds cool and peaceful to me."

"I think this room would look lovely in pale blue. This peachy color was Kenzie's idea. I've never been a fan. I think it clashes with the wood floors."

Laurel nodded. "Would you mind if I switched out your king bed for my full? It'd give me a lot more room for my favorite chair and ottoman right here."

"That's fine. Although I don't know where to put this huge bed. Unless Windy would like it in the attic. The other rooms on this floor already have queen beds."

"Windy might like it. But she's also offered us the extra space in her storage unit. I don't want to cram all my stuff into this room, so I'll probably take her up on it, or else I'll just donate it. It's mostly a lot of junk that I won't even miss. I'm sure we can find a place for this bed to go too."

"I really don't care what you do with it. Or with anything else in here. That dresser and bedside table can go. I just hope you and Windy do whatever works best for you. Make these spaces your own."

Laurel peered curiously at her. "You're absolutely certain you want to do this, Riva? No second thoughts?"

"Well, knowing me, I'll probably have second thoughts, but I'm okay." She stood and looked at the room that hadn't been used for a long time. In a way, it was sad. She tried to imagine it with color and life and furnishings. "My mind is made up, Laurel. I want to do this. And like I was just telling Marcus, I will probably look to rent the other two rooms up here too. But no hurries. I want to get the right women. So if you have any suggestions, I'm open. Windy seems a great fit."

Laurel came over to hug Riva. "Thank you so much for being open to this, sweetie. You have no idea what a godsend this is to me. That awful apartment was seriously depressing. The manager is lazy and negligent, and the rate increase made me want to pull my hair out. Coming to your house will feel like a new lease on life, a breath of fresh air. Thank you."

"You're welcome." As Riva backed away from the hug, she noticed Laurel's misty eyes. And Laurel was not a crier. Riva extended her arms and hugged her old friend again, with more enthusiasm this time. Laurel always seemed like the strong one, but underneath it all, this tough talking woman had a big soft heart. "Welcome to my home, Laurel. I probably should've done this a year ago."

"No, sweetie, you were still getting over Paul. It was a necessary season. No looking back."

"You're right." Riva firmly nodded. "It was a necessary season." But just like weather, she knew that seasons eventually changed . . . when the time was right. Apparently the time was right, and this was the beginning of a new season.

"Marcus offered to help us with painting and moving," Laurel said, grabbing the tape measure as she bent down to measure a wall. "He's very handy."

"That's nice. He seems like a good guy."

Laurel let the tape snap back into place as she stood. "He is a good guy," she confirmed. "And a bachelor too." Her brows arched. "According to Windy he's not even involved with anyone."

"Uh-huh." Riva kicked a dust bunny out of a corner. "These wood floors probably need a good scrubbing."

"I've been hinting around with Marcus."

Riva felt her brows arch. "Hinting around?" Hopefully Laurel wasn't about to play matchmaker with her. "About what?"

"Well, I wouldn't mind getting better acquainted with him. If I had a decent house with a real kitchen, I might've invited him for dinner."

"Oh?"

"Which might be something to consider, Riva. How will you feel about your tenants using your kitchen and inviting dinner guests over?"

Riva just shrugged. "That'd be okay. As long as we coordinate it somehow. In case I had plans, you know, to entertain." She felt hypocritical now. When had she last intentionally entertained anyone? Not since before Paul got sick. But seasons change.

"Yes, definitely. We might even want to post a social schedule on the fridge. Help keep us on the same page."

Riva studied Laurel more carefully now. With her short gray hair, university sweatshirt, and "mom" jeans, she wasn't the most stylish person. It was hard to imagine her actually on the lookout for an available man. But it sounded like perhaps she was. "So," Riva started cautiously, "how long have you been interested in Marcus?"

Laurel waved a hand. "Oh, I don't know. I've only just crossed paths with him casually. But Windy has mentioned that he was lonely. If I'd known I'd see him today, I might've spiffed up some." She tugged at her stained sweatshirt. "Not exactly date bait, am I?"

Riva chuckled. "I think you're pretty cute. And I admire your confidence to wear what you please." Riva looked at her own ensemble—the same as yesterday. "And I'm no fashion plate myself. I've had these clothes on for two days."

"But you always look pretty, Riva. Some of us have to work harder at it."

"Well, I don't know Marcus well, but he seems the type of guy who might look beyond appearances and see what really matters underneath."

"I think you're right." Laurel returned to measuring and Riva excused herself to go back downstairs. She wanted to check on Marcus but didn't want Laurel to think she was trying to put the move on a man that her friend already seemed to have set her sights on. Good for Laurel.

Riva was impressed at the progress her new tenants had made on their rooms in less than two weeks. Thanks to Marcus's help and the way Laurel and Windy worked together, they had painted the attic a creamy white and removed the old carpet to reveal the original wide pine planks. Windy instantly fell in love with the wood, especially since Marcus knew how to restore it. He'd spent one day sanding and the next day sealing the wood with a product that was supposed to be dry by now.

As Riva surveyed the attic from the doorway, she was amazed at the transformation. Thinking the gleaming golden floorboards might still be tacky, she kneeled down to touch them. Smooth and dry. And the off-white walls looked clean and bright. Even the high windows, recently washed, seemed to sparkle with light. All in all, the space was fresh and roomy and livable. Such an incredible change from the previous dark, gloomy attic that Riva had never really liked. But Windy adored it and had been chomping at the bit to move up here. And today was the big day.

Riva went down to take a peek at the ensuite Laurel had been working on. Painted a powder blue and cleared of all furnishings, it appeared ready for occupancy too. Windy's son Max and Marcus had been recruited to help. Just last night, Laurel had called to encourage Riva to make herself scarce by turning today into an errand day.

At first, Riva had resisted, but the more she considered it, the more it seemed like a good idea. It wasn't that Riva wanted to get out of helping her friends, but she didn't want to get in their way . . . and perhaps more than that, she didn't want to feel stressed by all the activity in her previously quiet home. She could imagine all the coming and going, up and down the stairs, banging into walls . . . moving bulky pieces into her house. Laurel was right. Best to get out of here until they were done.

So, already in her car, she spotted Marcus's familiar pickup pulling up. She backed up, eager to get her car out of the driveway for him. He called out a greeting and she waved to him, thinking about what a nice smile he had. As she drove down her street, she said a quiet prayer that the movers would have a good day—with no hurt backs or smashed fingers.

Riva's errands list was long enough that if she took her time, she might be able to stay away from her house for most of the day. She wanted to stock up on groceries, which would be the final chore since she needed perishables and it was too warm to leave things in the car. She also needed to get some cleaning items. She hoped to get some flowering plants and other yard things at the nursery. Her plan was to brighten up her yard by freshening up the pots that had survived the past years of neglect and winter freezes.

It might not be much, but it would be a start. And Paul, if he could see her, would be pleased. Serious gardeners might think that planting a few pansies and petunias was like putting lipstick on a pig, but it would lift her spirits to see some color abloom around and about her yard. Not only that, but it might also inspire her new tenants to get their hands dirty too. It would be amazing to get the outdoor spaces into shape.

She'd promised to leave her phone on just in case her new tenants had any questions, but she'd already told them where everything was located and to make themselves at home. Laurel and Windy were intelligent women. They'd probably get along better without her hovering about.

Still, a part of her felt slightly left out as she shopped for some household items and cleaning tools. As she loaded her purchases in the back of her SUV, she wondered how things were going at home. She was tempted to slip back to drop these things off and sneak a peek. But she was curious what she hoped to see. Was it how the move was going? Or was this about Marcus? And why was she thinking about him so much? Especially since she knew by now that Laurel had her eye on the friendly handyman.

Riva would never admit this to anyone, but she was more than a little curious as to how Laurel's plan for getting better acquainted with Marcus was going. Was Laurel's attraction one-sided or did Marcus have interest too? And, really, she couldn't blame Laurel for feeling drawn to the man. In the last several days, he'd shown himself to be thoughtful, helpful, kind, capable . . .

So many qualities that single women considered in a seriously great catch. Not Riva though. She was content being single. At least, that's what she always told everyone. And she meant it, didn't she?

As she drove to her favorite nursery, she pushed thoughts of whatever was happening at her house, and with the people there, far from her mind. Then as she strolled around the nursery, taking in the plethora of beautiful plants that would brighten her yard, she couldn't stop herself from filling first one wagon and then another! She knew she was going over her budget, but since getting the financial pad from rent money, her purse strings had been loosened a bit. Plus, she told herself, she was getting these things for her new tenants to enjoy too.

Not only that, but if Laurel's predictions were right, the tenant population in Riva's house should be on the increase soon. Already Laurel had directed an interested candidate Riva's way. Laurel's hairstylist Kitty Brinson had called Riva yesterday. Kitty owned a salon in town, and she'd actually been sleeping there at night. Apparently it was her only recourse to escape a bad relationship. But it seemed the city caught wind of this infraction and had given Kitty notice. They might ignore homeowners housing tenants, but business properties were strictly off-limits. Riva had invited Kitty to come check out the available rooms on Monday morning.

It wasn't until Riva was paying for her plants that she realized her SUV wouldn't have room for all of them, along with the purchases she'd just made and the groceries she still planned to get.

"Do you deliver?" she asked the cashier.

"Not on the weekends. But we can hold your plants for twenty-four hours. Or else schedule them to be delivered on Monday. But it's fifty dollars for delivery."

Riva considered. "I'll pick them up tomorrow morning."

"You got it." He handed her a pad. "Just write down your name and phone number, and they'll be safe in back."

She wrote it down, took her receipt, and thanked him. As she drove away, she remembered Old Red. Paul's classic '66 Ford pickup had been handy for chores like this. But she'd let it go shortly after Paul passed. It had made her too sad to see Old Red sitting forlorn and forgotten in her driveway. But now she missed the old beast. Maybe she should've kept it.

As she cruised through town, she realized she was hungry. Her breakfast of yogurt and toast had not stayed with her, and it was already past one. Spotting a parking place in front of a bistro called O'Malley's, she nabbed it and went inside. She'd never been in the bistro since it hadn't been open too long. Seeing only a few customers inside, she wondered if this was a good choice. But a woman with silver hair pulled back into a thick ponytail greeted her so warmly from behind the counter, Riva couldn't turn away.

"Welcome to O'Malley's." The woman gestured to a handwritten menu on the board behind her. "Can I get you something to drink?"

"Do you have iced tea?"

"We most assuredly do. Today's brew is black tea with a wee bit of lavender and fresh mint. 'Tis my favorite blend."

"That sounds nice."

"Aye, 'tis lovely."

Riva considered the woman's strong accent. "Are you Irish?"

"You're right about that. I'm Fiona Harris. My brother Ryan O'Malley and his wife Mae own this bistro." Her smile was bright, and her youthful face didn't seem to match the silver hair. "I try to help. You know, it's a bit rough getting set in a new restaurant in a new town."

"So, you and your family are new to Greenwood?"

"Aye. Ryan and Mae tried to make a go of it in Boston, but they didn't like city living so they bought this place last winter. It took them a bit to get it up and running, but it was a good time for me to come over to help some. I've been here since March."

"Well, I hope you like our little town. Welcome." She smiled. "My name's Riva Owen. I've lived here all my life."

"Greenwood seems a nice place. Not too big. Not too small."

"This is my first time here. What do you recommend?"

"'Tis all good. Today's soup is lamb stew and it's lovely. But our quiche is quite nice too." As she poured iced tea, she described their quiche options, and Riva went with the seafood one.

"And if you're still hungry, we have some bread pudding that's perfectly heavenly."

"I'll keep that in mind." Riva paid and thanked her.

"'Twas a pleasure to meet you, Riva." Fiona turned to greet the young couple just coming in. "I'll bring your order out to you when it's ready."

Riva sat at a table by the front window, slowly sipping her tea, which was delicious, and watching Fiona wait on customers. Such a friendly person. Riva would've liked to ask her more about Ireland, wondering if she'd left her homeland for good or just for an extended visit. Riva had wanted to get Paul to go to Ireland with her, and had even put it on their bucket list . . . and then it was too late. But it still appealed to her. Not that she could afford it now. And even if she could, would she want to go alone? Probably not. As much as she longed for independence, doing things alone was never as simple and easy as she thought it should be. And it usually made her miss Paul more than ever.

Chapter 6

From the bistro window Riva watched cars moving up and down Main Street. Everyone seemed to be in a hurry this afternoon. Everyone but her. She still had several hours to kill before going home. Hopefully she could drag out her stay here at O'Malley's before going to the grocery store. She should've told Fiona to take her time, but here she was coming with Riva's order.

"Here you go." Fiona set it down. "Would you like water?"

"No thanks." Riva took in the generous piece of quiche, a pretty fruit salad, and a crusty piece of bread. "That looks wonderful. Thank you."

"Do you enjoy music?"

"Music? What sort?"

"Live music, I should say. Specifically, Celtic folk."

"As a matter of fact, I love Celtic music." Riva mentioned some of her favorite groups.

Fiona's blue eyes twinkled. "I had a feeling." She produced a flyer with a photo of several smiling musicians. "This is my band." She pointed to the people. "Ryan and Mae and, of course, that'd be me there with the fiddle. We sometimes play here on the weekend. And some other venues as well. Our upcoming gigs are listed there. We've got a show here tonight. I hope you'll come listen . . . sometime."

"I'd love to. Thank you."

"And since you've lived here a long time, I thought I'd ask if you have recommendations for housing? Nothing too costly. I've been staying with Ryan and Mae, but their apartment is too small for three. I've got to find something else."

"Well, there's a real shortage of affordable housing here." Riva stared at Fiona for a long moment. She suspected the woman was older than she'd first assumed. Maybe early fifties, but it was hard to tell. "I, uh, I don't really know you. I mean, we just met. But I do have a very large home, and I have a couple rooms that I'm considering renting out." She explained how Windy and Laurel were moving in with her. "Right now, in fact. I'm trying to stay out of their way until they're done."

"My word! It was pure luck to meet you." Fiona's eyes lit up. "Would you consider renting to me? I can provide references from Bangor. Ireland, not Maine. And certainly Ryan and Mae will recommend me. I'm basically a quiet tenant, except for my music, of course. I do need to practice my fiddle and mandolin. But not loudly and never late at night."

Riva pointed to what looked like a wedding ring on Fiona's left hand. "Are you married?"

"I was. For thirty-one years."

"Goodness, you don't look old enough."

"We were wee babes when we wed." Her eyes grew sad. "I was almost twenty. Jamie a bit older. But my Jamie and me, we always said we grew up together *after* we got married. Sweet Jamie's been gone for nearly five years now."

"I'm sorry. I lost my husband too . . . not too long ago."

Fiona reached for her hand and gave it a warm squeeze. "I'm sorry for your loss, Riva." The bell jingling on the door drew Fiona's attention to a pair of teens entering the bistro. "Excuse me. I do tend to run on and on like a magpie. Better get back to work."

"Yes. No problem." Riva nodded, picking up her fork. As she ate, she wondered about this woman. Something about Fiona was extremely likable. But would she fit in well at Riva's house? What would Laurel and Windy think? She suspected Windy would like her. But Laurel? She'd be sharing the same floor with her. What if Laurel didn't appreciate the music? Maybe Fiona could practice somewhere else in the house. Whatever the case, Riva decided to leave Fiona her phone number with a note saying to call her for an interview. After all, Fiona would need to see the house. She might not even like it. But if she did, Riva would get a chance to chat with her further.

The bistro got progressively busier, and soon it was obvious that Riva's table would be needed by the elderly couple now placing an order up front. Although she'd considered ordering the bread pudding and a cup of coffee, Riva felt guilty for tying up the table while the couple waited. She took her little note to the counter and handed it to Fiona. "Give me a call," she mouthed as she moved toward the door.

Fiona nodded eagerly. "Thank you," she called back. "Come again."

As Riva drove to the grocery store, she noticed a flower stand on a corner and decided that her new tenants deserved some festive blooms to celebrate their first night in their new home. She used to get fresh flowers regularly. If not from Paul's garden, then from various spots in town, but she'd never seen this little kiosk before. She took her time and finally decided on a woodsy bouquet of sunflowers, purple delphinium, cedar greens, and Queen Anne's lace. "This is a lovely arrangement," she said as she paid the girl working the stand. "Very creative."

"Thanks." The girl handed her change back. "My mom's the floral artist. Anyway, that's what Dad calls her. I'll be sure to tell her you liked it." The girl's phone dinged, and she turned away to answer it.

Riva laid her flowers on the passenger's side. She checked her own phone, which had no calls, then continued on her way. It was just a little past three and seemed too soon to get groceries and go home. And yet, she was tired of being away and had actually hoped her new housemates would call. Her curiosity about what was going on at her house was growing. But no news was probably good news. So on to the grocery store. And then she would head home. If they were still moving, she would busy herself unloading things before taking a quick peek at their progress. And if no one wanted her around, she'd drive back to the nursery to pick up her plants.

Riva hated grocery shopping. It hadn't always been that way, but she'd never really enjoyed it. Paul, for some unknown reason, hadn't minded doing grocery runs. She'd often text him a list in the late afternoon while he was still in his law office, and he'd fill the list on his way home, often with a bouquet of grocery store flowers. And he never complained about it. Oh, how she missed that!

By the time she got home and unloaded everything from her car, Riva was tired. That return trip to the nursery could wait until morning. Not for the first time, she wondered how she used to have so much more energy. Was it aging? Or was it lingering sadness over losing Paul? She couldn't be sure.

Riva was just putting the last roll of paper towels into a high cabinet when she heard footsteps behind her. Turning to see who was approaching, she nearly tumbled off her stepstool.

"Whoa there." Marcus stepped up from behind, helping to catch her before she fell. "Easy does it."

Embarrassed at her clumsiness, she pushed away his hand as her feet hit the floor. "Thank you," she said curtly.

"Didn't want to see you splattered all over the floor." He looked amused. "You know most accidents happen at home."

"So I've heard." She folded the stool and stashed it by the fridge. "Sneaking up on someone is probably a good way to cause an accident as well."

"Sorry. I didn't know you were jumpy. Probably from living alone. Guess you'll have to get past it."

"Right." She watched as he pulled out a barstool and made himself comfortable at her breakfast bar.

"This really is a great kitchen." He rubbed his hands together as if he was hungry.

"Can I help you with something?"

"I came down for a drink of water. Helping Windy arrange and rearrange that attic, which is getting pretty warm, made me thirsty."

"Yes. Of course. Do you want something besides water? I got some sodas."

"No, water is fine. I would have gotten it myself but was feeling intrusive."

"Let me get it. Sorry for snapping at you." She rolled her eyes as she got down two water glasses. "I guess nearly falling startled me. Like a bad adrenaline rush."

"That's understandable."

She put ice cubes in the glasses, then filled them. "I'm usually super careful. The idea of being that old lady you see in TV commercials—lying helplessly on the floor, crying for help and wishing for an emergency necklace device—well, that image always makes me nervous."

He laughed. "You are not an old lady."

She set his glass on the table, then lifted hers in a toast. "Here's to that. But we're all getting older."

He clinked his glass against hers. "Then maybe the good news is that you're not alone. If you fall down, you have roommates to help you up."

She gave him a genuine smile. "That is good news. How are they doing?"

"Okay. Laurel's all moved in and looks happy as a clam."

"And Windy?"

"She's got that artistic temperament. Wants everything perfect. So much so that despite the sauna up there, she wouldn't even let me get her portable AC unit going for her. She has to figure out the perfect spot first."

"I'm glad to hear she has AC. I was worried about that." She sipped her water.

"Yeah. And that's why I'm hanging around. Plus, I wanted to ask if I could make a hole in the wall for its exhaust air. I'll make it look good. And you'll still be able to close it in winter."

"Sure, that's fine. I couldn't imagine anyone living up there on a hot day with no AC."

"The rest of your house seems comfortable."

"We got a heat pump with AC several years ago," she said, taking another sip of water. "Just one of the investments we made into this money pit."

"Money pit?"

"Well, there were a lot of things that needed attention before we knew what was ahead with Paul's illness and medical expenses. I guess if we'd known, we'd have done things differently."

He seemed to consider this. "I have a feeling Paul was glad for the fixes. It made this a better place for you."

"Maybe."

"I know if Anne had survived me, I'd have wanted to leave her comfortable."

Even if that left her in deep debt? Instead of saying that, she asked a question. "Anne was your wife?"

He simply nodded, toying with the flowers she'd arranged in a green vase. "Pretty." He attempted to straighten a drooping sunflower.

Taking the hint that he didn't want to talk about his wife, she picked up the flyer she'd laid on the breakfast counter. "I met a member of this Irish folk band today."

"Irish folk?" He sounded interested.

"Yes. And Celtic." She handed him the flyer.

"Cool." He nodded. "Wanna go?"

"Go?"

"And hear them perform." He pointed to a line. "They're playing at O'Malley's tonight at 7:30."

"Oh, right. I actually had lunch there today." She ran a finger around the moisture outside of her glass, trying to gather her thoughts. Was he just being friendly or was he asking her on a date? "To be honest, I'm pretty worn out. And I have to get plants from the nursery in the morning. I bought them and realized I didn't have room in my SUV. And besides that, I have my new housemates. I thought I should fix them dinner tonight."

"In other words, no?"

"Thank you for asking." She smiled. "Another time?" That was no sooner out of her mouth than she wished it wasn't. What about Laurel?

But his face had already lit up. "Great. I'll hold you to it," he said. "You mentioned plants at the nursery. I don't know if you noticed, but I do happen to have a pickup."

"Which you've been putting to good use today. I'm sure Windy and Laurel appreciate it."

"I couldn't have done it without Max's help."

"Windy's son?"

"Yeah. He's got a strong back. Fortunately for me."

"Maybe you and Max would like to join us for dinner," she offered. "It won't be anything fancy. Just spaghetti and salad and bread. But there will be plenty."

"Max is gone. Previous engagement. But I could go for a home-cooked meal." He tilted his head. "But I thought you didn't cook."

"I don't *love* cooking, but I do know how. And it's always more fun when there are people to cook for." She glanced at the clock. "I should probably get the meat sauce going. It's always better if it simmers awhile."

"Anything I can do?"

She strained her ears. "Sounds like Windy's calling for you."

"Maybe she's decided where to put her AC unit." He stood.

She picked up their empty glasses. "I want to go say hi to Laurel and check out her new digs." She set the glasses in the sink. "Then I'll start dinner."

"If the AC biz doesn't take too long, my offer to help is still good."

She gave him a skeptical look. "So, are you saying you're a good cook?"

"Nah, I would never make that claim. And if I did, September Wind would blow in and show me up."

She chuckled. "*September Wind*. I can't imagine growing up with a name like that. Although Riva was no walk in the park when my friends had names like Susan and Sandra and Pam." She pointed at him. "And August Storm?" She laughed. "Sorry."

"To be honest, it wasn't so bad once we moved to the commune. All the kids had weird names. By the way, do you know the meaning of your name?"

"It was my grandmother's name. She was Jewish and told me it was related to the name Rebecca and something to do with rivers. But that's about all I know."

"Well, I thought it was an unusual name, so I did some research," he said as they started up the stairs.

"And?" She turned to look at him.

"It has an interesting meaning."

"Really? What?"

"Riva means to join or connect."

"Interesting. I never heard that before."

"Ironically, it seems that's what you're doing now." He paused at the landing. "Joining with and connecting friends together in your home."

She considered this. After a year and a half of grieving and becoming somewhat reclusive, the idea of bringing people together felt like a hopeful sign. Like maybe she was going to live up to her name.

Chapter 7

Riva knocked three times on the ensuite door. She'd need to start referring to this space as "Laurel's room." When the door opened, she was greeted with a big smile.

"Come in, come in," her new housemate said jovially.

Riva paused in the doorway, gazing about. "Oh, Laurel, it's lovely. Your patchwork quilt with these pale blue walls is beautiful. And those old curtains look as good as new. They're still white."

"They just needed a careful washing."

Riva ran a hand over the comfy-looking recliner. "And this fits in here just fine."

"It all fits just fine." Laurel beamed at her. "What didn't fit is now in Windy's storage unit, thanks to Marcus and Max."

Riva admired the art and photos on the walls. "It's just perfect. Cozy and inviting and pretty." She hugged Laurel. "I hope you'll be happy here." She bent down to pet the black-and-white cat sunning himself on the wood floor. "And Fred too."

"We're already happy."

"To celebrate my new roommates, I'm fixing dinner tonight."

"Oh, you shouldn't go to that trouble for us."

"No trouble. Just spaghetti. But it feels festive to have people in the house again. I want to celebrate, and I'm sure you gals must be tired from a long moving day. I hope you're hungry." She checked her watch. "Dinner should be ready around seven. But come down sooner if you like. I plan to put out some appetizers. And I invited Marcus to join us as a thank-you for all his help."

"Wonderful. I was about to take a shower and clean up."

"Great. I'm going to check out Windy's space before I start dinner."

"It looks really great up there. I was almost envious until I remembered she'll have to go up and down those steep stairs whenever she needs to use the bathroom."

Riva considered this. "I hope that's not too much for her."

"I mentioned it, but she just laughed and said she needs the exercise."

"To each her own." Riva gave Laurel's room a last glance. "I really do love what you've done to this space. Feels good to see it pretty and occupied again. I think you've made the room happy."

Laurel chuckled. "Well, the feeling's mutual."

As Riva went up the attic stairs, she hoped that Windy was as spry as she sounded. Then she reminded herself that Windy was younger. Only a few years, but perhaps it made a difference.

"Hello?" Riva called through the opened door.

"Come on in," Windy yelled back. "Check out my cool pad."

"Pad?" Riva laughed as she went in. "That's a blast from the past." She looked around the room, surprised to see how much Windy had moved up here. Not that it looked overly stuffed. It was actually quite stylish and eclectic. Oriental carpets, oversized leafy green plants, interesting lamps, colorful upholstered furnishings with lots of interesting throw pillows. There was even an antique armoire and several other old wood pieces. "Wow." Riva nodded with approval. "This is very cool."

"And thanks to the AC, it's getting cooler," Windy told her.

Marcus closed a toolbox with a snap. "Just finishing up."

"I can't believe you had so much stuff in your apartment." Riva sat down in the bentwood rocker.

"Most of this was in storage," Windy said.

"Windy has been a treasure hunter in garage and estate sales for years now," Marcus said. "Squirreling away pieces."

"Well, I lost most of my stuff when I lost the house," Windy explained to Riva, "so I began to dream of the day I'd get a place of my own again. Unfortunately, that began to seem like an impossible dream." Windy's eyes sparkled with what looked like joyful tears. "Until now. Thank you."

Riva stood and patted her on the back. "You're welcome. And I'm really glad you're here, Windy. This feels like a new beginning for me."

"For me too." Windy looked around her room. "I just love this space."

"And your decor is such fun. It hearkens back to the seventies."

"To my hippie roots." Windy laughed.

"You know what they say about the apple not falling far from the tree," Marcus teased.

"Then what happened to you, *August Storm*?" Riva teased him back.

"You told her your real name?" Windy's brows arched.

He bristled. "My legal name is Marcus."

"Whatever you say, *Stormy*." Windy poked him in the arm.

"That's the thanks I get for all my help today?"

"Sorry, bro. Accept my humble gratitude, *Marcus*."

"Mine too." Riva turned to Windy. "By the way, you're both invited for dinner at seven as an expression of *my* gratitude." She gave the attic one last glance. "I really do love what you've done up here, Windy. I never dreamed it could look this great."

"Windy's always had a creative streak." Marcus grinned at his baby sister. "Even if she is an overgrown hippie child."

Windy socked him in the arm and he feigned pain, grabbed his toolbox, and made for the door. "I'm getting outta here before baby sis gets really rough." He winked at Riva with mischievous gray eyes. "No appreciation for my good help."

"Come down and help me with dinner, and I'll show you some appreciation," Riva told him.

"You got it." He nodded eagerly.

"Hope you like chopping produce."

"I'm a natural sous-chef."

"Perfect." She grinned at Windy. "I like a guy who can take orders."

Windy laughed. "Good luck with that!"

It turned out that Marcus could take orders—and he was good at chopping veggies. Before long, the meat sauce was simmering and the salad was tossed. Riva even had time to arrange an impromptu appetizer spread of crackers, cheese, olives, nuts, and smoked salmon. And it was only six o'clock.

"That looks good enough to eat." Marcus snuck an olive. "But your charcuterie board needs a good bottle of wine."

Riva opened the pantry where she and Paul used to keep a small assortment of bottles but only found red wine vinegar and olive oil. "Slim pickings here."

"Want me to make a run to the market?"

"Do you know much about wines?" she asked.

He shrugged. "I know enough to pick a decent bottle."

She crossed to the door that led to the basement. "Are you afraid of dark basements with lots of spiderwebs?"

He tilted his head to one side. "Any torture racks, skeletons, prison cells, or poisonous snakes down there?"

"Not that I know of. But I hate going down there myself," she explained. "The house has been in my family for generations, and my father was a connoisseur of fine wines. At least, he claimed he was. So when he and Mom moved to Arizona, they left the wine and a bunch of other things here with us."

His brows arched. "So you have a wine cellar?"

"I'm not sure you'd call it that, but yes, there are a couple of dusty old racks in the cellar. Paul and I rarely ventured down, and we kept the door locked when the kids lived at home." She opened the door and flipped on the light. "But if you're game and can tell whether a bottle is good or not, you're welcome to try."

"Your dad won't mind?"

She shook her head. "He passed about twenty years ago." She reached for a tea towel. "Take this to swipe away the cobwebs and dust."

"All right." He took the towel.

"And be careful on the stairs," she warned as he went down. "Holler if you need help. I'll leave the door open."

"If I'm not back by dinnertime, call in the troops."

Riva checked the kitchen clock. If he wasn't back by seven, she would be calling 911. Keeping her ears tuned to the stairs, she filled a large pot with water and salt and oil and set it on the stove, then she went over to yell down the stairs, "You okay?"

"I'm okay." He was already coming up. "And I think I hit the mother lode."

She stepped back as he came through the door with three bottles in his arms.

"Wow, you think those are any good?" she asked. "Paul and I were afraid to touch any of them after my dad died. How do you know if they've spoiled?"

"All these reds, and the others down there, get better with age. Some of the ports and merlots are more than forty years old. That could produce a lovely full-bodied wine."

"Or give us food poisoning?" She stared at the dusty bottles he set on the counter.

"We can tell by the aroma when we open them. I brought up three choices just in case some have turned to vinegar. Want to start with a merlot?"

She shrugged, presenting him with a corkscrew. "Whatever you think is best. You're the expert."

He took the bottles to the sink where he washed and dried them, then proceeded to open one. He held it out to her to sniff, but she just wrinkled her nose. He took a whiff, then smiled. "Smells just fine."

She got out four wineglasses, then sat down on an island stool, watching as he poured a sample before swirling it. "It needs to aerate," he explained, holding it up to the light and studying the liquid going around the glass. "But it looks and smells good."

"I'll let you be the judge of that." She munched on a cheese cracker, waiting for him to quit playing with his wine and take a test swig. Hopefully he wouldn't immediately crumple to the floor from poisoning.

Finally, he brought the glass to his lips and tried the old wine. "This is perfectly lovely." His victorious smile crinkled the edges of his eyes. "Not too full-bodied, but smooth and sweet. Fruity traces of berries or maybe cherries." He took another sip. "And chocolate notes."

"Chocolate notes?" She picked up the bottle and sniffed.

He held out his empty glass. "Please, sir, may I have some more?"

Amused at his Oliver Twist impression, she refilled his glass and then filled one for herself, taking a tiny sip. Not bad. She took another sip, this time letting it roll around in her mouth to really taste it. "Wow, this really is good. Who would've thought anything drinkable was in these dusty old bottles?"

"You know what they say." He raised his glass. "Wine and women . . . both get better with age."

Too embarrassed to respond, she took yet another sip, then pointed at him. "What about for men? What's their saying for getting older? What gets better with aging men?"

He seemed to consider this. "Old pickups?"

She chuckled. "Well, I'll admit I was admiring your old pickup today. Reminds me of one that Paul had." She set her glass down. "I do think I taste a smidgeon of chocolate," she told him. "And there's kind of a spicy taste too. What's that?"

"That is the sign of a very good wine." He clinked his glass against hers. "Here's to new beginnings in an old house . . . and to wine and women improving with age."

"And to helpful old dudes with cool pickups," she added.

They both laughed.

"Looks like the party is starting," Laurel said, joining them.

"Come have a glass of this wonderful merlot." Marcus shared about unearthing bottles in the cellar. "Very nicely aged."

"This house is just full of surprises." Laurel took the glass he offered. "I'm not usually a merlot fan, but I'll try it."

"I better get my pasta water boiling." Riva went over to the stove, listening as Laurel and Marcus discussed the merits of the merlot as well as other wines. It sounded like Laurel was a bit of a wine expert too. As Riva covered the pot, she noticed Laurel's attire. Sleek black pants and a silky turquoise top. For Laurel, this was very dressed up.

"You look nice," Riva told her as she returned to her stool.

"Well, you said we were celebrating." Laurel picked up a piece of cheese. "I thought I should dress for the occasion."

Riva glanced down at her own T-shirt and khakis. Both were a bit rumpled from her day of errands. And her hair was still in its original ponytail from this morning. But there was no time to spruce up now. She needed to get the pasta cooked and the table set. "I thought we should eat in the dining room," she told them while she removed plates from a cabinet and silverware from a drawer. "Since we're being festive."

"Need help?" Laurel offered.

"Nah, I got this. You stay and visit with Marcus and make sure my pasta water doesn't boil over." Riva carried the place settings out to the dining room, then hunted down matching placemats and napkins and got it all set. She even added a pair of half-used candlesticks to the table. She returned to the kitchen for matches and put some of the blooms from her arrangement in a smaller vase before returning to the dining room. Okay, it wasn't exactly elegant, but it was cheerful. And the first time since losing Paul she'd set up a meal in here. Baby steps, right?

She lit the candles, then lingered in the dining room for a long moment, fighting back tears as she remembered the last time she and Paul had dined in here over candlelight. It had been wintertime. There was a dusting of snow outside, and it had been just the two of them. He'd just gotten his diagnosis, and she'd fixed his favorite rib-eye roast with roasted vegetables. His awful treatments hadn't begun yet, but neither of them had much appetite anyway. And thanks to his new restricted diet, enjoyable dining experiences soon fell by the wayside.

Laughter from the kitchen brought her back to the present and, using the napkin from her place setting, she wiped her tears, then refolded it. It sounded like her guests were enjoying themselves. Riva was amused by how Laurel appeared somewhat smitten with Marcus. She couldn't remember ever seeing her usually serious and somewhat cynical friend acting so light and flirty. And she'd obviously taken great care to dress up tonight. Even her short gray hair looked more styled than normal.

Really, if true love was brewing, Riva was happy for Laurel. She'd been through a rough divorce and more than ten years of being single. Marcus could do a lot worse than a kindhearted, straightforward person like Laurel.

As she returned to the kitchen with dry eyes, Riva reminded herself she had no romantic aspirations. Although . . . if she wanted a relationship . . . a fellow like Marcus didn't seem half bad.

Chapter 8

The next morning, Riva got up extra early to finish cleaning up the dinner things from the night before. As she loaded the dishwasher, she felt happy to remember how they'd all enjoyed such a fun evening. It had been good to see friends gathered in her dining room once again, everyone enjoying the meal and companionship. After dinner, they'd all lingered at the table, having coffee and chocolate truffles that Windy had shared for dessert. But by the time they'd started to clean up, they were all worn out, and Riva suggested the mess could wait until morning.

She finished scrubbing the last pan as Laurel strolled in wearing plaid pajamas and a sleepy smile. "Good morning," she said, reaching for a coffee mug.

"Coffee should be ready soon." Riva set the pan aside.

Laurel sat at the island. "You're an early bird today."

"I felt extra energetic and decided to get a jump on the kitchen." Riva turned the dishwasher on.

"Last night was perfectly lovely," Laurel said happily. "Thanks for putting it together, sweetie. I'd hoped to get down here and clean up the mess before you woke, but you beat me to it."

Riva feigned disappointment. "Shoot, I should've slept longer."

"Ha ha." Laurel smirked. "Anyway, this reminds me of an idea I had yesterday. I think we should create a chore roster to post on the fridge."

"A chore roster?" Riva wasn't sure she liked the idea of keeping tabs on grown-ups. "Do we get gold stars if we do our chores right?" she teased.

"Make fun, but a roster can prevent serious misunderstandings. I used to maintain one at the grade school where I worked. It was the only way to ensure that someone besides me cleaned up the breakroom. You'd be surprised how lazy a bunch of teachers can be at the end of the day."

"Well, I suppose if you want to manage the roster, I won't complain." Riva gave the countertop around the stove a good swipe.

"Windy liked the idea. And if you get more tenants, I think you'll appreciate it too."

"Speaking of tenants, I met an interesting woman yesterday. She's looking for housing too." Riva got the flyer she'd attached to the fridge and showed it to Laurel. "That's her with silver hair. Her name is Fiona."

"A musician?"

"Yes. She seemed nice, and I gave her my number."

"I gave Kitty your number too."

"Yeah. Kitty already called. We scheduled a meeting for tomorrow morning."

"I'll warn you, Kitty is a real talker. I guess you have to be when you do hair, you know, to keep your clients entertained. So don't be overwhelmed if she goes on and on. To be honest, it'll be mostly about herself." She chuckled. "She enjoys dramatizing a bit, but it does pass the time while getting your hair done."

"Okay." Riva considered this. Having a chatterbox in her home didn't sound too good. "Hopefully Kitty knows how to be quiet too."

"Oh, I'm sure she does. She's been through a lot with her ex. I don't know her socially, but she's been cutting my hair for years, and she seems like a good person."

"You think she'll fit in with us here?"

Laurel shrugged. "It's hard to know. My guess is she's a bit younger than we are, but her hair and makeup are, well, rather youthful, so it's hard to tell . . . After hearing her conversations, I'm guessing she's close to sixty. Although I suppose she could pass for being in her forties."

"Lucky her."

Laurel pointed at Riva. "Well, you don't have anything to complain about. You still could pass for forties."

"It's the dark hair." Riva brought over the coffee pot and filled their mugs. "But the gray is on its way. I see new strands daily."

"My grays came with my divorce. A parting gift from dear Reggie."

"You wear them well." Riva sipped her coffee.

"Marcus told me he likes seeing women with naturally gray hair."

Riva raised her brows. "Oh?"

"He said it's a sign of maturity to allow yourself to go gray." Her smile was wistful. "I guess I'm more mature than I realized. But it's nice to be appreciated for it."

Riva studied her friend. "You really like Marcus, don't you?"

"He's a good guy." Laurel's pale blue eyes lit up. "I mean, I don't know him that well, but based on what I've seen and what Windy has told me, he's a genuinely good person. It's been a while since I could say that about any man."

"Well, I can understand why you've been skittish about men after the way things turned out with Reggie."

Laurel set down her mug with a frown. "You really think I've been skittish?"

Maybe that was the wrong word. "Well, hesitant, apprehensive, tentative . . . ?"

Laurel slowly nodded. "You're probably right, but I don't feel like that now."

"Good for you." Riva glanced at her pajamas and slippers. "I need to go to the nursery this morning. A bunch of plants are waiting for me. Guess I should get myself dressed."

"Need any help?"

Riva didn't know how to answer. The truth was she didn't need Laurel's help since Marcus was giving her a ride. It wasn't that she didn't want Laurel to know, but she wasn't sure how her friend would react. Hopefully she wouldn't see Riva as competition. "Nah, I think I've got it. But thanks." She refilled her mug and left to get dressed.

Since she planned to get dirty, Riva decided on old jeans and a T-shirt today. After all, she wasn't trying to impress anyone. Including Marcus. She pulled her hair into a messy pony, then tugged the tail through an old ball cap that once belonged to Paul. She was just buckling up some sandals when she heard a tapping on her door.

Laurel poked her head in. "Were you expecting Marcus this morning?"

"Yes. But he's early."

Laurel's brow furrowed. "Early for what?"

"Oh, he just offered his pickup to help me get my plants."

"Oh, right." Laurel moved out of the way with a worried expression. "He's waiting in the library."

"Thanks." Riva smiled at Laurel. "Don't worry, sweetie, this is just a friend helping a friend. Nothing more."

"Right . . ." But Laurel didn't look convinced.

"Maybe you can help me when we get back?" Riva pocketed her phone. "I plan to pot a lot of plants in the yard this afternoon."

"Well, I don't have much of a green thumb. Maybe Windy will want to help." Laurel held up a can of cat food. "Feeding time for Fred."

For some reason, Riva felt apologetic to Laurel. Was it only because Marcus was helping her pick up plants? That seemed childish. But having housemates might be similar to having siblings. Not that she ever had any. She knew that conflicts could arise when people lived under the same roof. Hopefully she could handle this.

"Ready to go?" Marcus asked as she joined him in the library.

"I am."

"Sorry to be early."

"No problem." She led the way outside. When they got into his pickup, he started the engine, then pulled out his phone. "Maybe we should make sure the nursery is open this early."

"Good idea." She waited as he typed in the address.

"Uh-oh. They don't open until ten." His mouth twisted to one side. "I haven't had any breakfast yet. How about you?"

"Just coffee."

"I know a great breakfast spot"—he put the truck in gear—"if you're game."

"As long as it can be my treat," she said. "To thank you for your help."

"You won't get any argument from me."

"I like your truck," she said as he drove down her hill. But even as she said this, she wondered why being in his pickup made her uncomfortable. Was it because it was so similar to Paul's? Like somehow she was being unfaithful?

"Thanks. I like it too. I have an electric car too, but this old beast is more fun."

"I can see it's a Ford, but what year?"

"It's a '64."

"Did you restore it yourself?"

"Yes. I thought it was just a hobby when I got it, but it turned into serious therapy after Anne passed. Guess it kept me off the streets and out of trouble."

"Right." Still feeling uneasy, she glanced out her window and suddenly wished she'd turned down his offer to help today. She could've gotten the plants by herself. What if this seemed like a date? And what if Laurel was hurt by it? And why was she making a mountain out of a molehill?

"Are you okay?" he asked.

"Huh?"

"You seem a little distracted today. Having any regrets about taking in your housemates?"

"Oh . . ." She considered this. "Maybe a little. I mean, I really like them and all. But I guess I'm realizing how different personalities living under the same roof could get, well, dicey. And I suppose I've gotten used to being alone."

"It'll probably be an adjustment, but the companionship might be worth it."

"I did enjoy our evening last night," she admitted. "I'm probably just overthinking things. I do that sometimes. More so after losing Paul."

"Sometimes it helps to talk things out."

"That's something I really miss. Paul and I used to talk things out. But being alone now, well, the decisions and changes and aging and life . . . it can get overwhelming."

"I know. I feel the same way sometimes."

"Overwhelmed?"

"Not exactly. Anne's been gone a long time, so I've had time to adjust. But I still feel like I need someone to talk to, someone I can run things past and make plans with. Like a few years ago, when I was deciding whether to retire from teaching or not, I remember wishing Anne could give her opinion."

"But you did choose to retire."

"Yes. And I actually felt Anne would approve. Early in our marriage, she always wanted me to work less and live more. She wanted me to consider early retirement, but I never felt ready. When I finally did retire, I didn't know what to do with my spare time."

"Besides helping your sister move or restoring old pickups?"

He smiled. "Yeah. But after my first year of retirement, I was surprised at how easy it became to fill my time. I don't regret retiring at all." He glanced at her. "I suspect you won't regret taking in housemates either. Give it time. After all, you're living up to your name, Riva. Connecting with people and bringing them together." He pulled up to a small café called Nellie's. "Have you ever been here?"

"No. I don't even recall seeing it before. Is it new?"

"I think Nellie has had it for a couple of years."

"You know her?"

"Oh, yeah. She's a good friend."

As Marcus opened the door for her, she was tempted to tease him for having a surplus of *good* women friends, but she thought better of it. After all, what was that to her? Some men just preferred female friends.

"Marcus, my man!" A heavyset woman wearing a gingham apron came around the corner to give Marcus a big hug. "I was just thinking I haven't seen you in a coon's age."

"Apparently I was thinking the same thing."

"Or else you were just craving your blueberry blintzes." She winked. "I just happened to make some."

Marcus introduced Riva as Nellie led them to a booth by the window. "We were off to the plant nursery before we realized they weren't open."

"And that we haven't had breakfast," Riva added.

Nellie handed them menus. "Well, you came to the right place."

"It smells like it." Riva smiled. "Could I get some coffee?"

"You got it." She pointed at Marcus. "You too?"

He nodded and, as Nellie left, they perused the menus. Once again, Riva felt nervous—as if she were on a first date. But she hadn't dated in forty years. She knew it was juvenile and that she needed to get over it, but this was all new to her. To calm her nerves, she made small talk, asking him about his career and then listening carefully as he told her about the challenges of teaching middle school.

"I used to coach too, basketball and baseball." He paused as a server set down their coffees and took their orders. "When Anne got sick, I quit coaching. Probably good timing. I was getting a little long in the tooth, and younger teachers were stepping up and probably needed the additional income that came with the gig."

"Did Anne have a career too?"

"She was a teacher's aide in a kindergarten classroom. The kids adored her." He sipped his coffee.

"I always liked children at that age. Wide-eyed and innocent but still interested and curious."

His expression turned somber. "Anne used to say almost that same thing."

"I thought I wanted to go into education. Maybe teach art."

"You're interested in art?"

"I've dabbled with it over the years. Nothing serious. And I never did finish a degree." She shrugged sheepishly. "Got married young instead."

"Did you ever work outside of the home?"

Her heart warmed at his words. "Thank you for acknowledging that working *inside* the home matters." She smiled. "And yes, I did work. After the kids were solidly in school, I played legal secretary at my husband's law firm."

"Played?"

"Well, I didn't have any law training, but I read a lot of books. My father and grandfather were both attorneys and our library was well stocked. So I read and read and taught myself a few tricks. I got pretty good at legal research eventually. Paul appreciated my help, and it kept my brain active."

"Impressive."

Riva felt herself relaxing as their food was served. Really, this was simply two friends having breakfast. Why had she been obsessing? By the time they were done, the nursery was open.

Before long, they had all the plants neatly loaded in the back of his pickup and were on the way home. "Any other errands you need to do in town?" he asked at a stoplight.

"The only other thing I want to do today is get all these plants in the ground. I didn't realize how many I purchased yesterday. And if the weather forecast is to be trusted, we're in for some super-hot days next week. I'm not much of a gardener, but I know plants do better in cool, damp soil. Especially before a heat wave swoops in."

"I'm pretty good with a shovel." He turned onto her street. "I'm not much of a gardener, but I can dig a mean hole."

She glanced at some of the larger plants in back. "I originally planned to only get plants to put in pots, but I guess I got carried away. I will definitely need some holes dug."

"I don't have anything else going on today—"

"Oh, I don't expect you to help me."

"I want to help. I only have a small deck at my condo, so I actually sort of miss the yard work."

"But I really don't want to trouble you—"

"I *want* to do this, Riva. Just let me."

"But Windy will probably want to help."

"Oh, sure, Windy loves gardening, but take it from me, my baby sister hates digging holes. She'd probably protest if she thought you turned me down. Just think, with me digging and you and Windy planting, we'll get it knocked out in one day. Before that heat wave starts." He jerked a thumb over his shoulder. "And you really did get a lot of plants, Riva. I'm sure it's more work than you think."

"Uh-huh," she mumbled as he drove up her street. She could imagine Laurel's expression if she saw Marcus offering his assistance. But maybe Laurel would want to help too. That might smooth things over. Not to mention getting things done. Because Riva knew she'd bitten off more than she could chew today. And she wasn't only thinking about the plants.

Chapter 9

Laurel, despite her claim to have no green thumb, really stepped up to help in the yard. Whether it was to be around Marcus or just to lend a hand, it didn't matter. By noon, Windy, Laurel, and Marcus had everything under control. Not only with planting but weeding and preparing beds and pots as well. Windy, the true gardener, took the lead.

"We need at least six bags of potting soil," she told Riva. "And probably that many bags of organic compost as well."

"I can take you to get it in my pickup." Marcus laid his shovel in the wheelbarrow.

"No, you can't, Stormy," Windy told him. "You and Laurel need to finish getting this raised bed cleaned up so we have a place to plant my veggie starts and seeds."

"I can get the dirt and compost in my SUV," Riva said.

Marcus tugged a key ring from his shorts pocket. "Here, Riva, just take my truck. It'll be easier to load and unload."

"And cleaner for your rig," Windy added. "Those bags sometimes break open, and the compost can really stink up a vehicle."

Riva took the keys from Marcus. "You're sure you trust me with your pickup?"

He grinned. "Hey, you're trusting me with your wheelbarrow."

She laughed. "Good thing I have comprehensive coverage."

At the end of the day, Riva's backyard was transformed, and the workers were dirty and tired and hungry. "Thank you all so much," Riva told them. "It looks amazing out here."

"Many hands make light work. Although that wasn't exactly *light* work." Laurel rubbed her back. "I can't wait to soak in the tub again tonight. What a treat to have a tub!"

"I never dreamed we could accomplish this much in just one day."

"Too bad we didn't make a video," Windy said. "We could have our own DIY yard-flipping show."

"With one episode," Laurel said.

"What about the front yard?" Windy asked.

"Thankfully that's smaller." Riva didn't even want to think about that yet.

"I can handle it on my own if you want, Riva," Windy said. "But at least now we have this gorgeous space to enjoy." Windy leaned the broom she'd been using by the door.

"It'll be fun to use the backyard again. I just wish I had the energy to fire up the barbecue and grill you guys some juicy T-bones," Riva told them.

"No, of course not." Windy patted her back. "Don't even think of it."

"But how about pizza?" Riva pulled out her phone.

"Suits me," Marcus said, and the women chimed in. So as they went inside to wash up, Riva ordered a couple of pizzas and several salads to share before heading to her own room for a quick shower.

In her bathroom, she was surprised to see what a mess she was. Her hair was sticking out all over, and there was dirt on her face. Her clothes and hands and feet were filthy too. She took a fast shower, promising her hands and nails further attention later, then dressed. She took a brush through her still-damp hair and was just slipping into flip-flops when she heard someone at the front door.

When she got there, Marcus was thanking and tipping the delivery worker. "I thought we should eat on your patio," he told her as he carried the pizza boxes. "To celebrate your yard's revival."

"Revival?" she echoed. "That sounds about right."

"I already set out some plates and things," he said. "I hope you don't mind."

"Not in the least. Thank you."

"I looked around for paper plates to keep it simple but couldn't find any."

"I don't like paper plates," she confessed. "I'd rather run the dishwasher."

"And I opened a bottle of sauvignon that was left over from my cellar foraging last night. I hope that was okay."

"Of course. That's a wonderful idea." She followed him out the French doors to the patio. "Oh, the temperature is just perfect to eat outside." She glanced to where the old table was neatly set with four places, a bottle of wine, and even a hurricane candle. "Wow, this looks great." She glanced at him. "I'm thinking you're a real renaissance man, Marcus. You're good at so many things."

He laughed as he poured a glass of wine and handed it to her. "Well, I've never been called that before, but I suppose I like a lot of different things. After all, variety is the spice of life."

With wine in hand, she sat down and looked around her orderly and attractive yard. "It smells so good out here," she murmured. "I don't remember it smelling this good before."

"I think it's the lilac bush in your side yard." He sat across from her. "As well as the freshly cut lawn and damp soil. But I agree it's a good smell." He lifted his glass. "Here's to lots of happy times spent out here."

She clinked her glass to his, then took a sip. "I feel sort of bad

I let it go while Paul was ill. And then I never came out after that. But seeing how pretty everything looks now, I'm sorry I didn't do this sooner."

"All things in good time." He nodded with satisfaction. "But I have to say, even though it was a lot of work, the results are well worth it." He glanced toward the house. "Are the other ladies joining us?"

"I think so." She peeked into a pizza box. "But we don't have to wait for them. I don't know about you, but I'm ravenous."

"Me too."

And so they both dug in. They were already going for a second piece each when Windy and Laurel came out. "Save any for us?" she teased as she sat next to Marcus, helping herself to pizza.

"We waited for you like one pig waits for another," Riva replied glibly. "That's what my grandma used to say."

"Looks yummy." Windy dished out some salad.

"Good thing you didn't dillydally too much or we might've polished it all off." Marcus filled two more wineglasses.

"Imbibing again?" Laurel's brows arched. "Riva, darling, I didn't know you were this extravagant."

"Blame it on me," Marcus said. "I thought it was a celebration."

"Here's to your new and improved yard." Windy toasted.

"Here's to lots of fun times out here with friends." Laurel smiled, her eyes fixed on Marcus. "I bet you're good with a grill."

He shrugged. "I'm probably a little rusty."

"You should taste his tri-tip," Windy told them. "He marinates it all day, then wraps it in bacon and cooks it on the grill. Believe me, it's delish."

They continued to eat and drink and visit, but Riva could tell the energy levels were down considerably from last night. Finally, they were done, and Riva couldn't help but let out a yawn as she gathered up the empty pizza boxes. "I won't tell anyone else what to do, but I'm exhausted. I plan to turn in early tonight."

"Me too." Windy was already stacking dishes from the table.

They both went into the kitchen, but Laurel and Marcus remained outside, visiting. Riva had overheard something to do with a school board issue and what they felt needed to happen.

"Those two have a lot in common," Windy said as she rinsed a plate.

"Yes. It just occurred to me they both worked for the school district."

"And Laurel seems to really like Marcus."

Riva paused from stuffing a box into the trash compactor. "So you've noticed that too?"

Windy laughed. "How could you not?"

Riva shoved the second box into the compactor, then closed it and turned it on. It growled and crunched.

"Plus, she told me yesterday that she was fond of him," Windy admitted. "And you saw how much she fixed herself up the last two nights. That's not like her."

"It's kind of sweet to see her smitten like this."

"Yes, she does seem a bit smitten, huh?" Windy gazed out the window, then lowered her voice. "I just hope she doesn't get hurt."

"By Marcus?"

"Well, she's putting herself out there. But if he doesn't feel the same . . . well, it could be tough." Windy rinsed another plate, then looked at Riva. "I wasn't going to say anything, but Laurel was not too happy when you and Marcus left in his pickup this morning."

Riva winced. "I was a little worried about that."

"I'm not mentioning it to trouble you, Riva. I mean, really, it's between Laurel and Marcus. But I thought you should have a little heads-up."

"Heads-up?" Riva knew what she meant but was surprised that Windy felt the need to say it.

"Well, you know that if you're not careful, well, you could be stepping into a romantic triangle."

"Oh, that's impossible." Riva rinsed her hands. "I have no interest in a romantic anything. And certainly not a triangle. No worries there."

Windy looked relieved. "Okay. Good to know. Enough said." She sighed, then gazed out the window again. "It's so pretty out there this time of evening. And even though you have no interest in a romantic anything, your yard feels rather romantic."

Standing behind Windy, Riva peered out at her backyard. With the candle still glowing on the picnic table and fresh plants happily tucked in here and there, it was magical and altogether lovely in the dusky light. If a person was in the mood for romance—and again, she was not—her own backyard wouldn't be such a bad place to start.

Chapter 10

To Riva's relief, Kitty Brinson wasn't as chatty as Laurel had described. As they had coffee in the library, Riva decided she liked the woman. She was a little quirky perhaps, and her platinum hair, hot pink lips, and short skirt were outside of Riva's personal comfort zone, but the woman seemed sincere.

"I want to be totally forthcoming," Kitty said finally. "I've had bad luck with men. So much so that I've sworn them off. But I have one hanger-onner. My ex seems to think he's going to get me back. I gave up my apartment because he kept showing up there. I sort of felt he was stalking me, so I started staying in my salon. I park my car at a friend's house, and she drops me at work. It seems kind of silly, but I feel safe there." She sighed. "And my finances are a bit of a mess, but rest assured I can afford what you quoted for that room."

Riva felt a tinge of concern. "Is your ex, uh, dangerous?"

"Oh, I don't think he's dangerous. Just obnoxious. And I'll have my friend drive me up here as well so my car won't be visible, just in case. In fact, your house isn't far from my salon. I could walk back and forth in good weather." Kitty's eyes got misty. "I have been feeling like I'm such a mess. I'm actually a pretty good businesswoman and have a good reputation as a hairdresser. It's just that I'm a terrible judge of character with men."

"You remind me of my roommate Shayla during my first semester in college," Riva told her. "Like you, she was blond and pretty. Men were always attracted to her, but they always turned out to be the wrong guys. And she never could quite figure it out. One night, she was in tears, and I suppose I was fed up, so I told her she was a jerk magnet."

"A jerk magnet?" Kitty looked amused.

Riva shrugged. "It was probably not a nice thing to say, but it felt true at the time. Shayla's appearance was kind of like Farrah Fawcett, who was a big deal at the time, and men seemed drawn to her like moths to a flame. But they tended to be superficial and only interested in a good time and some arm candy."

"I get that." Kitty rolled her eyes. "So what happened to Shayla?"

"She dropped out of college and married a jerk." Riva grimaced. "Well, he was a jerk at the time, and the marriage didn't last a year. But maybe the guy grew up. I'm hoping Shayla figured it all out. I lost track of her." Riva stood to get a book from a shelf. "Have you ever read Jane Austen?"

"I've never been much of a reader," Kitty confessed.

"Well, this Jane Austen book—*Pride and Prejudice*—has a character that reminds me of you. She's a secondary character, a younger sister of the protagonist of the story, but she's sort of a nineteenth-century jerk magnet." Riva studied Kitty. "I'll tell you what, if you promise to read this and then talk to me about it, I will rent you a room."

"Really?" Kitty's turquoise eyes got big.

"Absolutely." Riva smiled, handing her the book. "Maybe the book can help you improve your discernment about men."

"I'd like that. Good grief, you'd think I'd have figured it out by now, but I keep falling back into it." Kitty ran her hand over the cover. "Thank you."

Riva handed her a copy of the rental agreement she'd printed from online. "I'm having my tenants sign this rental contract," she explained. "My husband was an attorney, and I think he'd want me to do it like this, but I'm using the simplest one I could find."

"I don't mind a bit." Kitty slipped the papers into the Austen book and slid it into her Gucci bag. "Thank you for giving me a chance, Riva. I wasn't sure what a landlord would say if I confessed my bad luck with men."

Riva hoped she wasn't making a mistake, but for some reason she wanted to help Kitty. "The last page on the rental agreement includes the house rules I put together. You need to sign it too. It does stipulate no overnight guests. I hope that gives you some boundaries for any overly pushy male friends."

"Hopefully I'll be pushing the overly pushy ones away." She pulled out a checkbook. "Is it okay if I pay you with a check?"

"Absolutely."

"I'm kind of old-fashioned that way. Helps me to keep better track of my finances." She wrote out a check and handed it to Riva.

"Thank you." As Riva gave Kitty a house key, she heard the doorbell. "That's probably my next tenant interview. Did you decide which room you prefer?" She stood, pocketing the check.

Kitty shrugged. "They looked so similar, it doesn't really matter to me. I'm very minimalist, so I won't be moving too much in here. Well, except for clothes. I'm a bit of a clothes horse, but the closets are on the small side, so it's good motivation to do some sifting and sorting on my wardrobe."

"If you need to store anything, my basement has some room. But I'll warn you it's a little creepy down there, and there are steep stairs." Riva led her to the front door. "I'll introduce you to Fiona. Her family owns O'Malley's downtown. She may be occupying the bedroom next to yours and sharing the bathroom."

Riva opened the door and introduced the women. "Kitty owns Mirabella Salon," she told Fiona, then turned to Kitty. "Fiona is a musician from Ireland."

"We're a Celtic folk band," Fiona explained. "I play fiddle and mandolin, so I hope you won't mind if I practice sometimes. It won't be late at night."

"I love folk music," Kitty told her. "I won't mind at all."

"That is, if Riva decides to take me in." Fiona looked hopefully at Riva. "I brought references with me."

"Well, come on in and let's talk." Riva told Kitty goodbye and led Fiona inside for a quick tour of the house.

"It's a perfectly glorious home," Fiona said as they came back down the stairs.

"Let's sit in the library," Riva suggested. "Can I get you a coffee?"

"No thank you. I already consumed far too much caffeine this morning. I think I was nervous."

"I hope you're not nervous now that you're here."

Fiona frowned as she handed Riva her references. "I'm still a wee bit jumpy. Might be the caffeine . . . or because I'm so eager for you to like me so I can get out of my brother's flat." Her smile looked stiff. "And it would be wonderful to stay in your lovely home." She looked around the library. "Oh, my! You do have a lot of books."

"Do you like to read?"

"I must admit I'm not too well-read."

"Maybe we can change that."

"I used to read mystery books when I was young."

"I have plenty of those on the shelves." A moment later, Riva looked up from Fiona's references. "Well, this all seems in order. Can you tell me a little more about yourself? I'm curious as to why you left your homeland. I realize you wanted to be near your brother. But leaving Ireland, well, that seems like a big step."

"Ah, there were a multitude of reasons." Fiona pursed her lips. "For starters, when my sweet husband passed nearly ten years ago now, bless his soul, I was bitter lonely. To be honest, Jamie was a bit of a yoke, but he was truly good at heart—and a fine musician. He died suddenly. Made total hames of my life."

"Hames?"

"Ah, yes, it means he left me in a bit of a mess. Lots of pieces to pick up."

"I know how that goes." Riva thought of the medical bills she was still paying. "And I'm sorry for the loss of your husband."

Fiona nodded. "Earlier in the same year Jamie died, my big brother Ryan relocated to Boston. So I missed him too. And my daughter Claire was restless and bored with Northern Ireland and eager to see the world. She joined Ryan and Mae in Boston to help with their first restaurant there. Claire's thirty-two now, married, and lives in Louisiana. She and her husband Vance own a coffee house in New Orleans now. I considered moving down there, but I don't like the climate—or the snakes and alligators Claire tells me about. Oregon feels a wee bit like Ireland to me. And, of course, Ryan and Mae were already here. So when Ryan told me they needed a new fiddler, I decided to take the big leap and here I am now. I've been sleeping on their lumpy sofa bed these last three months."

"That's quite a story." Riva tried to imagine what it would feel like to make a huge life change at this stage of life. Fiona's references let her know the woman was almost the same age as Riva. For Fiona to reinvent herself in a different country was admirable and brave. Just taking in tenants was more than enough of a challenge for Riva. "Well, if you still want to live here, you're most welcome, Fiona."

"Thank you so much! Ryan and Mae will be thrilled to hear that."

"I'm curious though. Perhaps you don't know, but have you left Ireland for good? Will you remain in the US permanently?"

"That's a good question, but you're right that I don't know what the future holds. I have a visitor's visa for the time being. I'll see how it all goes and decide when that's up."

"I suppose I'm extra curious since I've always wanted to see Ireland. It seems like such an enchanting country. I had hoped to go with my late husband."

"Truly?" Fiona looked surprised. "'Tis a lovely place for certain, but your Oregon is so similar. Ryan has been good to take me sightseeing. I've been to see your gorgeous beaches and amazing forests and stunning mountains and such. It's a beautiful country, indeed. The farmlands and vineyards around here are so lush and green. It reminds me of my homeland. So for now, I don't feel terribly homesick. And I must say, the people here have been just grand."

Riva handed her the rental contract, explaining her desire to keep everything above board and legal.

"Not a problem." Fiona glanced over the contract. "Do you mind if I take it back to work to read? Then I can bring the signed copy back with a cashier's check a bit later."

"That's fine."

"And if all is well, when can I move in?"

"Anytime is fine."

"Today?"

"I don't see why not." They both stood and shook hands. "I'll give you a key when you come back." Riva walked her to the door. "I hope you'll be happy here, Fiona."

"I'm already happy here." She beamed at Riva. "You've truly got a beautiful home. Thank you for inviting me to join your family."

Riva smiled. "I guess we are sort of family. A makeshift family."

"Family is where you find it."

As Fiona went out, Riva wondered what kind of family they would make. Laurel and Windy seemed to be settling in nicely already. What would happen when they added Kitty and Fiona to the mix? Five women sharing the same home would probably cause some ups and downs. Hopefully they would all find the space and grace to live peacefully together. Either that or she'd consider taking a sabbatical . . . and perhaps head to Ireland?

Riva was still gazing out the foyer window when Windy, on her way out, explained her plan to fix dinner that night. "I already informed Laurel. I expect to have it ready by seven, and I won't take any argument from you."

"No argument, but it's possible we'll have more than just the three of us tonight."

"Is my big brother crashing again?"

"No. But our new housemates will probably be moving in later today. They both seemed pretty eager."

"And you like them?" Windy looked a little concerned. "They'll fit in okay?"

"I think so." Riva briefly described Kitty and Fiona. "We're all pretty close in age. I don't think I'd enjoy having younger, rowdier women living here."

"Yes, but being the same age doesn't always mean you get along with someone. But I'm sure if you like them, I will too." Windy jingled her car keys, then smiled. "Now I'm off to get a few groceries for tonight. Need anything?"

Riva said no, then went to hunt down Laurel. She wanted to tell her about the new tenants. After a trip upstairs and through the house, she finally discovered Laurel sitting in a lounge chair outside, a crossword puzzle book in her lap. Fred was sunning himself on the patio next to her. "I didn't know you were an outdoorsy gal." Riva scooted the other lounge chair next to Laurel's.

"Probably because I didn't get much opportunity before. My crummy apartment didn't have any outdoor space. I got used to being inside 24/7. Not healthy. I'm soaking in my vitamin D this morning."

"Good thinking." Riva rolled up her pant legs. "And I do understand feeling like a hermit. After Paul got too sick to do much, I let the yard go and quit coming out here at all." She leaned her head back and gazed up at the clouds drifting across the clear blue sky. "But when he was alive and keeping it up, this used to be my favorite spot to read on a summer morning like this."

Laurel stroked Fred's coat but didn't say anything.

"You're welcome to help yourself to books from the library anytime." She told Laurel how she'd insisted Kitty read *Pride and Prejudice*. "For therapeutic reasons."

"Wasn't that written like a couple hundred years ago?"

"Jane Austen is still surprisingly relevant today. She understood human behavior better than many modern-day philosophers."

Obviously unconvinced, Laurel just shook her head.

"Don't you remember the character Lydia in that book? The youngest flibbertigibbet sister who was overly focused on appearances . . . and a very bad judge of men. Well, she reminded me of Kitty—or vice versa. Can you see it?"

"To be honest, I never read any Jane Austen books."

Riva sat up straight. "Tell me it ain't so."

Laurel laughed. "You know I've never been the reader you are, sweetie."

"Well, if you're living in my house, you should change that. In fact, I was just thinking we should start a house book group."

"Really?" Laurel's mouth twisted to one side. "Well, that might be interesting. But would it be limited to this house or can we invite outsiders?"

"I don't know. It's not a fully developed idea."

"I understand. But if we opened it up to others, would men be allowed?"

"You're jumping way ahead of me now. Maybe you should plan it, Laurel. You're the organizer."

"Then I think we should include men. It would make discussions more interesting. And I'd like to invite Marcus to join us. He's a reader. What book will we start with?"

"I, uh, I have no idea. Maybe we shouldn't rush it. Just getting our new housemates and everyone acclimated might take a bit. Besides, summer is a busy time to start a book group. We should wait for fall when life slows down." Perhaps more truthfully, Riva wasn't ready to host a mixed group in her home. Plus, she suspected Laurel's interest in including men, particularly Marcus, was purely personal.

"You could be right." Laurel reached down to scoop up her cat, setting him in her lap. "After all, there are other activities to do in the summer. I was just sitting here, envisioning this space as a fun gathering place. We'll have to host some barbecues. We could hang paper lanterns and set up some music. I have a portable CD player in storage." She sighed. "It's been so long since I've practiced any kind of hospitality, I'm probably a little rusty. But your home is so perfect for entertaining. I really think filling the place with more happy people will help you to get past your grief."

"I'm getting past my grief." Riva didn't like the defensive snap in her tone, but she couldn't seem to help it. "Everyone grieves at their own pace, Laurel. That's something I learned in that grief group *you* insisted I attend."

"That's probably true. But you must admit you've been cheerier since opening your home, right?"

Riva slowly nodded. "It does feel good to have people around. For the most part anyway."

"What's that supposed to mean?"

"Only that I still need my alone time . . . in a quiet place."

"You have a big house, sweetie. I'm sure you have plenty of quiet spots to hide out in. And if you really need to hole up and don't want to be disturbed, why not post a sign on a door? We won't bother you. Fred and I will skedaddle if you want to sit out here on your own."

"No, my dear, you don't need to leave." She patted Laurel's shoulder and leaned back again. "It's been a while since I've really visited with you. We've all been so busy. Hopefully things will slow down, and we can all settle in." She shielded her eyes from the sun as she turned toward Laurel. "You heard that Windy is fixing dinner?"

"Yes. She wants to make chicken kebabs."

"Sounds good to me. Glad I caught her on her way out. I told her to plan on six guests tonight."

"Six?" Riva counted on her fingers. "You, me, Windy, Fiona, and Kitty. That's only five."

"When Windy told me she was making kebabs, I texted Marcus

the news. He told me Windy makes fabulous kebabs with a killer peanut sauce."

"Oh?" Riva tried not to react. "Six for dinner, then?"

"Yep. He said he'll be here with bells on." Laurel laughed. "I'd like to see that."

Riva wanted to ask Laurel about her feelings toward Marcus but just couldn't get herself to go there. In normal circumstances, she would. After all, that's what friends did. But for some reason, fishing for information about Laurel's romantic feelings in this situation felt intrusive and awkward. Especially after what Windy had hinted about avoiding a possible love triangle. No way did Riva want to go there with Laurel—or anyone. She flashed back to living in a college sorority, remembering how girls would get into horrible fights over guys. She knew she and Laurel would never kick and scream and pull hair like those sorority sisters. But even a mature cold war under the same roof would be a hot mess. Windy was right. Best to avoid it.

Chapter 11

It wasn't long before Fiona returned with her signed contract, a certified check, and several bags of belongings and instruments. "Take whichever bedroom you prefer," Riva told her. "Kitty didn't seem to care and she's not back yet."

"Oh, thank you. I like the pale yellow room. So bright and cheery."

Riva smiled. "That was my sewing room."

"You're a seamstress?"

"Only as a hobby. It's been ages since I did any mending, and I was never very good at it. I gave away my machine and all of that years ago."

"My sister-in-law Mae is a quilt maker. I admire her work but don't care to try it myself." She held up a violin case. "Music is my main hobby." She smiled. "Have you a hobby now?"

"Not to speak of. I used to dabble in painting a little." Riva cringed remembering the promise she'd made Paul that she'd take it back up after he was gone. A promise she had yet to keep. She forced a smile. "I'm glad to have you here," she told Fiona. "Please, make yourself at home. The woman in the ensuite across from you is Laurel and her cat is Fred. Windy lives on the third floor, and she's fixing us dinner tonight at seven. And Kitty, in the room next to yours, plans to move in today too. So this will be a busy place."

"Like a girls' dormitory." Fiona hoisted a bag strap over her shoulder. "It'll be just crack."

"Crack?"

"Ah, excuse me Irish. Craic means fun. It's C-R-A-I-C."

"Right. It'll be craic," Riva tried it out. "I hope you teach me lots of your Irish words."

"In no time at all, we'll get you all set to visit my homeland. It'll be grand."

As Fiona carried a load upstairs, Riva retreated to her own room. She knew the house would be busy with comings and goings today. That would create the kind of noise, or craic, that Riva wasn't used to anymore. Not yet anyway. And so she decided to spend a quiet afternoon in the bath with a book. It'd been a while since she'd enjoyed a peaceful soak in her big tub. Back before Paul got sick, she used to take an occasional "home spa day" in the master bedroom. Usually before a big event or date night. And although she had no big evening plans, she felt the need to do some pampering today.

She tried to remember how she used to do it. First, she'd forewarn Paul that their room was off-limits for a few hours, and then she'd turn on some soft music, give herself a facial, take a relaxing bath, followed by a pedicure and whatever other sort of beauty maintenance felt good. But she hadn't done a "home spa day" once since losing him. She was well overdue. And it would be a good distraction from the activity filling her house today.

As she soaked in lavender-scented water, Riva hoped she hadn't taken on too much. Four housemates? Three who were practically strangers. And one friend who was feeling a bit like a stranger too, thanks to Laurel's schoolgirl crush on Marcus. But without that rent money, Riva would be looking for a new place to live. As she ran a bit more hot water, she decided that no matter how it all turned out, she would be okay. If having renters worked, she would be grateful to remain in her home. If it didn't work, at least she'd know she gave it her best shot.

After her spa treatments, Riva sat outside her bedroom door for a while, reading and soaking up a little sunshine from the large windows. And then, feeling sleepy, she decided to take a nap. By the time she woke up, it was late in the day. She could hear random movements in the house and instead of feeling jumpy like she had a few days ago, she began to enjoy the sounds. It felt like the house was returning to life, happy to be filled with inhabitants again.

It was still warm out and, knowing they'd be dining outside, she decided to dress in something cool. She foraged in her closet until she found a sundress she used to wear for evening lounging on a warm summer night. But she hadn't worn it since Paul was alive. She held it up in front of her full-length mirror. Was the cheerful floral print too bright for a widow? She knew what her daughter would say. "Lose the widow's weeds, Mom" had been Kenzie's response to all the black and gray Riva gravitated toward. But in all fairness, she'd always worn darker colors. The rayon dress was comfy and cool, and the flowing skirt felt good against her legs.

Maybe it *was* time to shed the widow's weeds. She'd known for some time that Paul would hate seeing her trapped in dark shadows of grief, but she'd felt stuck and it had been easy to hole up in her big house, keeping people at a safe distance. But that was over now. She was entering a new era. New friends, new activities, new life . . . For the first time in several years, she felt hopeful. Maybe there really was life after death. And she didn't mean heaven. She knew there was life there and had been longing for it since losing Paul. But today, for some reason, she felt ready to embrace life on earth. At least for the moment. She had no guarantee it would last.

Her hair, still mussed from her bath, was a mess. She pinned it up loosely. Having it off her neck felt cooler but made her realize she needed something else. She opened her jewelry box and dug out a pair of dangly turquoise-and-silver earrings that Paul had gotten her for Christmas the year before he died. She still didn't know how he'd found them since he'd been housebound, but she suspected Kenzie had something to do with it.

Thinking of Kenzie reminded her that she hadn't updated her about the houseful of new roommates. And so she sat down and wrote a rather lengthy text explaining the situation, assuring Kenzie that her new tenants were good women. She described them as "friends," which might've been a stretch . . . or maybe it was faith. Because Riva believed they'd all be friends before long.

By the time she sent the text, it was nearly seven. Feeling strangely lazy—having guests for dinner but not lifting a finger—she wandered out into her quiet house. She heard voices in the kitchen and continued on through to discover Windy and Fiona working together to make a gorgeous fruit salad. Riva greeted them, plucking a piece of pineapple from the cutting board. "Looks yummy."

"I need to go check the barbecue." Windy paused to look at Riva. "Wow, you look pretty."

"Thanks. It's just an old summer dress. Thought I'd pull it out of hiding. Nice and cool." She suddenly felt self-conscious, like perhaps she should be back in her drab colors.

"Well, it's nice seeing you in something colorful." Windy waved a hand down at her own outfit, another colorful skirt she'd paired with a fringed top and several strands of beaded necklaces. "You know how much I like color." She laughed as she picked up a platter of veggies. "We will be festive tonight. Excuse me, ladies, I'm taking this outside."

"Need any help here?" Riva asked Fiona as Windy went out.

"Thanks, I'm just about done." Fiona set her knife aside. "I really like Windy. She is such a free spirit. And she seems a good cook too." Fiona turned to Riva, then smiled. "Oh my, you really do look lovely, Riva."

"Thanks." Riva shrugged. "I'm not used to fixing up much. Not that I did much. But with summertime, dinner, more people in the house . . . I thought it was time."

"I understand. After losing my Jamie, I never gave a wit about my looks. I'd go about in dowdy old things. It wasn't until I joined me first real band that I took any interest in my appearance. I told myself it was for the sake of the band, but after a bit, I figured it was for me too. Lifted my spirits."

"That makes sense." Although Riva wasn't sure that her spirits felt particularly lifted as she gazed out the window. Kitty was engaged in conversation with Marcus, with Laurel standing nearby watching. With her arms folded in front and her brow creased, she looked troubled. Meanwhile Kitty, with her platinum blond hair, impeccable makeup, golden tan, and slightly snug tank top, looked pleased as pink punch.

"Have you met everyone yet?" Riva asked Fiona.

"I met Kitty this afternoon. She seems nice. I helped her carry some bags and things into the house. That woman has a lot of clothes! She said she must keep up her image because she owns a hair salon." Fiona pushed back a strand of sleek silver hair and laughed. "She asked if I have mine done professionally, but I told her it was a gift from Mother Nature."

"A beautiful gift too." Riva rinsed off the cutting board.

"I met Laurel too," Fiona said, then she lowered her voice. "I've noticed how Laurel and Kitty are both fairly attentive to our only gentleman guest, but I didn't catch his name."

"That's Windy's brother, Marcus." Riva glanced out the window to see all four gathering in the eating area where Marcus was opening a bottle of wine.

"Shall we join the party?" Fiona picked up the fruit salad bowl.

Riva opened the door and waited for Fiona to pass. But as Riva went out, she suddenly felt strange. Almost surreal. It was as if she wasn't in her own home, or maybe she wasn't in her own skin. She wasn't even sure what bothered her, but something felt unsettling.

Was she simply adapting to her new tenants? Hopefully not having second thoughts again. Or would that be third or fourth thoughts by now? *Just remember*, she told herself as she shut the French door behind her, *having tenants is allowing you to remain in your home.* It was a good thing. And it was only natural that it would take time to adjust.

"There you are," Marcus said cheerfully to Riva. "We were just wondering when you were joining us." He held a glass of white wine out toward her. "I didn't raid your wine cellar this time. Windy said she wanted Sauvignon Blanc to go with the chicken."

Riva took the glass from him. "Thank you."

Marcus seemed to really see her now. "You look very nice," he said quietly.

"Thanks," she muttered, feeling even more self-conscious. "I see you've met Kitty, but I don't think you've met Fiona." She politely introduced them. "I think I already mentioned she's part of a Celtic band."

He shook Fiona's hand. "What instruments do you play?"

"Mostly the fiddle. But I play mandolin too. And the penny whistle. Also a wee bit of guitar, but I'm only a beginner."

"I bet you're a fast learner. And guitar's not that difficult. I play some," he said. "Not very well and mainly for my own entertainment."

"We should make music after dinner," she told him. "You can play my guitar, and I'll be on fiddle."

"And I'll dance!" Windy laughed. "But right now, dinner is ready. Everyone grab a plate and serve yourselves."

It was cozy with six diners at the round picnic table. It didn't escape Riva's notice that Marcus was flanked by Kitty and Laurel, who both seemed determined to catch his attention. Kitty was trying to talk baseball with him and actually sounded like an expert, but the moment she paused, Laurel jumped right in.

"Riva and I are talking about doing a book group," she directed to Marcus. "But Riva wants to ban men." Laurel playfully elbowed Riva.

"Ban men?" Marcus asked. "That seems a bit sexist."

"It's only that I thought we could start with just the women living here," Riva said in defense.

"But I'm not even a reader," Laurel said.

"I'm not either," Kitty admitted. "But Riva already gave me assigned reading."

"What book?" Windy asked.

"*Pride and Prejudice*," Kitty told her. "It was written hundreds of years ago."

"I love that one," Windy said. "I love anything by Jane Austen."

"Can that be our first book group book?" Kitty asked. "That way I wouldn't have to read two books."

"Since Windy and I both already read it, I think we should choose another title," Riva told her.

"Yes," Laurel agreed. "Something that appeals to everyone. Not just women."

"Meaning men don't read Jane Austen?" Marcus reached for the breadbasket.

"Have you?" Laurel asked.

"As a matter of fact, I've read more than one Austen book."

"My brother's always been a voracious reader." Windy passed the salad dressing. "We didn't have a big selection of books on the commune where we grew up, but he'd scrounge them up somehow. I even caught him reading Nancy Drew books. I never let him hear the end of that."

They all laughed.

"Hey, Nancy Drew was better than some of the religious propaganda they forced on us." Marcus shrugged. "I learned to make the best of things."

"So, it was a religious commune?" Riva asked.

"Were you in a cult?" Kitty's eyes grew wide.

"Not exactly," Marcus told her. "They started out as a traditional commune where everyone had jobs to keep it going. But then a new leader took over, and it got overly fundamentalist. At least for me."

"For me too," Windy agreed. "I was twelve when Marcus escaped. I couldn't wait to get out."

"Did they try to brainwash you?" Laurel asked.

"Not exactly. But the leaders used the Bible to beat us." Marcus's tone was light, but his expression was serious.

"They hit you with a Bible?" Kitty asked.

"Not literally." Marcus chuckled before growing somber. "They had a special stick for that." He looked at Windy. "Remember the rod?"

"Yeah, spare the rod, spoil the child."

"That's child abuse," Kitty said.

"Probably." Marcus sighed. "But we don't really need to go there now. Although, it might help some to understand why I used books, even Nancy Drew, to escape."

"Speaking of books, I love the idea of a book group," Windy said. "Admittedly I became a reader later in life than my brother, but I do love to read."

"I used to like reading," Fiona said. "I probably don't do as much as I should anymore, but a book group might help me get back to it."

"When will we start it?" Windy asked. "And what will our first book be?"

"I, uh, I'm not sure." Riva bit her lip. "I thought maybe we should wait until fall."

"Why wait?" Marcus asked. "Summer is a good time to read. Nothing like a good book in a cool spot on a hot day." He turned to Riva with a smirk. "I'm just feeling left out that you want to ban men."

"I think we should take a vote," Laurel declared. "Maybe three votes. First, for whether or not to ban men." She held up one finger. "And a second vote for when we should start, and a third vote to choose a book. What say ye?"

They all chimed in that a vote was a good idea, and Laurel began lobbying to include men. "A male perspective would make it more interesting," she said.

"I have a male bandmate who likes to read," Fiona told them. "I'm sure he'd like to come to our group."

"I think having guys would make it more fun," Kitty added.

"Let's take a vote," Laurel said.

"I'll assume the vote is for members of the house only," Marcus said.

"That seems fair," Riva said. But when they voted, the majority was clearly for having men. Not wanting to be the only objector, Riva raised her hand.

"It's unanimous," Laurel told Marcus.

Fiona winked. "You're in like Flynn."

"Does that mean I get to vote and lobby now?" Marcus asked Riva.

"Of course." She smiled stiffly. "And I know from experience that when you say you're going to wait to start something, it often doesn't get started at all. I think we should go for it, ladies. Even if all we do is the reading and don't actually meet until later this summer."

Laurel called for another vote and again it was unanimous.

"Now for the title choice." Marcus pointed at Riva. "Since this is your idea, I bet you have some suggestions."

Riva's mind went blank. "I, uh, I don't know. It should be something both men and women will enjoy."

"Have any of you read Tolstoy?" Marcus asked. "I've read some, but not all."

"Tolstoy?" Riva blinked. "That seems a bit daunting for our first book."

"Fitzgerald?" Windy suggested.

"Fitzgerald might be a bit overwhelming too." Fiona glanced at Kitty. "Especially to people who haven't been reading a lot."

"And a little depressing," Riva added.

"What about James Joyce?" Fiona suggested. "I always wanted to read *Ulysses*."

"How about something easy?" Kitty turned to Marcus. "You say you're a reader, but have you ever read one of those steamy romance novels?"

Marcus cleared his throat. "Can't say that I have."

"Can't say or *won't* say?" Kitty teased, making the others laugh uncomfortably. "The only reason I mentioned it is because some of my clients bring books like that to my salon and, honestly, they can't seem to put them down. I'd love to hear a guy's perspective on one of those."

"I think we should ban bodice rippers," Riva said.

Kitty's brows arched. "Bodice rippers?"

"A friend of mine called them that." Riva wished she'd never brought up the book group idea. It seemed to be taking on a life of its own. "I'm starting to reconsider Tolstoy now," she told Marcus. "What about starting with one of his short stories? That might not be too intimidating."

"I don't know." He glanced at Kitty and Laurel. "Maybe we should get something lighter and more compelling. We don't want anyone to lose interest in reading because we picked something too heady."

"Since you both mentioned Tolstoy, I got to thinking of a novel I wanted to read last winter," Windy said. "Has anyone heard of *A Gentleman in Moscow* by Amor Towles? It made all kinds of bestsellers lists and has even been adapted for TV."

"I want to read that too," Riva told her.

"So do I," Marcus chimed in. "I heard it's a compelling way to learn about the Russian Revolution. And not too heavy."

"Sounds good to me," Fiona said.

Marcus looked at each of them. "Is that four votes for Towles?"

"What about our nonreaders?" Riva looked at Laurel. "Are you abstaining?"

"I'm willing to give the Russian book a try if you think it's that good," Laurel said to Marcus. "So we definitely have a majority."

"I think I'll abstain," Kitty said. "My head is spinning at the thought of having *two* books to read now."

"Being in our book group isn't mandatory," Riva told her. "It's supposed to be fun."

"Fun?" Kitty frowned. "To be honest, I kinda feel like I'm back in English lit class in high school. And I took that class by accident. I was never real academic." She took a sip from her wineglass. "But Windy said the book is a TV show? Are we allowed to watch that instead?"

"I think any book we choose should have to be available in movie form," Laurel said. "Just in case we don't have time to read."

Kitty put on a sly expression. "True confession," she began, "I read a couple pages of *Pride and Prejudice* today, but it was just too wordy for me so I googled it, hoping I'd find a summary, you know, so I could cheat. Well, I discovered it's a movie. I think Hugh Grant is in it. He's not too difficult to look at." She giggled. "So that's my backup plan. You know, in case I'm too busy at work . . . or whatever. I can spend an evening with Hugh Grant. Might not be as fun as *Notting Hill*, but it can't be as dry as the pages I read today. I hope you don't mind." She looked hopefully at Riva.

"I guess I don't mind . . . if you really can't manage the book. But spoiler alert, Hugh Grant isn't in *Pride and Prejudice*. He's in *Sense and Sensibility*."

Kitty frowned. "Hopefully there's a hottie in *Pride and Prejudice*."

"I know I brought it up, but isn't movie watching considered cheating?" Laurel asked.

"I don't know. It's not like we're making rules." Riva winked at Kitty. "But did I tell you there'll be a test?" They all laughed.

"Oh, man." Kitty rolled her eyes. "You academics kill me."

"Ever heard of CliffsNotes?" Marcus chuckled.

"Or maybe you and I can meet separate from the group," Laurel used a teasing tone with Marcus. "You fill me in on the Austen books you've read, and I'll attend group and pretend I read it."

This resulted in more laughs, and although Riva felt partly

amused, she was also exasperated at the resistance. Didn't Kitty and Laurel understand that reading was good for the mind? And why was Marcus catering to them like that? Or was Riva being too rigid here? Wasn't the goal to encourage her housemates to enjoy reading and books?

"I think Kitty and Laurel make a good point," she said. "Book group should be more about stories and the individual ways we interpret those stories. Whether that happens through film viewing or book reading shouldn't matter. I don't want to force people to read. It should be fun. I've imagined people gathered together to discuss how art imitates life and life imitates art . . . and all kinds of things. I want to hear how others relate to various story elements based on their individual experiences. That's what makes it fun."

"Well said." Marcus clapped.

"Here, here." Kitty lifted her wineglass. "Here's to book group being fun."

Although Riva believed what she'd just said, and she lifted her glass with the rest of them, she still felt a little uneasy about their book group, even if it was a few months away. But perhaps the uneasiness was about Kitty. The more Riva got to know this flamboyant, outspoken woman, the more she questioned how she could possibly fit into Riva's rather quiet life . . . and peaceful home. And, unless she was mistaken, Laurel was having similar concerns.

Chapter 12

As Riva and Laurel helped Windy clear the table and clean up, Fiona brought out musical instruments for some after-dinner entertainment. Marcus was strumming on guitar, trying to keep up with Fiona on the violin, and Kitty was using some kind of flat drum to accompany them.

"If discussing book group reminds Kitty of high school, then the musical trio out there reminds me of kindergarten marching band." Laurel's tone was cynical as she rinsed a serving platter.

"What do you two think of Kitty?" Windy asked quietly.

"She's different and lively." Riva tried to sound nonchalant.

"She seems like a free spirit. She could be fun," Windy added.

"I think she's opinionated and full of herself." Laurel dried the platter. "I'm sorry I recommended her to live here, Riva. I obviously didn't know her as well as I thought I did."

Riva didn't know how to respond. Instead, she pointed out the window where Kitty was dancing about and hitting the drum with her hand like an oversized tambourine. "Well, she definitely dances to a different drummer." Riva put the last of the leftover food in the fridge. "And speaking of that, we should probably go back out to enjoy our entertainment."

"You mean face the music?" Laurel threw down her dish towel.

Windy opened the window above the sink. "Hey, Fiona is really good. Listen to that, ladies. My feet are itching to do some dancing."

As Windy headed outside, Riva lingered in the kitchen with Laurel. "Are you going to be okay with Kitty?" she asked her old friend.

"Oh, sure." Laurel shrugged. "I've known women like her before. You just have to set boundaries and not let them push your buttons."

Riva wasn't really sure what that meant, but she nodded. "I just don't want all of us to get off on the wrong foot. House-sharing might be trickier than I imagined."

"Oh, I'm sure it will be." Laurel paused in front of a little mirror by the door, fluffing her hair and checking her teeth before going outside. Riva considered doing the same but didn't like seeing Laurel becoming slightly focused on her image. She never used to be that way. But Riva knew it was for Marcus and in a way it was cute. But it was also unnerving. Would her old buddy emerge unscathed from all the competition? Leave it to a man to stir things up like this.

As Riva joined the musical throng on the patio, she suddenly imagined Marcus as some kind of swarthy, chauvinistic sheik with a harem of women catering to him and dancing about to seek his approval.

"Come dance with me, Riva." Windy held out her hands with a wide smile.

"I'm not much of a dancer," Riva admitted. But Windy had her by the hand now and was leading her about, telling her what to do and how.

"You're doing great." Windy swung her around, nearly making her tumble.

"Until I fall on my face." Riva laughed. "But I'll admit, it's fun."

"I can teach y'all how to line dance." Kitty set down her drum. "But we need the right kind of music." She told Fiona to play something more upbeat. "And, Marcus, you won't be able to keep up on that guitar so put it down and join in the lesson." She winked at Marcus. "There might be a test later."

Before long, they were all attempting to line dance to Fiona's fiddle music. And although Riva was having fun, she felt a growing aggravation inside of her. She couldn't fully grasp what it was about. Sure, Kitty was a bit irritating and Laurel wasn't being herself. But all in all, they were having fun, and Fiona's music was delightful. Finally, she couldn't contain whatever was going on inside and had to excuse herself from the group.

As she went into the house, she hoped they'd assume she was off to powder her nose, but she had no intention of going back outside tonight. Something inside of her felt seriously off, almost on the verge of anger. But what did she have to be angry about? Behind the closed door of her bedroom, she kicked off her sandals and listed all the good things that had come her way this past week.

She had enough money from her renters to pay both her taxes and insurance right now. That alone should make her want to dance. Plus, she had some very interesting housemates to liven up her otherwise drab world. Her house had gotten fixed up a bit by her new tenants. Thanks to them, her backyard was functional and getting better each day. Even tonight, the space looked more festive since someone had strung paper lanterns through the trees. She stuck another finger up when she remembered that Windy had fixed a delicious dinner for them. Despite their differences, they'd even managed to organize her book group. And right now, everyone was out there having a very good time. What was wrong with her?

She sat down in the chair by her bed, picking up a wedding photo she kept on her bedside table. She just stared at it. They'd been so young and innocent back then, vowing their love to last until death parted them, figuring they'd be about a hundred by then. But they vowed again, after Paul got sick, that their love would last throughout eternity. She remembered the times he'd say those words. Weakened by the brutal illness and useless treatments, numbed by pain pills, walking the fine line between living and dying, he would hold her hand and say, "I'll love you forever."

She would always echo those words back to him. How could she not? She would absolutely love him forever! But she suspected that loving someone was easier from up there than from this side of eternity. Not that she fully knew what *up there* really meant. But she did believe in an afterlife. She believed in a God who loved them so much that he'd prepared a beyond-imagination beautiful place for them.

But sometimes, down here in dirty earth shoes, she felt disillusioned and not very loving toward herself or anyone. At the moment, she felt left out and left behind and sad. Similar to when she'd had measles in second grade and missed out on her class field trip to the zoo—times about a thousand! And she couldn't imagine that Paul could feel like that up in heaven. He was probably having a fabulous time. She should be happy for him instead of having a pity party for one down here.

She'd experienced something of a vision not long after Paul's death. It had come in a flash one night. It was this amazing image of him all healed and whole. He seemed better than he'd ever been on earth, even in youth. He appeared strong and wonderful, actually glowing. And with wide open arms, she knew he'd be there to welcome her home . . . when her time came. It had been heartwarming and unspeakably sweet. But tonight Paul felt so far away, and she just flat-out missed him. And it all felt so unfair.

Perhaps that's what had made her angry. Her husband was missing . . . meanwhile everyone was having such fun in his backyard. She wanted to have Paul right there with her and felt unable to enjoy herself without him.

But he was gone.

She remembered the stages of grief that they'd talked about at the grief group and the way she couldn't relate to ever feeling angry. Well, that's exactly how she felt now. Not a raging fury but a slow burn that stole any happiness she might've experienced tonight. To enjoy an evening of food and music and dancing in Paul's favorite place—without him there—had just felt wrong. And she supposed she'd even felt guilty. And that had made her mad . . . angry even.

Even so, it didn't really make sense. After all, Paul was up there dancing in heaven. Isn't that what everyone told her after he passed? So why shouldn't she be dancing down here? Except that she just did not feel like it. Not anymore. Perhaps she never would. And she doubted that anyone or anything could change that in her.

She laid the wedding photo face down on the bed and clenched her fists. "Oh, Paul!" She felt hot tears pour down as she stood. "Why did you have to go so soon? Why aren't you here with me? Why am I left alone and broken?" Pacing back and forth in her bedroom, she felt guilty to think of the party going on out there. She was being a neglectful hostess. But it wasn't her party. Not really. Windy was the cook. And the other housemates could play host. Riva locked her bedroom door, silenced her phone, and flopped onto her bed with a choked sob. Why was this still so hard? It had been almost eighteen months, and she felt just as miserable as she had that cold December day when Paul had slipped away.

Lying on her back, tears still streaming down the sides of her cheeks, she stared up at the slowly turning ceiling fan overhead, watching it go round and round with blurry eyes.

"I still love you, darling," she finally whispered. "I will love you forever . . . but right now I feel like I'll miss you forever too." Then, without getting back up to brush her teeth, wash her face, or even change into pajamas, she closed her eyes . . . and cried herself to sleep.

Chapter 13

Although Riva felt better in the morning, she still felt a little off-balance. It was barely six, and the house sounded quiet when she tiptoed out. As she walked through her house, everything appeared to be in order, including her kitchen. It was all spotless, and suddenly it felt a little surreal. Like last night never happened, or maybe it was that life had gone on without her. Like maybe she hadn't even been missed.

She quietly made coffee, then carried a steaming mug outside to see if everything was in order out there as well. It all appeared tidy and picked up. Even the tables had been wiped down. Well, at least she had responsible housemates. Hopefully they weren't too offended by her mysterious absence. Or perhaps they were having so much fun, they really didn't miss her.

"Good morning." Riva startled to see Windy, wearing a floral nightgown, coming outside with a coffee mug. "Do you want to be alone?"

"No, not at all." Riva set down her mug and moved a lounge chair to catch the morning sunshine. "Pull up a seat if you'd like."

After they were both situated in the sun, Riva mentioned how clean everything was—even the yard.

"Well, I suspected you weren't feeling too well last night, so I wanted to be sure it was all cleaned up before morning."

"Thank you."

"It was my pleasure. Really." Windy sighed. "It's so lovely being in a home like this. I can't thank you enough for letting me rent your attic."

"You're still happy up there?"

"It's like a slice of heaven."

Riva frowned. "I was thinking a lot about heaven last night. To be honest, I don't know what to expect when we get there."

"But you do believe you'll get there?"

"God willing and the creek don't rise." Riva attempted a smile. "Yes, I do believe I'll get there. Last night I hoped it would be sooner rather than later." She looked intently at Windy. "You told me a bit about losing your husband. I'm sorry. I forgot his name."

"Bill."

"Yes. And I know it was a traumatic death with the car wreck and all. Can you remind me how long since he died, Windy?"

"Almost seven years."

"Please tell me, it does get better, right?"

"Of course. But it takes time. And it's different with everyone." Windy sipped her coffee. "My first year was a nightmare. I cried all the time. And then dealing with everything, selling off the real estate business, paying overdue taxes, dealing with lawyers . . . It was all so exhausting. I felt like I was barely keeping my head above water and then I found out about all the debt Bill had never told me about. I lost the house and my daughter moved across the country—so, well, my second year wasn't much better."

"Oh, my. I'm so sorry. I probably shouldn't have even asked."

"I don't mind." She brightened. "I'm so much better now. After I lost everything, it turned out to be the best thing ever."

"Seriously?"

"Yes. I felt so free. Oh, I admit living in that awful apartment wasn't so great. I missed my house and my garden. But I was determined to move on. I returned to my hippie roots and shopped thrift stores and bought houseplants and tried to fix up the apartment. It was okay at first. I got hired part-time in the Hummingbird Gallery, which was wonderfully therapeutic."

"I didn't know you worked there. I love that gallery."

"I quit after Bill's social security kicked in for me. I wasn't quite so destitute, but I still volunteer there sometimes just for the fun of it. Having those monthly checks gives me a bit more freedom. Of course, I still dream my ship will come in and the lawsuit about the accident will pay off, but the insurance company keeps going back into appeals and God only knows how much my lawyers will take if it ever gets settled. And I'm okay with that." She smiled. "I really am."

"How long did it take until you felt really happy again? I mean, you seem to be genuinely happy now." Riva felt almost envious.

"For the most part, I am happy, but I still miss Bill at times. Usually it's when I'm alone in the middle of the night, or if I hear a certain song. In those moments, it's not painful like it used to be. It just brings forth an old longing, more like nostalgia than grief. Bill wasn't perfect by any means, but he did love me, he was a good father, and he tried to be a good provider. I just wish he hadn't overextended his investments." She sipped her coffee. "But on the other hand, if he'd been better with money and I still had my house, well, I wouldn't feel as free as I do now." She grimaced. "I hope I didn't overshare. I've been told I do that sometimes."

"Not at all. It was good to hear. Kind of like being in a mini grief group."

"So, was that what happened to you last night?"

Since Windy had been so forthcoming, Riva shared about her own dark night of the soul. "I had a good cry and actually feel pretty good today. Although I don't really feel happy. I think what caught me most by surprise was the anger. That's a stage of grief that I missed . . . or skipped. But it sure did hit me last night. I got so mad at myself—and at life in general—because I couldn't enjoy the party."

"I remember feeling like that." Windy told Riva about a time when she'd been invited to meet friends at the coast. "Bev and Larry had rented a beach cottage. I hadn't been over there since before losing Bill, but it had been almost two years by then and I thought I was okay. Well, something triggered me, maybe it was seeing Bev and Larry together, or thinking how Bill had loved the ocean, I'm not sure. But I fell apart and ended up leaving my friends a note and driving back home in the middle of the night."

Riva felt both comforted and worried. "I wonder how long it'll take to get past this . . ."

"Past what?"

They both jumped to see Kitty had slipped out there unnoticed. Dressed in striped pajama shorts and a pink T-shirt, she looked rumpled but pretty.

"Good morning, girls," she said cheerfully. "Am I interrupting?"

"Not at all. We're just swapping sob stories." Riva tried to sound light.

"Sob stories?" Kitty pulled a chair over and sat down with a curious expression. "Sounds depressing."

"Riva had a rough time last night," Windy explained. "Her husband has been gone just over a year."

"Almost eighteen months," Riva supplied.

"That's why you left the party?" Kitty's brow creased as she slid an emery board out of her T-shirt pocket. "That seems silly."

"I know it sounds silly, but something just got to me and I guess I needed some alone time." Riva didn't really want to go into it again. Not with Kitty, anyway. She didn't get a safe sense of empathy from the woman. Maybe she just needed to know her better.

"Oh, I get that." Kitty frowned at a perfectly manicured thumbnail. "When I lost my Danny, I was a hot mess. I cried for weeks."

"Was Danny your husband?"

"Yes, my first husband. The second husband was the jerk."

"And Danny passed?" Windy put a hand on Kitty's shoulder. "I'm sorry. How long has it been?"

"Oh, Danny didn't die. We just split up. But that was after I gave him almost twenty of my best years. Later on, when I considered going back, he'd already taken up with a twentysomething bimbo who only wanted a sugar daddy. She didn't even stay with him for a year. I think it's because he was drinking like a fish by then. But I was glad about that."

Riva was confused. "Glad that he was drinking?"

"No. Glad that the bimbo left him high and dry." Kitty began to smooth out the edge of another hot-pink nail.

"Oh?" Windy glanced at Riva.

"Our breakup was probably for the best anyway," Kitty said lightly. "Of course, I didn't think so at first. After all, Danny came from a wealthy family. And it was nice not having to go to work or worry about money. Fortunately, my divorce settlement was enough to buy my salon and set me up. And it allowed me to have some fun." She checked her nail, then filed a bit more.

"How long ago did you and Danny break up?" Riva asked.

"It's been close to ten years now. About the same as Laurel. She and I were comparing notes last night. We have a similar story." She laughed. "Well, similar but different. Laurel's divorce settlement was pathetic. I don't know how she even got by."

Riva bristled. "Laurel's had a hard go of it."

"You can tell just by looking at her." Kitty nodded knowingly. "A drab woman like that who's let herself go . . . even when she comes into my salon, she always insists on just a haircut, nothing else. I keep trying to talk her into highlights and layering, but she just laughs. Poor thing."

"Laurel isn't one to fuss over her appearance," Windy said, clearly defensive of her friend.

"Obviously." Kitty set down the emery board. "Good grief, her face alone speaks volumes on that."

"Her face?" Riva studied Kitty more closely. She'd been trying to calculate the woman's age. Based on the information they'd just been given, Kitty wasn't much younger, but her blond mane was thick and her flawless skin looked so youthful, it was hard to tell.

"Not only her face," Kitty clarified, "her drab hair, pudgy figure, boring clothing. Well, it all tells me this is a woman who's pretty much given up on life."

"Oh, I don't think that she's given up on life," Riva said. "Whatever happened to growing old gracefully?"

"I guess that's okay if you want to look like Grandma and live alone with your cat. But it's not for me."

"I think you're being a little hard on Laurel." Riva worked to control her tone. "There's a lot more to her than that."

"I agree," Windy chimed in. "And if anything, I've seen her making a comeback since moving into Riva's house. She's got a new interest in life, and it hasn't hurt her to become friends with my brother. Amazing how the right man can bring a woman back to life." She glanced at Riva. "Don't you agree?"

"Yes, I think Laurel's doing better than ever."

"Someone should tell her face." Kitty laughed.

Riva stifled the urge to punch this woman or change her name to Catty. "What would you suggest she do with her face?" she asked Kitty through gritted teeth.

"Hmm. Good question. If she came into my salon and gave me creative freedom, I'd encourage her to get a good facial with an aesthetician, for starters. See if there's anything she can do about those deep wrinkles. Maybe some Botox. Although the best resort is plastic surgery. It's spendy, but with the right surgeon, well worth it." She patted a cheek. "I've had everything done." She pushed her already full lips into a pout. "Which is one reason I ran through my divorce settlement and found myself hard up for cash."

"What about alimony?" Riva asked.

"That sort of ended with my second marriage. What a piece of work that guy was."

"And that marriage is over too?" Windy's brow creased.

"It was over before it began." She looked at Riva. "I told you I have bad luck with men."

"Lydia in *Pride and Prejudice*," Riva whispered to Windy.

Windy nodded. "Are you involved with anyone now?" she asked Kitty.

"Not to speak of. Oh, Lance still comes around." Kitty turned to Riva. "Total deadbeat, thinks he can bully money out of me."

"Do you have any children?" Windy asked.

"Thank God, no. Wouldn't that be a disaster?" She stood, patting her trim waistline. "Otherwise I'd probably have a pouch. I've seen other women my age who were moms. Everything just sags." She fluffed her hair.

"Well, I wouldn't trade my children for no sags," Windy declared.

"My children are worth it too." Riva felt the need to count to ten before she decked her new housemate, wondering how hard it would be to break the rental contract.

"Well, I didn't mean to put down your kiddos, but at this stage of the game, I think it's important to look our best. Don't you gals think so too?" She scrutinized them for a moment, then smiled. "You both look pretty good . . . considering."

Riva wondered what Kitty would say about them if they weren't listening but kept quiet. It was amazing how much more you could learn about people if you kept your mouth shut and observed.

"Thanks, I guess. But at this age, appearances are way less important to me than they once were." There was a sharp edge to Windy's tone. "I try to focus on things that matter more to me. Like living my best life, having good friends, being happy."

"Oh, yeah, I totally agree with that," Kitty said quickly. "I just happen to think my chances of getting all that are better when I look my best." She pointed at Riva. "Yesterday you gave me that little pep talk. You told me I was attracting the wrong men. It was hard to hear, but I think you're right." She turned back to Windy. "Can you believe our little house mother actually called me a jerk magnet?" She threw back her head and laughed.

Windy looked dumbfounded and Riva felt irritated. Really, did Kitty think of her as the house mother?

"Anyway, I'm taking your advice, Riva. And I must say, unless I'm wrong, your big brother won't fall into the jerk category, Windy."

"Marcus is definitely not a jerk," Windy said.

"That's exactly what I thought. He seems to be a perfectly marvelous man." Kitty's eyes sparkled in the sunlight. "He's interesting and fun-loving and seems to know a little something about everything. He can even dance." She grinned at Windy. "He is quite a find."

Windy nodded with a dubious expression.

Kitty checked her phone. "And if I'm going to meet up with him today, I better get showered and dressed."

"You have a date with Marcus?" Windy asked.

"Not yet." Kitty laughed. "But hey, the day is young."

After she left, Windy and Riva exchanged glances, but Riva felt tongue-tied and torn. Had she made a mistake in letting Kitty rent a room in her house? Or was she just being judgmental now? "I, uh, I don't know what to say," she finally muttered.

"You and me both."

"I, um, sure hope Kitty fits in here."

Windy released a loud sigh. "Me too."

"Do you think this thing with her and Marcus will get serious?" Riva felt rising concern for Marcus now. Like they'd put him in an awkward position.

"I wasn't going to say anything, but you might want to hear what happened after you went to bed last night."

"Something happened?"

"I suppose I was sort of on hyperalert. Kitty was obviously putting the moves on Marcus. But I know my brother. He's used to that. After all, he's good-looking and genuinely nice and a bachelor. A lot of women think he's a good catch. Not that he ever gets caught. To be honest, I think he kinda enjoys the attention."

"A confirmed bachelor?"

"I used to think so, but he's softened up some with age. But I also know he's got discerning taste."

"Right." Riva tried not to look as interested as she felt. "So, what happened last night?"

"Well, as you know, Laurel has already expressed her interest in Marcus. And Marcus has been polite and friendly to her. Just like he is with everyone. Including Kitty. Anyway, Laurel's not dumb. She could see Kitty moving in on her territory last night. And believe me, there were some awkward moments after you left. Kitty's social skills are, at best, interesting."

"You can't say she lacks confidence."

"She does seem to love herself." Windy's nose wrinkled. "Well, as you just saw, she's not very careful with her words, and she seems oblivious when she offends someone. After last night, I think we can assume Laurel will be looking for a new hairdresser."

"Well, that's not such a big deal." Riva shrugged. "I thought maybe something really went awry."

"Depends on your perspective. It bothered me to see Kitty tweaking Laurel. It made me uncomfortable. So I started to clean up, and Fiona stopped playing music to help me. I think she felt uncomfortable too. We were trying to give the gentle hint, as in the party's over."

"Uh-huh?"

"After Fiona and I went inside, Marcus picked up the guitar again. His adoring audience of two was watching, and I'm not sure what happened, but the next thing we knew, Laurel stormed into the kitchen, slamming the door so loud behind her, I thought it would shatter. Then she called Kitty a bad name, not that Kitty could hear her, but I won't repeat what she said. And then she stomped up the stairs."

"Oh dear." Riva didn't like the sound of this.

"I know. Awkward. Not long after that, Marcus came in, said his goodbyes, and went home."

"What did Kitty do?"

"She was all chipper and cheerful. Just like this morning. She happily headed off to bed." Windy paused, glancing around. "So Fiona gathered up her instruments, and I went upstairs. On my way up, I could hear Laurel and Kitty talking. They were sort of arguing about past bad relationships, like who had the worst of it. Kitty pointed out how Marcus was different, and Laurel started getting louder. I was about to go up and interrupt them, you know, before it got too out of control." She paused to sip her coffee and perhaps catch her breath.

"And?" Riva waited impatiently for the rest of the story.

"It sounded like Laurel was trying to calm down and act mature, so I thought I should wait a bit and let them work things out. But then Kitty started to taunt poor Laurel. It was similar to what she just said to us, telling Laurel to get Botox or see a plastic surgeon. She told Laurel if she fixed herself up enough, she might trap a man. But not Marcus. That's exactly what she said."

Riva closed her eyes, shaking her head. "You gotta be kidding."

"I wish. About then Fiona came up the stairs. She had all her instruments, and I was trying to clue her in and lighten her load, but I dropped the drum, and they heard us upstairs. Laurel called Kitty another bad name and another door slammed. We went on up, and Kitty met us on the landing, looking like sugar wouldn't melt in her mouth. She gushed about the food and the music and thanked us for a wonderful evening. She said she loved living here, then she hugged us both good night."

Riva's eyes popped open. "Oh my." She could imagine Kitty wanting to make alliances within the household for her own purposes. "This is a little unsettling."

"Yeah. Kitty's a smooth operator."

"I feel sorry for Laurel."

"Me too." Windy shook her head. "I can sort of understand Kitty thinking the way she does. After all, she works in the beauty industry. Her whole livelihood is about appearances. So much so that she can't see what really matters."

"I'd hoped reading *Pride and Prejudice* might help." Riva grimaced. "But she may be too far gone for that."

"I still can't believe Laurel was the one who wanted Kitty to live here."

"Poor Laurel. She wanted us to be the new Golden Girls, but it looks like Kitty's got something more like Charlie's Angels in mind."

"Yeah, and she's Farrah Fawcett."

"And she'd probably like one less angel around here."

Chapter 14

To Riva's relief the next two days passed quietly. Laurel's nose was definitely out of joint over Kitty, but with Kitty being gone at work during the day, Laurel seemed to get over it. Or else she focused her angst on creating order. Concerned about housemates using their own foods, she decided to organize the fridge, labeling spaces to keep things separated. "I hope you don't mind," she told Riva as they were fixing breakfast Thursday morning. "But after some of my yogurts went missing, I thought it was necessary." She frowned. "And I'm pretty sure I know who took them."

"I think this is a great idea." Riva removed her own carton of orange juice and filled a glass. "Thanks for doing it. You're so good at organization."

"Hard to forget all those years of keeping the middle school office and most of the faculty on the same page."

"Well, I appreciate it." Riva closed the fridge. "Five women living together might be a bigger challenge than we expected."

"How are you feeling about it all?" Laurel refilled her coffee mug. "Having second thoughts?"

"Honestly?" Riva sat down on an island stool and sipped her juice.

"Yeah, honestly. Do you wish you hadn't opened your home up like this?"

"I'm torn. Of course, I'm relieved to be able to keep my house, but I'm also concerned about the, uh, mix of personalities."

"Specifically Kitty and me?"

"Oh, Laurel. I love you. I've known you for so long. I'm glad you're living here." She took another swig of juice.

Laurel's brows arched. "But you'd like to kick Kitty to the curb?"

Riva chuckled. "Not exactly."

"Well, I wouldn't mind . . ."

"Let's just be thankful she has the salon to keep her busy during the day."

Laurel winked. "Believe me, I am."

"Having Fiona and Kitty working does make the house quieter during the day . . . I do appreciate that." Riva finished her juice and rinsed her glass. "I can't imagine how it would be if all five of us were all in the house day in and day out. That's probably the only reason I'm not having serious second thoughts about this."

"I'm curious. If you needed to kick someone out, would you be tough enough to do that?"

"Kick someone out?"

"You know, for breaking rules, not abiding by the contract."

Riva considered this. "Well, it would be tricky. I mean, it's a legal contract, but I know that landlord-tenant disputes can get messy."

"So, what would you do?"

Riva thought about it for a moment. "I suppose I'd try to reason with the tenant. If necessary, I'd consult an attorney." She grimaced. "But I sure hope it never comes to that." She put her glass in the dishwasher, then turned to Laurel. "Are you thinking about Kitty?"

"Well, she does seem like a misfit here." Laurel frowned. "I really blame myself for recommending her. I realize now that Kitty the salon owner is a whole different person than Kitty the roommate. Not only that, but I'm also sure she's scared off Marcus."

"What makes you think that?"

"Have you seen him since our last dinner party?"

"No . . . but it's only been a couple days. I'm sure he's got better things to do with his time than hang out here."

Laurel crossed her arms over her chest. "Windy told me he's laying low on purpose. Doesn't want to rock our boat."

"I can appreciate that. Our boat's already rocky enough." Riva studied Laurel. "So how are you doing? I know you and Kitty are at odds. But are you okay?"

Laurel leaned against the counter. "I guess so. I've been thinking a lot about how Kitty and I have had similar luck with men and how we are both attracted to the same guy. To be honest, it's hard to admit I have anything in common with that woman. But we're not the same."

"No, of course not."

"After my divorce, I learned to push men aside, decided I didn't need one. Kitty's not like that. She needs male attention and seems willing to get it at any cost. I just don't like her setting her sights on Marcus. He's too good for her." Laurel pounded a fist into her palm. "But he's too nice to tell her to take a hike."

"But you're not," Riva teased.

"That's true. But I am determined not to engage with that woman. It'll take some real self-control, but I plan to keep my mouth shut."

"Good for you." Riva patted her on the back. "I don't like to judge anyone, but it's my observation that, whether it's intentional or just habit, Kitty is very good at pushing buttons."

"Narcissists usually are."

"Narcissists?"

Laurel nodded. "I noticed some books in your library about narcissism."

"Oh, yes, I remember Paul researched that for a client a few years before he passed. I read some on the subject too."

"Well, I started to read one book and you know what I think?"

"What?" Riva asked nervously.

"Kitty sounds like a classic narcissist."

Riva considered this. "That's a pretty difficult personality type . . . hard to live with."

"I'll say."

"But I can't kick out a tenant for having a difficult personality type."

"Obviously."

"Is reading the book helping you? I mean, to deal with Kitty?"

Laurel shrugged. "My plan is to avoid Kitty, not deal with her. But I suppose the book is helping me to understand her a little better. And there are some tools we can use."

"Such as?"

"Right now, I'm focused on distancing and diversion."

"I get distancing. How does diversion work?"

"For one thing a narcissist loves attention and compliments. So next time Kitty goes after me, I'll try to divert her by feeding her ego."

"Interesting." Riva wasn't so sure. Kitty might be shallow, but she wasn't stupid.

"Also, we need to put up boundaries for her."

Riva was confused. "What kind of boundaries?"

"Personal boundaries. According to the book I'm reading, you have to step away from them, not let them get to you." Laurel looked determined.

"Do you think that really works?" Riva studied her friend. "When emotions run high, some people have difficulty stepping away."

"That's probably true, but we need some tools. And from what I've learned from that book, and from this experience, narcissists are not easy to live with." She reached across the counter for her mug. "And since we can't kick her out, I guess I'll need to learn how to survive, preferably with my sanity still intact."

"Sounds like a good plan." Riva smiled. "I admire how you're taking the high road on this."

"Better than running." Laurel grimaced as she put her mug in the dishwasher. "I've decided I won't let her drive me out, Riva." She removed a can of cat food from her shelf in the pantry. "If you'll excuse me, Fred is waiting for his breakfast."

"Give Fred my regards." Riva filled her coffee mug, then went outside where she spotted Windy working in the backyard. "You're at it early." She went over to see what Windy was doing with the raised bed.

"I'm transplanting these seedlings." Windy pointed out the tomatoes, beans, cucumbers, and squash. "I'd been babying them inside, but all threat of frost is gone, and it was time to get them into the ground."

"Looks like you've got your work cut out for you."

Windy nodded, wiping the sweat from her forehead with the back of her arm. "I saw you talking to Laurel. How's she doing?"

Riva told her about Laurel's research into narcissism and Windy just laughed. "Leave it to Laurel to want to figure this all out. I doubt it'll be that simple."

"I know." Riva sat on the edge of the raised bed. "Laurel thinks Kitty has scared Marcus off from visiting here. Do you think that's true?"

"He did mention something like that to me. But he's not scared. Just being cautious. I suggested he bring a friend or two next time he comes to dinner. I mean a male friend. And mostly for Kitty's sake. Give her someone besides Marcus to zero in on."

"Do you think he'd do that? Bring friends?" Riva tugged a stray weed out.

Windy held out the bucket of yard waste toward her. "He said he'd think about it."

"Not that we need to have lots of dinner parties."

"I enjoy having a table full of guests. It makes cooking even more fun, but if you're not comfortable with—"

"No, no . . . I'm okay. I just don't want it to be too much work for you . . ."

"Or for a fun evening to evolve into a knockdown drag-out brawl between Kitty and Laurel." Windy reached for a spade. "We could become the local WWE."

"Sounds entertaining."

"We could sell tickets." Windy chuckled as she dug a hole.

"I guess another dinner party might be a good test for Laurel's new theories about living peacefully with a narcissist."

"Good point. So do you mind if I plan another get together for Saturday night? I've been thinking about seafood."

"Sounds good."

"Maybe Marcus will dig up some available bachelors by then. We could tell Fiona to invite her guy friend from her band if she likes as well. The more, the merrier."

"I hope you're right." Riva made a stiff smile. She didn't think it sounded that good, especially after her awkward exodus at their last gathering, but if Laurel could face another social evening, Riva figured she should at least try. "Let me know if I can get anything or do anything to help," she told Windy. "We shouldn't leave it all on you."

"Laurel already offered to help delegate tasks, including the shopping. You know how she loves charts and assignments. If you're not careful, she'll take over the whole house."

"I'm not sure I mind." Riva felt somewhat relieved. "Despite what Kitty said, I don't plan on playing the house mother." She wrinkled her nose.

"And you shouldn't have to."

"Right." Riva stood. "Happy gardening."

Windy set down the spade and reached for a seedling packet. "Hey, are you going to the grief group today?"

Riva considered this. "I, uh, I don't know. I hadn't really thought about it." The truth was she had never planned to return to the group, had felt she didn't need it.

"I just thought after that rough night of feeling shook up by your anger . . . well, it might be helpful. I heard there's a special guest speaker today. I'm not sure what the topic is, but it might be good."

"Are you going?"

Windy stretched, reaching her hands upward. "I think gardening is more therapeutic for me at this stage of the game, but if you want someone to go with you, I could—"

"No, no, that's okay." Riva shook her head. She didn't need handholding. "I'm not sure it'll do me any good, but it probably won't hurt. Besides, I don't have anything else planned."

"I think my car has you blocked in, but I can move it."

"Don't bother. It's such a gorgeous day. I'll walk." Riva figured she could walk down the hill extra slow, be late to the meeting, "not want to interrupt," and then continue into town for a cup of coffee.

When Riva got to the library, the doors to the meeting room were closed and, for a moment, she just stood there, trying to decide whether to wimp out or go in.

"Let me get that." A hand reached past her, opening the door. She turned to see Marcus, grinning like the cat who caught the canary. "After you," he said quietly.

Feeling trapped, she went in ahead of him. Today the chairs were arranged in rows, which felt a bit less intimidating. She took a seat in the back and Marcus sat next to her. As she settled in, she caught random phrases from the middle-aged woman in a business suit at the front.

". . . compassionate comfort . . . the right to a peaceful end-of-life experience . . . educate loved ones . . ." The woman continued talking, but Riva's mind was on alert.

She glanced at Marcus. His jawline looked stiff, and his brow furrowed. Was he as confused as she was? Wasn't this supposed to be a grief group? It felt like a class on assisted suicide. She fidgeted with her purse, removing her phone, and wondering if she could feign an urgent message that forced her to leave early. Or did she need an excuse? Why not just walk out? After all, she was a free agent. She glanced toward the closed door. As a man up front asked the speaker a complicated question, she stood and made a beeline for the door.

Feeling breathless and somewhat claustrophobic, she exited the meeting room and practically sprinted from the library. Outside, in the clean fresh air, she walked quickly, or maybe she ran, about a block before she stopped by a concrete bench and sat down, inhaling a steadying breath. What was wrong with her? She was well-aware that assisted suicide was perfectly legal in Oregon, but it had never been a topic she'd felt the need to delve into. And, really, she didn't see how being educated on it could possibly help her move past her own grief. If anything, it just made her feel worse.

"There you are." Marcus stood over her. "Are you okay?"

She forced a wimpy smile. "Yes, yes, I'm fine. I just decided I didn't want to be there."

"Was it the topic?" He sat down next to her.

"Probably . . . I don't know. I don't think I wanted to be there in the first place. Honestly, I don't see what today's topic has to do with me. I thought this was supposed to be a grief group. I didn't expect for some expert to stand up there and tell me how to die or how to let someone else die." She felt tears stinging. "Been there, done that."

"Uh-huh." He rubbed his chin. "And yet it must've pushed an emotional button with you."

She looked at him with blurry eyes. "Well, maybe it did. I don't know. I guess I'm not as far along in my grief as I think I should be. It's been eighteen months, and I feel like I should be almost done by now."

"I'm not sure we ever get done." He sighed. "It's been six years for me, and I'm still dealing with it."

"You are?"

"Sure."

"You really loved Anne, didn't you?"

He hesitated. "I did . . ."

She was confused. "What happened?"

"It all just sort of changed."

"Sorry, I shouldn't have asked."

"No, I don't mind. I thought I was going to grief therapy today too. Windy had encouraged me to go. I'm not even sure why."

"She encouraged me too . . . told me there was a speaker . . ."

"To be honest, it kind of pushed my emotional buttons too." He pursed his lips and looked toward the sky. "Anne actually mentioned something like this once. She knew it was legal in Oregon, and she confessed to wanting to exit her life."

"Oh?" Riva studied him, trying to determine how much she should react.

"I know she was trying to come to grips with her illness and wanted to escape it. I didn't agree though. I've always believed that God gives us our earthly lives and that we should wait for him to take us home in his timing, not ours."

"That's what I believe too."

He nodded. "I suspected as much. But Anne always lived life on her own terms." He let out a troubled sigh. "Sorry, that's another story."

"Were you with her when she passed?"

He shook his head grimly.

"Did that make it harder for you?"

"To be honest, I'm not sure. It's . . . complicated. And like I said, it's kind of a long story." He looked directly at her with sad eyes. "One I've never fully told. Not even to Windy."

"If you need to talk"—she placed a hand on his forearm—"I'm listening." For a long time, they both just sat there. Riva was worried that her offer had been intrusive. She knew stories about losing a spouse were personal and intimate, and she barely knew Marcus. What right did she have to his story? She was about to backpedal and apologize for being nosy when he began to speak.

Chapter 15

Riva listened closely as Marcus shared. He explained how he was close to forty by the time he was discharged from the Air Force and done with college. He met Anne shortly after starting his first teaching job at a local middle school. "Anne was an administrative aide there. But she didn't really like working with teenagers. Maybe because she wasn't that much older than they were. I actually thought she was a student at first." He paused to smile at a couple walking by with two small children.

"I think I was drawn to her youthful free spirit, although I'll admit her beauty pulled me in too. I couldn't believe someone like her was interested in an old codger like me. At first I thought it was because I'd encouraged her to finish her degree and become a kindergarten teacher. But then we got married and I helped her to actually do it." He cleared his throat. "But after nearly fifteen years of what I thought was a happy marriage, Anne got really restless. She called it her midlife crisis . . . and at the same time I was actually considering an early retirement and travel. Anyway, Anne was done with teaching, done with marriage, done with me, it seemed. She left me to spread her wings. I assumed that was the end of our marriage and that she would file for divorce.

But she didn't. I was pretty miserable. Then, not even a year later, she got a diagnosis for leukemia . . ."

"Oh, wow."

"She was still on my health insurance and begged me to take her back so she could get treatment. Of course, I welcomed her back. She apologized for hurting me and was very grateful for my help. We got her the best medical treatments available. She wanted to survive, but she hated how the chemo and radiation made her lose her hair and feel so sick. And who could blame her? After more than a year, her cancer was winning. Anne was worn out and fed up. That's when she brought up the idea . . . of physician-assisted suicide. I was not onboard and I told her so."

Riva nodded. "Sort of like what the speaker just said about family members' objections and why it needs to be the patient's right to decide?"

"Uh-huh. I guess those words struck a bad chord with me. Like you, I don't want to judge anyone. And I didn't want to impose my standards on Anne, but I wasn't ready to condone it. I was mostly just confused. Anne was going downhill fast that spring and when school let out for summer break, I assured her I would devote my whole summer to caring for her. And I did. I worked with hospice to monitor her care, to keep her out of pain. I did all the housekeeping, shopping, laundry . . . everything. I made her special smoothies and did whatever I could to help her. But she wasn't getting better. Then one day, after the hospice nurse arrived to help her bathe, Anne handed me a detailed list for the grocery store. I should've been suspicious since she had no appetite, but her favorite foods were on the list so I thought maybe she was rallying. By the time I got home, Anne was gone. The nurse was still there, explaining how Anne had died peacefully. That helped some, but I felt so let down. It felt like Anne had intentionally sent me out of the house because she knew she was dying. And that really hurt." His eyes were filled with tears now.

"Oh, Marcus, I'm so sorry. That must've been so hard on you.

But maybe it was her way of sparing you that pain of seeing her . . . go." Riva remembered her own last day with Paul. "It's not easy."

"Yes, I'm sure you're right. But after all I'd done, taking Anne back and caring for her, I just felt sort of tricked. I know that must sound selfish, but the truth is, I was a mess. I was even pretty angry for a while." Tears trickled down his tanned cheeks, and Riva didn't know what to say or do. So she hugged him. He held tightly to her, and they embraced for a long moment. She could feel his sobs, or were they her own? It was hard to tell. Finally, she felt him relax, and she released her hold on him and sat back.

"Are we having our own mini grief group here?" she asked as she fished a couple fresh tissues from her walking purse, sharing one with him. "I came prepared."

"Thanks." He blew his nose. "And thanks for listening."

"I'm so sorry for all you went through," she said.

"Thanks." He blew out a deep breath. "I never told anyone all that before."

"I can understand how today's topic would stir up old feelings."

"Especially unresolved ones."

"Are they unresolved?" she asked.

He paused for a moment before answering. "I'm not sure. I suppose I thought they were. Good grief, it'll be six years next month. But I think what still bothers me is that I can't remember if I ever told Anne that I forgave her."

"For leaving you?"

"Yeah, and to be honest, I'm not sure I had forgiven her at that time. I mean, when she died I think I was still working on it. Have you heard the quote that it's easier to forgive an enemy than a friend?"

She nodded. "Probably even more true with a spouse who hurt you."

"I know. But I still feel bad to think she left this world with my unforgiveness weighing on her."

"But she must've known, Marcus. I mean, you took her back,

you took care of her. If actions speak louder than words, she'd have to have known."

"Maybe so. But if I'd only known she was about to go, if she hadn't sent me out with that list, maybe I'd have been there and I could have told her . . . before it was too late."

"Maybe you still can. Why can't you tell her now?"

"Now?"

"Yeah. A friend sent me a poem after Paul passed." She pulled out her phone. "I keep it in my notes to read sometimes. I haven't read it recently. I guess maybe I should." She pulled it up.

"Want to read it now?" he asked.

She looked at him. "Do you want to hear it?"

"Please."

"It's called 'Death Is Nothing at All' by Henry Scott-Holland." She started to read. "'Death is nothing at all. It does not count. I have only slipped away into the next room. Nothing has happened.'" She continued with a part about speaking to the departed in the same way, saying their name without solemnity or sorrow and enjoying the jokes they once shared. And finally, she read the last line. "'How we shall laugh at the trouble of parting when we meet again!'"

"Do you believe that?" he asked. "That you will laugh over your husband's parting?"

"I try to believe it." She slid her phone back into her bag. "I'll admit that sometimes I believe it more than others. But I do find it reassuring."

"So you think I can just tell Anne that I've forgiven her? That I forgave her?"

Riva shrugged. "I'm no expert on this, but I can't see that it would hurt to try."

"I guess I'd like to think about that some. I don't think I can do it right now, but I'm open to the idea." He stood, then reached for her hand. "At the moment, I'm distracted by my stomach. I feel more hungry than sad. In exchange for your helpful grief counseling, can I take you to a late lunch, or have you already eaten?"

She let him pull her up. "I haven't eaten since breakfast."

"O'Malley's is just a couple blocks away. You in?"

"In like Flynn, as Fiona would say."

As they walked toward O'Malley's, Marcus made small talk, but Riva was still mulling over his sad story about Anne. What an awful way to say goodbye . . . to not even have the chance. At least she'd had a better parting with Paul. That was something to be thankful for.

Fiona's brows arched as Marcus and Riva came into the bistro. Not wanting Fiona to assume this was a date, Riva quickly explained the unplanned meeting at the library. "We sort of skipped out on grief group today," she confessed, "and then realized we were both hungry."

"Hunger and grief?" Fiona shook her head. "'Tis a bad mix for certain."

After placing their orders and sitting down, Marcus asked Riva about her own experience with Paul. "If you need to talk, I'm a good listener too."

"Since you shared your story, I'll tell you a bit of mine. The condensed version. Who knows, it might help me to sort some things out." She took a deep breath before diving in. "Paul was diagnosed with small cell lung cancer, which is the worst kind. He'd never been a smoker, but both his parents smoked like chimneys when he was a child. Anyway, it took us by surprise. He'd seemed in great health and rarely went to the doctor. But he did have some shortness of breath that he attributed to aging. Other than that, he had no pain or symptoms. If he hadn't gone in to have his heart checked, which was my suggestion due to the shortness of breath, we might not have even known about the cancer."

"I've heard lung cancer can be very stealthy."

Riva sipped her water, preparing herself to continue. "Anyway, by the time we got his diagnosis, it was similar to Anne's . . . he was in the final stages of lung cancer. He retired from practicing law, and we threw ourselves into finding the best medical treatment. I was so optimistic. I really thought we could beat it. I even took him to the Mayo Clinic. I thought our insurance would cover the treatment, but it didn't. Since Paul was self-employed, our insurance was less than stellar. After the first year of doing everything we could to win the battle, we were told it was hopeless . . . and our savings were depleted. Short of a miracle, his condition was terminal."

Marcus grimaced. "I know how hard that was to hear."

She just nodded. "For the next year, it was all about maintenance. My job was to just take care of him. He got sicker and weaker, and it got harder. I hate to admit it, but it almost felt like my life was ending too. As if, instead of just being put on hold, my life was over. I suppose it might've just been exhaustion. As you know, caregiving is tiring."

"That's an understatement."

"It's weird to think I've never really told anyone this part of my story before, but it really did feel like I was dying. Or maybe I just wanted to die." She paused as Fiona came over to set down their orders and refill water glasses. And then, more eager to tell her story than to eat, Riva let it spill out, explaining how hard it was to assume all the household responsibilities once he was gone, including the things that Paul used to do.

"The extra work combined with the physical aspects of helping Paul with everything, well, it just seemed to take over our whole world. Hobbies or anything outside of the house fell to the wayside. Frankly, even if I had the time, I didn't have the energy. Other than Laurel, who kept pressing into my shrinking world, bless her heart, I quit socializing altogether." She sighed. "To be honest, I feel like I sort of did die then."

"You still feel like that?"

She shrugged. "I think I sometimes do. Like the other night, after dinner—with the music and dancing and all—it felt kind of . . . surreal. Like I was enjoying myself and then I couldn't. I just had to get away."

"I get that. I think we can get stuck in our grief sometimes. Especially if we don't make a conscious effort to get unstuck."

She picked up her fork to try her salad, then stopped. "I guess what caught me off guard most of all that night was how angry I felt. I never really believed in the anger stage of grief. Didn't think I needed to go through it. I couldn't even relate." She forked into a cherry tomato. "But I felt angry that night."

"We all grieve differently, but I got lots of experience with the anger stage unfortunately." He bit into his roast beef on rye.

She stared curiously at him. "Are you past it?"

He nodded as he chewed. "I think I am, but I guess it could sneak up on me. Kind of like it did on you. But hopefully it's behind me by now."

"Well, that's encouraging." She took a bite, still mulling over her own unexpected anger issue, wondering how often it would take her by surprise. "I couldn't really figure out what my anger was about. I mean, it came at me so hard and fast. It was pretty unsettling. And embarrassing."

"Embarrassing?" he asked.

"Well, hiding out in the house when you were all outside having such a good time. I felt like a party pooper!"

"I *was* curious where you'd gone, but no one else seemed to notice or mind."

She wondered if that was supposed to be encouraging but couldn't help musing that the other women, particularly Kitty, were probably glad to reduce the female population that night.

"Want to know what I've learned about anger?" He wiped his mouth with his napkin, then sipped his soda.

"Absolutely."

"My theory is that most anger is the direct result of feeling a loss of control." He took another bite.

"So I was angry because of a loss of control? Control of what?"

He swallowed. "Well, when you get right down to it, there is very little—if anything—in this life that we can control. But going through the death of a loved one really seems to drive this home. It did for me. It's like you do everything you can, practically kill yourself doing it, and they still die. You can't stop it or control it. And that makes us angry."

"I get that," she said, pushing her food around her plate. "But I still don't know what triggered me that night."

"Maybe you felt a loss of control in that social situation. Think about it, you've taken in all these tenants, some you barely know, and they are living in your home. The home you've had to yourself since Paul passed. It's like you had a little control, but now you have all these roommates . . . maybe that feels like a loss of control."

She considered this. "Well, that kinda makes sense. But I don't recall feeling like that, resenting my housemates. Not on that particular evening, at least. I'd been having a good time." She picked up her water. "Come to think of it, that might've been the problem. I felt guilty for having fun. Like my life was supposed to be over with. Like after Paul died, I should've been buried with him.

"I think I was frustrated because it felt wrong to enjoy myself," she added. "I felt guilty. Like I was a dead person, and dead people shouldn't have fun. And that made me mad and disgusted at myself for being such a pathetic mess. I suppose that made me feel just plain angry." She pounded a fist on the table for emphasis. "It felt terrible."

"That makes total sense. So how are you feeling right now? Are you feeling guilty for enjoying yourself? Does that make you angry? I don't know about you, but I'm having a good time right now." His eyes twinkled. "I'm enjoying your company, Riva, and I don't feel angry or guilty."

"Thanks. And in honest answer to your question, I'm not quite sure how I feel. Not guilty exactly . . . maybe a little uneasy. But I have enjoyed your company, Marcus. Even exchanging sob stories has been encouraging. It's good to know I'm not alone. I suppose that's why I went to the grief group. Even if we did end up playing hooky."

"I think we had our own support group. I know I feel better. I hope you do too."

She smiled. Sincerely this time. "I do feel better. I appreciate your insight and how you're further down the grief trail than I am. Your journey was definitely different and, honestly, it sounds like it was a lot harder. But seeing you're past it, or nearly there, is encouraging." She paused as Fiona returned to the table.

"Anything else for you two?" she asked brightly.

After they declined, she handed them both a flyer. "This is the new schedule for our band." She pointed to the first gig. "We're playing at The Brewery Friday night—that's tomorrow. In case you're interested. It's our first time playing there. It's a grand venue, but they cater to a crowd that's a bit younger and rowdier." Her expression suddenly looked concerned. "The owner there is fretting we won't pull in enough traffic so I'm begging everyone I know to come and show support."

"I'd love to come," Marcus told her.

"And you, Riva?" Fiona looked hopeful.

"I, uh, I don't know."

"Afraid to get out and have some fun?" Marcus teased.

She sat up straighter, feeling slightly defensive. "As a matter of fact, I'm ready to have some fun." She nodded at Fiona. "Count me in."

"Brilliant." Fiona beamed. "I'll save a table right in front for you two."

As Fiona returned to the counter, Riva was already questioning herself. Going out on Friday night was way out of her wheelhouse. Did this mean she and Marcus were going there together? Like on a date? Because that wouldn't fly with Laurel . . . or Kitty. Maybe it was best to pull the plug before it turned into a feud among friends.

"Are you okay?" Marcus peered at her curiously. "You look troubled."

"Maybe a little."

"Don't you think you deserve an evening out, listening to good music with good company?" His eyes twinkled.

She studied him. Did he think this was going to be a date or was he just teasing her? She was probably overthinking this whole silly thing. "That's not it," she began slowly, trying to think of a graceful way out of what could be an awkward mess. "It's just that Fiona said she was begging *everyone* to go. That makes me think my housemates will all be there too . . ."

"Is that a problem?" he asked.

She shrugged, hoping to appear nonchalant. "I hope not." But underneath her calm veneer was worry. She wasn't sure how she'd react if Laurel or Kitty got worked up over seeing her with Marcus. "It's just that I wouldn't want them to think we were, uh, on a date."

"Don't worry. It won't be a date," he assured her. "Just a couple friends going out to hear some music. And if your housemates come along, we'll all just be there in support of Fiona and her band. Right?"

"Of course. You're right." She forced a smile, trying to feel reassured that she and Marcus were on the same page. Although the whole idea still made her uneasy. She knew that Laurel could read anything she wanted into this. Not to mention Kitty. But maybe it didn't matter. Maybe Riva just needed to lighten up.

Chapter 16

Although Marcus offered to drive her home, Riva wanted to walk. She told him she needed some time to clear her head, but mostly she didn't want Laurel to witness Marcus dropping her off. Oh, she knew it was juvenile to worry about something so small, but she just didn't want to create any more stress within her precarious household. As she walked up to the house, she was glad to be alone because Laurel was in the front yard with a hoe. And to Riva's surprise, Laurel had a half full bucket of weeds and crabgrass, and the bed alongside the front porch looked much better.

"Laurel," Riva exclaimed, "I'm surprised to see you out here. You told me you hate yard work. This looks great."

"I thought I did. But that day in the backyard helped me see that it's not so bad. And it's good exercise. Plus, Windy asked me to help. Since she's probably doing more than her fair share of cooking, it only seemed fair." She stood up straight, using a foot to scoot the bucket of debris. "This time of day, with the shade, it's not too hot. But progress is kinda slow going."

"Well, I appreciate the effort. I'm going to put on some shorts then come back out to help you. Can I bring you out something to drink? Water? Soda? Tea?"

"I'd love water. Thanks."

After changing, Riva went to get some water to take outside and found Windy in the kitchen, chopping veggies. "Whatcha making?" she asked. "It's very colorful."

"Mexican chopped salad." Windy cut an avocado in half.

"Looks yummy." Riva filled two tumblers with ice.

"It's really cool and refreshing on a hot day. You can eat it like salsa with tortilla chips or like a salad. I'm serving it with grilled halibut tonight."

"Oh, Windy, it sounds delicious, but you're spoiling us." Riva filled the glasses. "We really should be taking turns cooking."

"That's what Laurel was just telling me so I sent her out front to weed." Windy grinned as she peeled the avocado. "Seems like a fair trade to me."

Riva held up the glasses. "That's where I'm headed, to help her."

"See, we're all pulling our weight." She wrinkled her nose. "Well, for the most part."

Riva paused before saying, "Meaning Fiona and Kitty aren't doing their share?"

"Well, I get that they both work. Fiona's music takes some time too. And to be fair, Fiona is stepping up. She's brought home groceries and helped me in the kitchen."

"But Kitty?"

Windy shrugged. "Well, I hate to sound like a tattletale, but Fiona hinted that Kitty is not too tidy."

"Not too tidy in what way?" Riva took a sip of ice water.

"Well, for example, the bathroom Kitty, Fiona, and I share. I didn't realize that Fiona has been cleaning up after Kitty every morning. But she decided to skip it yesterday and today, so I have seen what a mess it's been. Since Laurel is in charge of the chore roster, I thought about mentioning it to her, but there's already bad blood between those two."

Riva nodded, biting her lip. "Right. Let's not rock that boat if we don't need to."

"So I have a suggestion, if you agree."

"What?"

"How about if Fiona uses the bathroom down here to get ready for work. I know she'll keep it clean in case you need it for company or whatever. But since she goes to work early and doesn't always have time to clean up after Kitty, well, it might simplify her life. And then she can shower upstairs in the evening. Fortunately, she likes to shower before bed."

"I love that idea, but that doesn't solve the problem of Kitty's untidiness."

"That's true," Windy said. "But I don't mind calling Kitty on it. And if it's mostly just her and me using that bathroom, it'll be easier to make her toe the line."

"And if she doesn't comply?"

Windy sighed. "Then I suppose the house mother will have to chime in."

Riva cringed inwardly. Confrontation had never been her strong suit.

"But let's just hope things get better." Windy squeezed some lime juice onto her chopped veggies.

"Thank you for all you do here." Riva put a hand on her shoulder. "You're a natural peacemaker."

Windy sighed again. "Well, I'm not sure you realize what a godsend you've been to me by letting me live here."

"That's what you keep telling me. You know, that godsend thing works both ways. I love having you here, Windy." Of course, Riva wasn't sure she loved having all her other housemates.

Windy rinsed a knife. "I never told you about my dark night of the soul."

"What do you mean?" Riva took another sip of her water.

"Well, it was just a couple days before I met you at the grief group. I'd given notice for my apartment but knew I had no place to go. Anyway, I've been volunteering at the houseless shelter for a couple of years now, cooking dinner for them once every other week."

"Even this time of year?"

"Yeah, they don't have people overnight but still offer meals and clothing and a few other things. Anyway, that's why I'm usually busy on Tuesdays."

"That's so cool. I would love to help you sometime."

"I will definitely take you up on that offer. So anyway, I had spent the evening there and was getting ready to go home, but I stopped to help this woman who'd been staying there for a couple of weeks. The first time I met Mrs. Marshall, I assumed she'd come to volunteer, but it turned out she was houseless. As I was leaving, I saw her outside the facility. We talked a bit, and she seemed lost and confused and didn't think she belonged in the shelter. By then I knew she had no family and had lost her husband's pension and later her house. Other than her monthly social security stipend, she was broke."

"That's sad."

Windy nodded. "So I helped her back inside and got her into the sleeping area where someone else helped her get ready for bed, but as I walked home, I got to feeling like that woman was me. You know, in about ten, maybe twenty years. And I kept obsessing about this all night. Really, other than a few years, what made me any different from Mrs. Marshall?"

"What makes any of us any different?"

"Friends? Family?" Windy shrugged. "But that night, I felt so alone . . . I just couldn't imagine what the rest of my life was going to be like. It seemed so bleak and dark and hopeless."

Riva sighed. "That's so sad."

"The next morning, I was pretty down, but as I did my morning devotions, I remembered it was grief group day, so despite my gloomy perspective, I forced myself to go. And that's the same day I met you."

"You were feeling gloomy that day?" Riva blinked. "I thought you looked so bright and cheerful. You were dressed so colorfully, and your smile was so warm."

"Because I've learned that helping others always makes me feel better." Windy's eyes looked misty. "The hardest part of this story is that I learned Mrs. Marshall died that night."

Riva let out a gasp. "I'm so sorry."

"I never told anyone about that whole thing, not even my brother. But it made me determined to move in here, determined to make the most of the years I have left. So even dealing with someone like Kitty, and I'll admit she gets on my nerves, doesn't feel as daunting as it might've."

Riva set down the water glasses and hugged Windy. "Thanks for sharing that with me. It makes me even more glad I went to the grief group that day."

"Speaking of grief group, how did that go today?"

"Oh, my . . . that's a story for a different time." Riva picked up the water glasses. "I should probably get this out to Laurel. Don't want her to faint from thirst."

"Dehydration can be dangerous." Windy nodded. "But I'll hold you to telling me your story later."

Riva agreed, then went outside. She found Laurel sitting on the porch, fanning herself with a garden glove. "What took you so long?"

Riva handed her a water. "Sorry. I was talking to Windy."

"Thanks." Laurel took a long sip, then ran the cool glass across a flushed cheek. "Despite the shade, it's getting awfully warm out here. I needed a break."

"Maybe it's quitting time." Riva sat down next to her.

"Perhaps. What were you and Windy talking about?" Laurel asked.

"Nothing much."

"Or maybe it's none of my business." Laurel looked down with a sad expression. "It's hard to know boundaries, you know, with five women sharing a home. I'm still getting my bearings. I don't want to push my nose in where it doesn't belong. From what I've heard, I have a knack for that."

"Who said that?"

"Well, Kitty for starters. But I think I've offended Windy and Fiona with my charts. Just last night, before going to bed, I overheard Kitty telling Fiona that I was a dictator."

Riva shook her head. "Helping us be organized is not dictatorship."

"I don't know. I think I need to back off some. I know I've always been a bossy, outspoken, independent woman, but I think it was easier to wear that cloak when I was younger. Lately, I've been questioning myself. I don't want to become a grumpy old curmudgeon. Besides being miserable, it's not terribly feminine."

Riva frowned. "Feminine?"

"I know that sounds strange coming from me. But lately I've wondered . . . do I really want to spend the last part of my life alone?"

"You're not alone." Riva touched her arm. "You have friends."

"Thank God. But you know, Riva, some women our age get married . . ."

"Yes, of course." Riva didn't know what to say. Laurel was obviously thinking about Marcus, dreaming of something more than just female friends.

"But I suspect that most men our age are not seeking out women who are overly assertive and pushy." She sighed. "Bossy old women are probably not a hot commodity in the dating world."

"Oh, I don't know. It takes all kinds." Riva studied her discouraged friend carefully. Laurel was the oldest woman in the house, which seemed worthy of respect, and she'd always been the "strong" friend in Riva's life. Despite the rough road Laurel had been down, she always seemed to rise above it all, helping others along the way. "Really, Laurel, I think your assertiveness has served you well. I would hope you wouldn't try to reinvent yourself to attract a man. Think about it, would you really want someone like that anyway?"

Laurel finished her water, then just sat with a thoughtful expression. "No, I suppose I wouldn't want that." She turned to Riva. "But at the same time, I don't want to be alone."

"Like I just said, you're not alone. You have friends."

"Friends like Kitty?" Laurel rolled her eyes.

"Friends like me." Riva hugged Laurel. "And I hope you don't change yourself just to catch a man. But if you decide to make changes because you want to, because it's good for you, then I will cheer you on."

"Thanks, Riva." Laurel tipped her head toward the street before standing. "Trouble this way comes."

Riva looked out to see Kitty, on foot, coming up the hill toward the house.

"Excuse me," Laurel said. She already had the front door open. "But I'm trying not to engage with that one."

As Laurel disappeared into the house, Riva wanted to follow, but Kitty was eagerly waving to her, calling out "hello," and Riva knew it would be rude to walk away.

She waved back as she went down the steps, heading toward the spade and bucket Laurel had left next to the path. She bent down to continue the weeding. If Kitty wanted to chat with her, she would have to do it while helping. But when Kitty got there, in her heels and snug skirt, she only remained there long enough to complain about her aching feet.

After Kitty went inside, Riva considered the assortment of women now inhabiting her house. Their commonality was being unmarried, home-challenged, and "of a certain age," but could they possibly be more different from each other? How long would it take for this friendly faction of females to turn into a combative cast of contemptible characters? And if and when they did, where would Riva go to hide?

Chapter 17

After a scrumptious dinner, Riva insisted on cleaning up. She told the ladies she wanted to do it alone, but Windy remained behind. "I want to do some prep work for Saturday's dinner," she told them.

"That reminds me"—Fiona pulled a folded flyer from her pocket—"don't plan on me for dinner tomorrow night. And Riva too. Right, Riva?"

"Uh-huh." Riva set a stack of plates in the sink.

"The Brewery?" Laurel's tone sounded skeptical. "Isn't that a pretty wild place on a Friday night?"

"I've been there a few times on Fridays when they have live music. It's usually a bunch of twentysomethings acting like high school kids," Kitty added. "I don't mind going out with a younger man, but those boys are too young for me. Count me out."

"That's why I was trying to get some older folks to come," Fiona said. "In case the youngsters don't care for our music. We don't want to flop on our first night there."

"Well, I'll go," Windy offered. "I'll be your date, Riva."

"Great." Fiona set a platter by the sink. "I've already reserved a table for her and Marcus. You can sit with them."

"Riva and Marcus are going?" Laurel's brows shot up. "When did this happen?"

"We ran into Fiona today," Riva said nervously. "Marcus and I happened to meet up at the grief group today and then, well, we saw Fiona and she told us about the show. It's no big deal." She looked at Laurel. "And trust me, it's not a date."

"Then you won't care if I join you," Kitty chirped.

"No, not at all." Riva felt like a phony but didn't know what else to say.

"Then I'll go too," Laurel declared. "That way we'll all be there."

"Fabulous." Fiona clapped her hands. "And I'll go practice my fiddle for a bit. Don't want to keep anyone up late tonight."

"Want to bring it down here?" Riva asked. "It'd be fun to clean up to your music."

"Really?" Fiona beamed. "I'd love to serenade you. Music is meant to be enjoyed. Anyone else?"

"I'm beat," Laurel told her. "I plan to take a relaxing bath in Epsom salts to soak off my aches and pains from all that yard work today."

"It must be such a drag to get old," Kitty said glibly.

Laurel humphed as she left the kitchen, and Riva held back the urge to scold Kitty. Good grief, Laurel wasn't that much older than her. Based on Kitty's story, she couldn't be more than ten years younger than Laurel. She might do Botox and face lifts and whatever people did these days to preserve their youth, but the clock would eventually catch up.

By the time Riva finished cleaning the kitchen and Windy was done food prepping, Fiona had stopped playing her fiddle and switched over to her phone for an online music provider that was tuned into other Celtic Irish folk bands. "For inspiration," she told them. "This is what we want to sound like someday."

"Based on what I've heard from just you playing alone, your group probably already sounds like them." Riva hung up her dish towel.

"Yeah, I can't wait to hear you all together." Windy closed the fridge. "This music makes me want to dance."

"Then let's dance!" Fiona grabbed both their hands and before long she had them jigging and clogging and step-dancing around the kitchen.

After dancing to several lively numbers, Riva sat down on a stool. "This is too much fun, but I need a break."

"Me too. I'm knackered." Fiona turned off the music and gathered her things. "But after that practice, I expect you both to cut loose on the dance floor tomorrow night."

"I can't wait." Windy got herself a glass of water. "That's good exercise."

"Well, I'll warn you guys," Riva said, "dancing in my kitchen is one thing. Dancing out in public is something else."

"We'll just see about that." Fiona grinned. "Good night, ladies."

After Fiona left, Windy turned to Riva. "I understand about your inhibitions."

"My inhibitions?" Riva frowned. "I thought I was being rather uninhibited just now."

"Yeah, in your kitchen. But beyond this house? Don't get me wrong, I get it. I felt totally shut down and closed-up after Bill died. But then, after I lost my house and everything, and I started to embrace my hippie roots, I learned to let my inhibitions go."

"That's admirable, Windy. For you, anyway. But I honestly doubt I'll ever get to that place . . . I mean, letting all my inhibitions go." To be honest, she wasn't even comfortable with the idea of being that uninhibited. It frightened her.

"Which is exactly the reason you must come to my drumming circle with me," Windy told her.

"What's a drumming circle?"

"It's a group of women who gather once a month to play drums."

"I don't even know how to play a drum."

"No one really knows how. It's more like an instinct. Something you do. We just let go and go with the flow. It's more than just drumming though. It's a whole spiritual experience. Cultures for thousands of years have drummed and made music together. For women to gather like that, well, it's surprisingly empowering—and such a cool release."

Riva considered her next words carefully. "That all sounds interesting, but I really don't think it's for me."

"How can you possibly know that if you won't even try it?"

Riva thought about it.

"Come on, Riva, live dangerously for once." Windy laughed. "Not that a bunch of women with drums are dangerous. But go ahead and take a risk. It might feel good."

Riva really didn't enjoy feeling inhibited, but playing drums with a bunch of strange women? Seriously? "Would I need to dress, well, like you do?"

Windy looked down at her tie-dye T-shirt and embroidered bellbottom jeans. "No, of course not. You dress in whatever's comfortable to you. All you need to do is come with me and be open to the possibilities."

"When is it?"

"Saturday morning at ten."

Riva took a deep breath, then slowly let it out. "Well, okay, I'll try it. But only if you promise not to be offended if I don't like it. Okay?"

"I promise." Windy slapped her on the back. "But I'm pretty sure you'll like it."

Riva turned off the kitchen lights and followed Windy out. She picked up the novel she'd set on a table by the stairway. "Have you started *A Gentleman in Moscow* for our book group yet?"

"I reserved a copy at the library, but it won't be in until next week."

"I barely started it, but I'm already pulled in."

Windy smiled. "I'm not surprised. The synopsis I read of the book reminded me of you."

"How's that?"

"Well, it's about a guy who's kind of trapped, right?"

Riva frowned at the book cover. "Trapped?"

"Isn't he sort of imprisoned in a Moscow hotel?"

"Well, yes . . . I suppose he is trapped. And that reminds you of me?"

Windy shrugged. "No offense, but when I first met you, I thought you seemed kind of trapped here in your beautiful old home."

"Oh?" Riva barely nodded.

"Anyway, I think it'll make for an interesting book group discussion." Windy started up the stairs. Then, cupping her mouth, she lowered her voice. "Do you think Kitty will participate?"

"I don't know. I suppose if she finds the TV show . . ."

"And if Marcus comes." Windy gave her a sly wink. "That'd get her here."

They said good night and Windy continued up. But as Riva carried the book to her room, she wondered. Perhaps Windy wasn't too far from the truth about Riva being somewhat trapped in her home. Did others really see her like that? *Trapped and inhibited?* She'd never thought of herself like that when she was younger, and she really wasn't ready to be seen that way now. Hadn't she been making a lot of changes recently?

Hadn't she invited strange women to share her home? She'd gone to grief group twice. For Pete's sake, she'd just danced in the kitchen! And, although it wasn't a date, she'd had lunch with Marcus today and had even agreed to go The Brewery tomorrow. Not to mention she'd just agreed to go beat on a drum with Windy. Really, that didn't sound too trapped and inhibited to her. Compared to that stormy dark night when she'd felt so frightened and alone, well, she'd come a long way, baby!

By Friday afternoon, Riva was nervous. She wasn't sure if it was her imagination, but the whole house felt charged with a strange kind of energy. At first she thought it was coming from

Fiona, who'd been in the library practicing some lively tunes on her mandolin, but even after Fiona left to meet up with her bandmates for dinner, the energy remained. It reminded Riva of a buzzing beehive. She could hear movement upstairs and occasional exchanges between her housemates, and then someone was calling her name.

"I'm in the kitchen," she yelled back.

"Riva," Laurel said as she came in with an armload of clothes. "I need help."

"Help?" Riva put the tea pitcher back in the fridge. "If you want the laundry room, I'm sure no one is using it right now."

"Not that kind of help, darling." Laurel tossed her pile onto a stool. "Wardrobe help."

"Oh?" Riva frowned. "I'm not exactly a fashion diva, Laurel."

"I like your taste. And you're far more fashionable than I am." Laurel held up a bright red blouse. "I usually wear this at Christmastime, but Kitty always makes fun of how drab I dress, so I thought maybe this would punch it up." She pulled a heavy silver necklace from her tunic pocket. "With this?"

Riva slowly nodded. It really did look like holiday wear. "Uh-huh. What else do you have there?"

Laurel went through several options that screamed "I'm a retired school secretary." Riva grimaced.

"I think maybe you're trying too hard," she told Laurel.

"What do you mean?"

"Well, The Brewery is more of a hipster place. I bet most everyone will be in jeans and T-shirts."

"But Windy will be wearing one of her colorful ensembles. I know because I asked her. And I saw Fiona. She looked so cute and youthful in her denim skirt, lacy blouse, and cowboy boots. And who knows what Kitty will be wearing—probably something short and tight and cut low."

Riva set her iced tea aside. "Well, I doubt you want to go as Kitty's sidekick."

Laurel rolled her eyes. "Just shoot me now."

"Can we go through your closet together?"

She brightened. "Sure. I'd appreciate it."

Riva picked up half of the clothing pile and followed Laurel up to her room. Together, they went through her sparse closet. Finally, Riva turned to Laurel, giving her a long hard look. "You know what I think?"

"I'm not a mind reader."

"I think you need to discover your own style."

Laurel rolled her eyes. "I have no style, darling. That's the problem."

"Right." Riva pushed Laurel toward the bathroom and in front of the mirror. "Your short gray hair, which is very becoming, suggests you're a classic."

"Classic?" Laurel smiled. "I like the sound of that, but I have no idea what it means."

"You look best in classic styles. Not frills or fads."

"Well, I've never liked frills or fads, so you could be on the right track." Laurel tilted her head to one side. "But how do you know all this?"

"I took a class once. Another lifetime ago. I wanted to rejoin the workforce after the kids were in school, and I felt like I needed a makeover, you know, to ditch the mommy clothes." Riva went back to the closet and pulled out a navy-and-white striped boatneck top. She held it up to Laurel. "This would be a good look on you."

"Yeah, for going out in my yacht."

Riva chuckled. "Take me along. But, really, I've always thought of you as sort of sporty too. A sporty classic."

"I used to be sporty, back in my previous life. I was on the women's softball team for years. And I loved tennis and golf back when I could afford such luxuries."

"Maybe it's time you found a new sport," Riva suggested. "Lots of gals our age are playing pickleball."

"So I've heard. But at the moment, we're talking about tonight. Are you suggesting I wear workout clothes and tennis shoes to the show, maybe an eighties sweatband on my forehead?"

Riva smiled. "Not exactly." She pulled out a western-style chambray shirt and held it up to Laurel. "This color matches your eyes."

"That's a men's work shirt." Laurel frowned. "It won't even stay snapped over my bustline."

Riva slid a sleeveless white top under it. "Then wear it like a jacket over this shirt."

"That's pretty plain." Laurel shook her head. "And not very feminine. I wanted to look, well, attractive . . . you know, to the opposite sex. That looks like I should go shovel dirt."

"You're not using your imagination. We put the right scarf with it and that silver chain in your pocket and your black jeans." Riva fished around a bit more and found a red paisley scarf from a basket. "Here, just try these together, Laurel. You might be surprised."

"I don't know." Laurel looked doubtful as she carried the items to her bathroom to change. Riva sat on the recliner, and Fred leaped onto her lap, snuggled in, and cranked up his purring.

"You're a happy camper, aren't you?" She stroked his coat. "You like your new home?"

"What?" Laurel called back.

"Conversing with Fred," Riva told her.

After a few minutes, Laurel emerged, and Riva was impressed. "Oh, Laurel, I love this look on you. Stylish but classic. Feminine but not too silly or girly. I think you look great. How do you feel?"

"I like it. I don't know how you could imagine it like this, but I really like it." Laurel checked herself in the closet's full-length mirror. "I feel younger."

"You look younger. Now, all you need are some silver earrings, something simple like hoops. And a bit of lip color, maybe even some mascara, and you'll be rocking it." Riva gently pushed Fred aside and stood.

"Thank you." Laurel hugged her. "You're a true friend." She pointed to Riva's leggings and baggy T-shirt. "Is that what you're wearing tonight?"

"No, these really are my work clothes. I haven't even showered yet, and I was cleaning and doing yard work earlier." She smirked. "Gotta keep up with the chores roster."

"Unlike some people." Laurel scowled.

"We're still getting the kinks out." Riva shrugged. "Anyway, I guess I should get ready."

Riva was just going down the hallway when she heard footsteps and turned to see Kitty emerging from her room. "Hi there." Riva forced a smile, trying not to blink at Kitty's over-the-top ensemble. The low-cut turquoise top, floral miniskirt, and high-heeled shortie boots brought to mind seventies disco, or maybe it was *Pretty Woman*. "You certainly look festive." She waited at the top of the stairs.

"Thanks. I'm in a festive mood."

"Leaving for The Brewery early?"

"I'm meeting friends for a light dinner beforehand." She slid her purse strap over her shoulder, then cocked her head to one side. "Is that what you're wearing?"

Riva smiled. "No, I was just going down to shower and change." She stepped aside to let Kitty pass. "I have to give it to you, Kitty," she said as she followed her down, "not all women our age can pull off a short skirt like that. Your legs are amazing."

"Well, aren't you sweet." Kitty paused at the foot of the stairs, striking a pose. "My yoga class is paying off. That and a new tanning cream I started carrying at the salon." Her brow creased as she studied Riva. "You might want to try some."

"Thanks." Riva cringed inwardly. "I'll think about that."

Kitty flipped a strand of Farrah Fawcett hair over her shoulder and called back "See ya later" as she left. To Riva's relief, the house felt peaceful again. She didn't blame Kitty exactly, but more and more she felt this youth-chasing woman was a misfit in a house that would be better suited to growing old gracefully. *And graciously*, Riva reminded herself. Maybe Kitty needed them.

Chapter 18

Worried that Marcus might show up to take her to The Brewery, Riva had texted earlier, informing him that Laurel offered to drive her and Windy. As in, hint hint, this is not a date. But as the three women walked into the pub from the parking lot, she felt a strange flutter of expectation at the thought of seeing him there. And that bothered her. She didn't *want* to feel that way . . . shouldn't feel that way.

Although she'd pondered over her own wardrobe choices tonight, she had finally decided on a black linen sleeveless shift dress and sandals. Rather plain and boring but comfortable and cool enough to withstand the occasional hot flash, which she hated to admit still took her by surprise. To spice up the dress, she'd belted it with a long, fringed scarf and put on an old squash blossom necklace that Paul's mother had given her many years ago. According to Kenzie, who planned to inherit the necklace one day, these were a hot ticket item nowadays.

The look Riva had been going for tonight wasn't completely clear, but Windy had proclaimed her as "boho chic." As the three of them walked into the pub, all looking distinctly different from each other, she didn't feel too out of place. Perhaps it was her imagination, but she felt like maybe a couple of heads had turned as they walked in. Not that she wanted that. Or did she?

Marcus was seated by himself at a table up front, but he quickly stood when the three approached him, warmly greeting each of them. "You ladies all look lovely." He pulled out a chair for Laurel. "Fiona was just here. Their guitarist is running late, so they'll start up in about fifteen minutes."

"Looks like a mixed crowd," Riva observed. "Not all young folks."

"Fiona's flyers must've worked," Windy added.

Marcus pointed to his glass of red wine. "In case you didn't know, they don't only serve beer here. And I have to admit their house red isn't half bad."

He offered to get them all a glass and while he was waiting at the bar, Kitty walked in. Riva wasn't even sure how she knew their housemate had arrived. Maybe she could feel the room buzzing, or maybe it was the male heads turning, but somehow she could tell. She watched as Kitty went straight to Marcus, sidling up to him in a flirtatious way that had never come naturally to Riva . . . and she hoped never would!

"That woman is such a narcissist," Laurel mumbled.

"Really?" Windy's pale brows arched.

"I've been reading up on it." Laurel's eyes were fixed on Kitty and Marcus. "Believe me, I think Kitty pretty much checks all the boxes for narcissism."

"Laurel is an armchair psychiatrist," Riva teased. "Next she'll be diagnosing me."

"I've already done that." Laurel smirked. "You're a repressed widow who feels guilty for having fun of any kind."

Riva blinked but didn't respond.

Laurel seemed to regret her words. "Sorry, I didn't mean that to sound like a dig, Riva. You know I love you. It's just that, well, you must admit that you've had a hard time getting back into the swing of things."

"Why does everyone keep saying that?" Riva frowned. "I mean, look at me. Here I am at a pub . . . party girl, *woohoo*." She forced a tinny sounding laugh.

Laurel pointed at her. "Dressed in black. Widow's weeds."

"I happen to like black. I always have. And I got this dress years ago. Long before Paul got sick. It is not widow's weeds."

"I think Riva looks fabulous tonight," Windy said. "Sophisticated but artsy. And that necklace is killer. Where did you get it?"

Grateful for the segue in conversation, Riva told the story of how her mother-in-law had given the family heirloom to her on her thirtieth birthday. "It almost seemed like an apology for being so against our marriage at the beginning," she added. "I guess I finally proved that I wasn't just a flibbertigibbet out to ruin her precious son's legal career. Eleanor had always said Greenwood was small potatoes and that Paul should take his practice to some big city or perhaps become a congressman or something. She felt I was holding him back."

"Were you?" Windy asked.

"Paul never had those kinds of aspirations. He didn't even like big cities. And he loved helping people with legal troubles." She sighed. "Just one of many things I loved about him."

"He was a truly good man," Laurel agreed.

"I wish I'd met him." Windy paused as Marcus and Kitty, carrying drinks, joined them.

"I'll go back for mine now," Kitty said in a sassy tone. "I had to tell the bartender how to make a mojito, and I think he's into me now." She giggled.

"That bartender looks young enough to be your son," Laurel pointed out. "Maybe even her grandson," she muttered quietly to Riva.

Kitty threw back her head and laughed. "Hey, I have no problem with younger men." She poked Marcus in the shoulder. "Unless someone better comes around." She strolled off now, swinging her hips in a way that would look ridiculous on most women but somehow worked for Kitty. She'd probably had years of practice. Riva watched her with wide eyes, then checked to make sure her jaw hadn't dropped.

"That's quite a gal." Marcus grinned as he picked up his drink. "Ya gotta appreciate that youthful spirit."

"Oh, we do," Windy told him, then wrinkled her nose. "Except she makes the rest of us feel a bit old and dowdy at times."

"Well, that's just ridiculous." He lifted his glass high. "Don't forget that women and wine get better with age. Here's to you lovely ladies."

They all took a sip, and soon Kitty was headed back with her drink in hand. They were one chair short, so Marcus got up to get one from another table. While he was carrying it over, Kitty took his chair and scooted closer to Laurel to leave an empty spot between her and Windy. Marcus slid his new chair into place and sat.

"Isn't this cozy?" Kitty said, moving her chair even closer to his. She held up her drink. "Here's to hoping Gerard followed my instructions." She took a sip and seemed to think about it. "It could be worse, but I'm afraid he might need more lessons."

"Well, this is a brewery," Marcus reminded her. "I'm surprised they even serve mixed drinks."

"Apparently they don't serve many." She turned to Marcus. "Have you ever had a mojito?"

"Not that I can recall."

She held her drink out to him. "Try it. Tell me what you think."

"Uh, no thanks." He held up his wineglass. "This suits me fine."

She took another swig. "Well, I think it's a little on the bitter side. And I can't taste any mint."

"Maybe you should go back and lodge a complaint," Laurel suggested.

"Nah." Kitty waved a hand. "I can rough it. Besides, looks like our music is about to start." She took another long swig. Apparently, her drink wasn't that bad.

Riva looked toward the small stage where a young man was announcing the band. And then Fiona, three men, and another woman came out, yelled a greeting, and began to play a lively tune. The crowd seemed to get right into it. Some were even clapping along with the beat. Riva felt relieved for Fiona. Maybe advancing age wasn't a drawback when it came to music. After all, think of the years of experience these musicians must have under their belts. Pretty soon people were on the dance floor, and Riva wasn't surprised to see Kitty grabbing Marcus by the hand. "Come on. You can't sit here with four unattached women and think we won't get you out there."

The three of them watched as Kitty tugged Marcus out and then, not enjoying this scene, Riva turned her attention back to Laurel and Windy, commenting on the quality of the music.

"They are really good," Windy agreed. "My toes are tapping."

"I'm surprised you don't want to dance," Riva said to her. "You were so good in the kitchen the other night."

"I wouldn't mind dancing." Laurel sounded wistful.

"Then come on, girlfriend." Windy reached for her hand. "Let's you and me cut the rug."

"Cut the rug?" Riva laughed.

Windy held out a hand toward her. "Come on, you come too."

"I'd rather be a spectator for the moment," she said.

"She's inhibited and repressed," Laurel told Windy in a teasing tone.

Windy nodded. "Well, the night is young, Riva. We'll get you out there."

Riva watched them go, then took a deep breath and had a sip of wine. This whole thing was way out of her comfort zone, but at least she'd made the effort to come. She knew her friends were partly right. She was somewhat inhibited and repressed. She knew it was related to what she'd told Marcus when they'd skipped out on the grief group. Her two years of caring for a dying man—her best friend and true love—had changed her. Made her older, sadder . . . inhibited. At the moment, she wasn't even sure that, despite her recent efforts, she could ever undo that change. Maybe it was like aging—inevitable. When no one was paying attention, it just happened.

After that number ended, another began, and the dancers started up again. Riva tried to feign amusement as she continued to look on, like she was pleased to be here and highly entertained by the merrymaking going on out there. But truth be told, she felt irritated. Oh, the music was good . . . Fiona's band was very talented. But she felt so out of place right now. A complete misfit. And she wondered if there was a way to make a graceful exit. Maybe she could leave a note on a cocktail napkin or send a text or just vanish and let them wonder. It wasn't dark outside yet, and her house was less than a mile away. The thought of fresh clean air and a nice walk on a warm summer evening was tempting.

She glanced around the room, which was growing increasingly more crowded, and decided to make a fast break. If anyone noticed her absence, perhaps they'd think she'd gone to the ladies' room. But she was barely out of her chair when Marcus cut off her escape.

"Heading for the dance floor?" he asked hopefully.

"I, uh, I was actually getting ready to sneak out," she confessed.

He looked concerned. "Are you feeling okay?"

"Yes, I'm fine." She cringed. "Just a little out of place."

"That's because you should be dancing." He held out a hand. "Come on. Give it a try. Save me from another dance with Kitty."

"Where did she go?"

"Getting herself another mojito." He smiled. "Come on, Riva. Live a little."

"Okay." She felt a mixture of reluctance and nerves. Part of her wanted to dance with Marcus. Part of her wanted to run. The song playing was a little less lively than the earlier tunes, and Marcus took her hand and, with a hand behind her back, began to lead her in a two-step. He was a good dancer, and after a bit, she felt herself relax. By the time the song ended, she was actually smiling.

"Fun, eh?" he asked.

She nodded. "Surprisingly. My roommates gave me dancing lessons the other night. I think it's paying off."

"Go again?" he asked as the next song started.

"Okay."

And so they danced a second time. And then a third. But when she caught a glimpse of their table, she noticed Laurel sitting alone. "I think I need a break," she told Marcus between songs.

He looked surprised. "Tired?"

"Worried about Laurel. She looks unhappy."

He looked toward the table. "Should I ask her to dance?"

"Yes! She would love that."

With Marcus and Laurel two-stepping together, free-spirited Windy dancing by herself, and Kitty dancing cheek to cheek with a young guy in a cowboy hat, Riva was alone at the table again. She didn't really mind. Or that's what she told herself. But the truth was she felt awkward and out of place. She didn't belong in a pub like this, where singles came in the hopes of making a good connection. Especially if it was a temporary one.

Everything about today's world felt like that . . . temporary . . . disposable. Use it, lose it, throw it away. How many of these couples would still be together tomorrow? Maybe that's how they preferred their relationships. Noncommittal. Easy come, easy go. She watched as carefree younger people flirted, danced, drank, and mixed with each other happily. How could an old widow, still in love with her husband, possibly fit in? Clearly she didn't belong here.

Chapter 19

Riva was just planning another escape when Windy spotted her sitting alone and came over. "Come on, Riva." She tugged her to her feet and out to the dance floor. "I need a partner and your dancing isn't going to improve by sitting on your hind end all night."

"I danced a little, but I probably need more lessons," Riva said defensively. "Although I prefer the privacy of the kitchen."

Windy laughed. "Just pretend you know what you're doing and you'll be fine."

After a couple of songs, Riva almost felt like she'd broken through, or broken the ice, but it seemed it was possible to have a fun evening after all. Really, why did she obsess over such tiny things? It was good to move with the music, to follow Windy's lead, to dance with abandon . . . to be part of something bigger than herself.

Windy was just twirling Riva when Marcus and Laurel moved closer, and suddenly Marcus grabbed Riva's free hand and gracefully swapped partners so that Laurel was partnered with Windy and Riva was partnered with him. She didn't mind the switch, but couldn't miss the look of concern, or perhaps envy, in Laurel's eyes. Of course, now Riva regretted the dance floor trade-off.

At the end of the song, Riva was about to excuse herself from Marcus when Kitty stepped up and tapped her on the shoulder. "Mind if I cut in?"

"Not at all." Riva smiled in relief. Especially since they were playing a slow dance number now. Good timing to go sit down. That is, if Marcus would let go of her hand. "I, uh, I need a break anyway."

"Of course you do." Kitty's tone was placating as she moved close to Marcus. "Most of you older folks just don't have the stamina to keep up."

Marcus, still holding Riva's hand, nodded. "I need a break too."

"Not until you dance with me," Kitty insisted, tugged his hand free from Riva's. "Remember you promised me another dance? I'm claiming it now."

Without sticking around to hear Marcus's response, Riva returned to the table where Laurel was glowering and Windy looked a bit flushed and tired.

"We don't have to stay here all evening," Riva told them. "It looks like Fiona's band is a hit with all ages. I doubt we'd be missed."

"But I'm still enjoying the music," Windy told her.

"What about you?" Riva turned to Laurel. "Wanna go?"

Laurel shrugged. "I was having a good time . . . that is, until someone moved in and ruined it."

Riva wasn't sure if Laurel was referring to her or Kitty, but she didn't want to find out. "Well, maybe I wanted to prove that I'm trying to escape my inhibitions."

"You don't have to try *that* hard." Laurel's tone was snarky.

"Did Kitty actually cut in on you?" Windy asked Riva.

"Sort of."

"Sort of?" Laurel sniffed. "Looks to me like Marcus is enjoying himself."

"I think he's being polite," Riva told her. "He wanted to take a break and Kitty wouldn't let him."

"Do you think Kitty could dance any closer to him?" Laurel

asked. "And that outfit she's wearing"—Laurel scoffed—"does she think she's fifteen?"

"It's what I was thinking too," Windy admitted.

"I keep wondering how old that woman is," Laurel said. "She has to be at least midfifties, and that's if she was still a teen when she married the first time."

"Maybe you should check her driver's license," Riva teased.

"Good idea." She reached for Kitty's oversized purse.

"I was kidding." Riva gasped as Laurel unzipped the bag.

"Laurel." Windy's tone held warning.

"Lighten up, you two. She won't see me."

"I refuse to witness this." Riva stood. "I'll be in the women's room."

"Me too," Windy said, following her.

As they washed their hands a moment later, Windy and Riva made eye contact in the mirror. "I admire that Laurel is a pretty gutsy lady," Windy said, "but sometimes she worries me. I'm concerned what will happen if she pits herself against someone like Kitty."

"I know what you mean." Riva dried her hands. "Kinda like Wile E. Coyote about to catch the Road Runner, but there's a keg of TNT waiting for him."

"I never watched cartoons as a kid, but I caught up when my kids were small. I assume Laurel would be the determined but unfortunate coyote and Kitty's the lucky Road Runner who always gets away but makes sure Wile E. gets blown up or crushed." Windy fluffed her auburn curls.

"Yep. Road Runner always comes out on top. Of course, he's got the legs to run."

"So does Kitty."

"Look, Windy, I might sneak out of here. I think I've had more than enough music and dancing for one night."

Windy adjusted her beaded necklace. "I'm proud of you for doing as well as you have, Riva. I hope you don't feel bad about when we tweaked you about inhibitions. It's just that we both want to see you break out of your shell."

"I'm okay. But I'm not so sure Laurel agrees with you. She might prefer I stay in my shell. At least, when it comes to Marcus. I'm afraid she might consider me competition and classify me with Kitty. But I swear, I'm not after Marcus."

Windy turned to look directly at her. "I didn't want to mention it, but I think Laurel's concerns over Marcus are not too far off. And I don't mean with Kitty. I know my brother pretty well, and I can tell when he's interested in someone." Her brows arched as she pointed to Riva. "And if you can't see it, you must be in denial."

Riva took a deep breath. "Marcus is a very nice man, and I value his friendship. But that's all there is to it. Honestly, Laurel needs to understand I'm not out to catch him or any other man. I don't even know why I came here tonight. It seems places like this are just a setup for romance hunters."

"Romance hunters?" Windy chuckled. "Never heard it put like that before, but you're probably right. Though I don't think everyone here is on the hunt. Some came for the music. And just because you dance with someone doesn't mean you have to go home with them."

"Well, that's a relief." Riva rolled her eyes. "Anyway, if you could help Laurel to understand that my only interest in Marcus is friendship, I'd appreciate it. Because, honestly, that's all there is to it."

"For you, anyway." Windy had a knowing look as she pushed the restroom door open, but Riva stopped her. She wasn't quite sure what Windy was hinting at, but she could guess. And it just seemed to confirm what Riva suspected. Now she knew what she had to do. She would call it a night before her friendship with Laurel was stretched to a breaking point.

"I'll just walk home," Riva told Windy. "Can you make my excuses to the others?"

"You're really sure you want to leave?"

Riva firmly nodded. "The noise and closeness in here is getting to me, and I can tell I'm on the verge of a headache." She hugged Windy. "You stay here and have fun."

"All right . . . as long as you're sure you'll be okay walking home alone."

"A cool stroll in the fresh evening air is just what I need. Good medicine."

"If you say so." But Windy didn't look convinced as Riva made her getaway. Out on the dusky street, Riva felt a bit guilty for faking a headache. Though if she'd stayed inside any longer, she might've gotten one. On the sidewalk she could hear the band playing a folk song on the outdoor speaker. They really were good. As she walked away, the music growing fainter behind her, she felt a twinge of regret, or maybe it was a sense of failure. It should've been a simple thing to have remained there, to be with the others as they enjoyed the evening without feeling guilty, torn, or conflicted. It was as if something was broken inside of her, or else just stuck. Maybe her friends were right. Maybe she truly was inhibited . . . or perhaps she was simply a wimp.

It felt strange but good to be home without anyone else there. Riva put on some calming classical music and strolled from room to room. After a while, she was feeling slightly bored and perhaps missing her housemates just a little. With nothing else to do, she decided to go to bed. After all, it was almost ten and she'd had a long day. As she brushed her teeth, she hoped everyone was still having a good time.

She rubbed moisturizer into her face, wondering if she would ever have the social fortitude to make it through a whole evening out with friends. "You are a wimp," she told her reflection in the mirror. "Okay, maybe you're not a wimp. Maybe you just prefer a quiet evening at home. And maybe you should quit talking to yourself." Well, unless she could think of something positive to say . . . She stared at her reflection. "At least you gave it a try," she finally said. "Baby steps are okay." She smiled and turned off the light. As her grandma used to say when Riva was young and impatient, "Rome wasn't built in a day."

Riva could hear voices in the house and knew her housemates were home, but the voices sounded loud . . . and angry. She went to her bedroom door to listen. It seemed the disagreement was between Laurel and Kitty—no big surprise—and poor Windy was trying to referee. Riva considered going out to help Windy but remembered what Paul used to say about domestic disputes. Best to stay away. And so she just said a silent prayer for the women, asking God to restore peace in her home. But as loud angry footsteps stormed up the stairs, voices still raised, she suspected peace would not come easily.

She cracked open the door. It sounded like Windy was trying to calm Laurel down. Feeling guilty for being such a coward, she tiptoed out. "Everyone okay?" she asked tentatively.

"No, we are not okay," Laurel spat back.

"I'm sorry," Windy said. "Did we wake you?"

"I wasn't in bed yet." Riva looked at Laurel. "What's wrong?"

"Kitty is wrong. All wrong. That woman is a conceited nightmare that someone should kick to the curb."

Riva blinked. "Wow, I didn't think you were a violent person."

She glared at Riva. "You never should've let her move into the house."

Riva wanted to point out that Kitty had come here at Laurel's recommendation but suspected that wouldn't help this situation. "What happened?"

"I do not care to talk about it," Laurel growled. "I'm going to bed." As she stormed up the stairs, Windy exchanged glances with Riva. She lowered her voice, offering to tell the whole story.

"In the library," Riva directed.

After they closed the doors behind them and sat down, Windy began. "It probably started shortly after you left. Kitty kept urging Marcus to dance with her and, to defer her, he danced with Laurel. And even with me. In the meantime, Kitty was consuming more mojitos. I suggested we call it a night, but Laurel was enjoying Marcus's attention. Consequently, Kitty was getting more jealous. At one point we were all just sitting at the table, and Kitty started to pick on Laurel, poking at her age and appearance and whatever . . . trying to get her goat. But Laurel was handling it like a lady. I was really proud of her."

"What went wrong?"

"Marcus made a comment about you—how you were smart to leave when you did. He wanted to go home too. Of course, Kitty had to question him on that, saying how both you and Laurel were over the hill. Then she began to flirt with Marcus shamelessly. We could tell she'd over-imbibed, but she was literally throwing herself at my poor brother, telling him he'd have more fun with a younger woman. And then, she took advantage of your absence by slamming you."

"Sounds like a good time was had by all," Riva said sarcastically.

"Well, Marcus got fed up. He spoke up in your defense, which made Laurel madder. I think he knew it was hopeless, so he decided to leave. I followed his lead, telling Laurel if she wanted to stay, Marcus would take me home. But Laurel wanted to go with me. The three of us were in the parking lot when Kitty came running after us, saying she needed a ride. She grabbed onto Marcus."

Riva nodded. "No surprise there."

"Don't be too sure. Laurel started to tell Kitty to back off. And Kitty, probably thanks to the mojitos, came unglued. I actually thought it was going to become a physical fight right there in the parking lot. Kitty's voice was so loud, people were actually watching." Windy frowned. "Pretty wild scene. Like a couple of adolescents in the high school parking lot. I was embarrassed for both of them. Mostly for Laurel. She wanted to keep her cool, but Kitty kept pushing her buttons."

"Oh my. What happened then?"

"Marcus grabbed Kitty by the arm and said he'd take her home. Of course, she liked that, but poor Laurel was fit to be tied. She ranted all the way home. I was trying to calm her down before we got inside, but then Marcus dropped Kitty off and it started up again. They were being so loud in the driveway, I had to get them inside. But honestly, Riva, I've never seen anything like it. Two women their age acting like juveniles."

Riva took in a slow breath. "If I'd known having housemates would be like this, I'm not sure I'd have gotten into this."

"I'm so sorry." Windy looked almost tearful. "I hate fighting and wouldn't blame you for turning all of us out, but I'm so grateful to live here, Riva."

"I know you are. And I'm grateful you're here. I just don't know what to do about Kitty and Laurel."

"I think Marcus feels guilty too. I'd been nagging him to bring along some of his single male friends. I'll tell him he can't come to dinner tomorrow night unless he brings at least one other fellow with him. It's not like this house is his personal harem."

Riva smirked. "Is that every man's secret dream? To have a houseful of women fawning over him. Not that we all are. But maybe it feels like that to him."

"To be fair, I can tell he hates it as much as we do. It's like he's stuck between a rock and a hard place."

"He's not the only one." Riva frowned. "Well, it seems clear that Kitty is the spoiler. If she didn't live here, I think we'd be okay. The question is, how will I get rid of her?"

"That's a good question." Windy let out a yawn. "Why don't we sleep on it?"

"Good idea. And I need to pray on it." Riva stood.

Windy got to her feet. "And don't forget you promised to go to drumming session with me tomorrow."

Riva cringed. "Tomorrow?"

"Think of it as therapy. It'll help you break out of your shell and escape your inhibitions."

Riva held back an eyeroll. If anyone else mentioned her inhibitions tonight, well, she might just let loose and deck them. And then she'd see how they felt about her being overly repressed!

Chapter 20

For the first half of Windy's drumming session, Riva felt awkward, out of place, and tempted to sneak out. The problem was she'd ridden with Windy, and it was about a five-mile walk back into town—and more than ninety degrees outside. Not that this old barn was much cooler, and it was getting warmer by the minute. She wondered how these other women, about fifty of them, weren't overheating as they danced around the barn, chanting and singing and playing their drums. Windy's cheeks were flushed and her brow glistened, but she appeared to be having the time of her life.

Riva suspected if Fiona had come, she'd be enjoying it too. But she'd been called to work at the last minute. Riva hadn't even left the folding chair she'd sat in when they first arrived. The chairs were still circled, but very few were occupied. Instead of feeling like a wallflower, she was starting to feel conspicuous for not participating. But like Windy had told her, she was supposed to do only what she was comfortable with.

Realizing she might feel more at ease mixing with the women, she abruptly stood and joined the throng. After a few trips around the circle, she began to relax some. She beat her borrowed drum with more enthusiasm. And after several more loops, she started to enjoy the sound and movement and music. Was this what it felt like to cut loose and not worry about what others thought of her? She used to be free-spirited and easygoing back in her youth. But after marrying young, having kids, and reinventing a career track, well, her grown-up responsibilities had taken over and changed her. Finally, caretaking for Paul had sealed the deal. Drained of any ability to simply have good old-fashioned, unrestrained fun, she'd resided to growing old. Gracefully? Or truth be told, she'd given up.

Riva paused from drumming to really see the women around her. From gray-haired earth muffins to young women in yoga pants, they were all from different walks of life, but they seemed to share one thing—a happy abandonment. She wanted that too. So if dancing around, beating a drum, and howling like a she-wolf could free her from her "inhibition" trap, she'd try it. Maybe it was just what the doctor had ordered.

By the time the session ended, Riva knew she would come back again. She felt strangely energized and refreshed and more connected to her heavenly Father. "That was amazing," she told Windy as they got into her VW Bug later on. "Thank you for bringing me."

"I noticed it took you time to warm up, but then you were really present."

"I feel like I got over some kind of obstacle or wall. Who knew pounding a drum could be so inspiring."

"And liberating." Windy nodded. "When I first started going, I was trying to find myself. I had gotten so confused . . . I was trying so hard to fit into a traditional role that I think I swept my unconventional childhood under the proverbial rug. But my traditional world had been vanishing too. When I lost Bill and my house and my job, I started to feel pretty lost. And invisible."

Riva pointed to Windy's tie-dye shirt and flamboyant leggings. "You don't look invisible to me."

Windy laughed. "I suppose clothes make me look more visible, but that's not what I mean. There was something deep inside me that made me feel like I was slowly disappearing. I was worried about getting older, being alone, having no home. More and more I felt invisible, like the vanishing woman."

"I guess I sometimes feel invisible too. But I think I've gotten used to it. Maybe even comfortable with it. I assumed it was just part of aging. Especially in our youth-worshiping culture. Older women tend to blend into the woodwork."

"If they choose to. But I think we can live differently. We can keep embracing life. Just because we're older doesn't mean we can't have fun."

"Like last night with Laurel and Kitty?" Riva teased.

"Okay, that wasn't exactly fun. It could've been though."

"Speaking of that, did you come up with any brilliant ideas for how we can convince Kitty to move on?"

"Get her married off?" Windy chuckled.

"Right . . . that might take some time."

"Evict her?" Windy suggested, tapping her chin. "No. Maybe we need to go about it more creatively."

"Creatively?"

"Yes. Find out what gets under her skin and devise a way to dish it out."

"Such as?"

"Like if she wants peace and quiet, we'd become noisy. Although I don't think that she'd care. And if she were a neat freak, we could create messes. But I got a sneak peek in her room the other day, and the woman's a slob."

"I have a feeling that Kitty would be better at getting to us than we could ever have luck getting to her."

Windy nodded. "I remember a Melanie Griffith movie where this guy, I think he's played by Michael Keaton. Anyway, he's this lowlife who moves into this couple's basement and starts to drive them absolutely wild. His goal is to take their house from them, and it gets pretty gnarly."

Riva cringed. "I hope you're not suggesting that Kitty would do something that depraved."

"No, of course not. But it was a creepy movie." Windy turned down Riva's street, revving her VW's engine to climb the hill.

"I think your first idea was the best." Riva waved to a neighbor walking their dog.

"Huh?"

"You know, to get Kitty married off."

"Well, don't expect Marcus to help us with that." Windy chuckled. "Poor guy got so exasperated with her last night, if there'd been a bus running, he might've tossed her right under it."

"Your brother is too much of a gentleman to do that."

Windy parked in the driveway. "Maybe, but if he gets pushed too hard . . ."

"I felt kinda guilty leaving Kitty and Laurel home alone in the house when we left." Riva got out. "But the place appears to still be standing."

"I bet Kitty has a hangover today. She's probably not feeling energetic enough to torment Laurel."

"Speaking of energetic." Riva stretched her hands skyward, inhaling deeply. "Drumming made me feel ready to take on something."

"Like Kitty?"

Riva wrinkled her nose. "Let's not push it." She pointed to the front yard, still in need of some attention. "I meant energetic enough to pull some more weeds."

Windy put her car in park. "Don't get overheated. I heard we'll be close to triple digits today."

"Good point. Maybe I'll wait until a cool morning." She opened the front door. "Do you need any help with dinner tonight? Or have you changed plans?"

"You mean due to our feuding roomies?"

"Or the heat."

"Fiona already invited some of her bandmates, and I told Marcus he has to bring at least one friend. Plus, I've made salads and have seafood all ready to grill. So as far as I'm concerned, we're still on." Windy looked up toward the house and then lowered her voice. "Maybe we'll get lucky and Kitty will have other plans. She seemed to make a number of young male friends last night. Cross your fingers. She could have a hot date."

Riva crossed her fingers.

"And if not, we'll just let the good times roll. Right?"

"Yeah, right." But Riva wondered what it might really take to get Kitty to seek alternative housing. She didn't want to do anything underhanded. Perhaps she just needed to be the adult here and talk face-to-face with Kitty. Riva would gently explain her incompatibility concerns with the other tenants. She could offer Kitty two weeks' notice, refund her last month's rent, as well as return her full security deposit regardless of the condition of her bedroom and hall bath, which based on Windy's descriptions, was less than pristine. But she didn't want to throw a wrench into tonight's dinner plans. Maybe this conversation could wait until tomorrow.

Riva was relieved not to cross paths with Kitty for the whole day, and when she went to help Windy with dinner preparations, Kitty was still nowhere to be seen.

"Do you think she's okay?" Riva asked as she wiped down the backyard table. "Should anyone check on her?"

"Fiona saw her leaving earlier. She thought she was headed to her salon."

"Have you talked to Laurel?"

Windy nodded. "Yes, she was just down here offering to help."

"How did she seem? I mean, after last night's turbulence." Riva shook out a gingham tablecloth, then smoothed it over the table.

Windy bit her lip. "To be honest, she seemed a little stressed. I think Kitty's taking her toll on poor Laurel."

"Just one more reason to encourage Kitty to move on." Riva cringed to imagine that conversation. What had made her think she could be a landlord?

Windy fanned herself with a hand. "It's still awfully warm out here. Do you think our guests can handle it?"

"It should be cooling off soon. How about I make a gallon of ice water with lemons to put out here? And we used to have a backyard fan. Maybe I can hunt it down in the garage."

"Good idea." Windy looked around. "I think things are under control out here. I'm going to make a fresh pitcher of iced tea."

Glad to be out of the heat, Riva went to the garage to see if she could unearth the fan Paul had gotten for days like this. While poking around, she found her old box of art supplies. Paul had made the box for her when the kids were small. She opened the lid to see everything still neatly in place, just like she'd left it. Maybe this was the "new thing" she wanted to take on. How long had it been since she'd dabbled? She set the wooden box by the door, promising herself to look into it later.

Finally, she found the fan behind a stack of tires. She dusted it off, then set it up near the picnic table in back. Then, remembering how Paul used to water everything down, including the pavers, to cool things off on evenings like this, she decided to do the same. As she turned on the hose, she thought of Paul and how he would approve. How he'd be happy to see her out here enjoying the yard again. Like maybe she was coming back to life.

Feeling grimy and rumpled by the heat, Riva took a quick shower, then pulled out a lightweight dress she hadn't worn in ages. She held it up in front of the mirror and frowned. Was it too youthful? Was the Hawaiian print too bright? Or was she just being overly cautious? Remembering her energy today after drumming, she decided it was time to embrace another challenge. She slipped into the dress, enjoying the cool feel of cotton. In fact, the dress itself made her feel happy. It represented good carefree times in past summers. Perhaps it was just what she needed tonight. Because she was determined to have a good time.

She could hear voices in the house as she left her room. Marcus and Windy and a tall gray-haired man were visiting in the foyer. "There she is now." Windy waved Riva over. "Come meet Marcus's friend Wes Walker. Wes, this is Riva."

"Pleasure to meet you, Riva." With a wide smile on his face, Wes shook her hand. "I was just telling Windy this is a gorgeous old house. Amazing woodwork. I'm guessing it was built in the late 1800s?"

"1898," she told him.

"Wes's an architect," Windy supplied, leading them toward the kitchen.

"Retired architect," he said. "But I can still admire a work of art like this."

"I've never heard it called that, but I don't disagree." Riva watched as Marcus put a bottle of white wine in her fridge. It was kind of cute the way he already knew his way around her house.

Windy stood in front of the French doors leading to the patio. "It's still pretty warm out there, but we've got ice and drinks set up, and Riva has a fan running to create a breeze."

"No problem for me," Wes told her. "I like a warm evening." He opened the door, waiting for Riva to pass through. "What an inviting backyard."

"We've all been working on it. I sort of let things go after my husband passed. Windy is our landscape director. She's got a real green thumb."

"My sister is quite a gal," Marcus told Wes. "She gardens and cooks and even volunteers at the Hummingbird Gallery."

"You're an artist?" Wes asked Windy.

She shrugged as she filled a glass with ice water. "I'm more of a dabbler."

"Me too." Riva told them about rediscovering her old art supplies today. "Maybe we should dabble together, Windy."

"I'd love that." Windy filled another water glass, handing each of the men one. "We should stay hydrated," she told them.

"What mediums do you ladies dabble in?" Wes asked.

"Watercolors." Windy handed Riva a water glass. "Particularly flowers and plant life."

"Watercolors are too challenging for me," Riva admitted as they took seats near the fan. "Maybe I'm just too much of a control freak. I prefer acrylic for painting. I think I'll start with pencil sketching when I get started up again. Maybe work up into pen and ink." She glanced at Wes. "I'm not an architect by any means, but I always enjoyed drawing interesting structures like bridges and old houses and beach town shanties. I've always wanted to draw this house in pen and ink."

"You should do that," Wes encouraged. "There's so much detail to capture. Gingerbread and roof angles and leaded windows . . . it'd make a good subject."

They visited for a while, until Windy said she needed to get things ready in the kitchen.

"Need help?" Riva offered.

"Nah. It's mostly all done, and Fiona already offered to do KP." Windy looked at her brother. "Can you fire up the grill for me?"

"You got it." He stood.

While Marcus fiddled with the grill, Wes and Riva chatted. He was an interesting guy, but he also seemed interested in her. He was just asking about her children when Laurel came out. She glanced all around, as if looking for something . . . or, more likely, someone.

"It's just the three of us out here," Riva called out. "Come join us. Get yourself a glass of water. Windy wants to be sure we stay hydrated."

While Laurel assisted Marcus with the grill, Wes asked Riva another question. "How long have you lived in this beautiful house?"

"It's been in the family since my grandparents bought it," she explained, "but I've pretty much lived here my whole life. My parents moved in to help with my grandmother after Grandpa died. I was only three. Then I wasn't here during college and my first few years of marriage, but then my parents moved to Arizona and Paul and I moved in here."

"Did you tell him how your fear of getting rid of books kept you here?" Laurel called out in a slightly teasing tone.

"What?" Wes looked puzzled.

"My library," Riva explained. "My grandfather and father were both attorneys, like my late husband, and the book collection in the library is, uh, quite large. Partly due to them and partly because I'm a bookaholic. The idea of selling my home and the chore of packing or selling all those books—or burning them like my daughter suggested—was a little disturbing. It sounds silly, but it's one reason I decided to take in renters . . . so I could remain in my home and handle the expenses."

Laurel came over to sit by Riva. "I just hope that you're not regretting having your renters here."

"Yeah, I'm curious how things went last night." Marcus sat down too.

"What was last night?" Wes asked.

"A squabble between housemates." Riva glanced at Laurel. "But maybe you don't want to talk about it."

Laurel shrugged. "Where is she, anyway?"

"She who?" Wes asked.

"Our housemate who's been a little difficult," Riva told him. "I guess I should warn you in case she shows up."

"Is she coming tonight?"

"No one seems to know."

Laurel groaned. "Well, if she comes and opens her bag of tricks, I will perform a vanishing act."

"What does this woman do that's so bad?" Wes asked with curiosity.

Riva grimaced. "It's hard to describe."

"Let's just say Kitty is used to getting her own way," Marcus told him. "And if she's had too much to drink, like she did last night, well, she can get even pushier."

"That's putting it mildly." Laurel frowned. "She likes to be the center of attention. Particularly with eligible males. Or maybe it doesn't matter if they're eligible or not."

"Fair warning," Marcus said in a somber tone, "if she shows up, I'll be trying to distance myself from her tonight."

"You and me both," Laurel added.

Windy and Fiona came out with food to put on the grill, followed by a couple of men Riva recognized from Fiona's band last night. Introductions were made and Riva complimented them on their musical skills. She turned to Wes. "I hope you can hear them sometime. They're so talented."

"Fiona hinted that we might need to sing for our supper," a man named Brad told her. "And we just so happened to bring our instruments, so if you want a little merrymaking after dinner, just ask."

"I'll ask right now," Riva told him. "That'd be wonderful."

When the seafood was grilled and Kitty still hadn't shown up, Windy suggested they eat without her, and soon the eight of them were seated at the table. Interestingly enough, they alternated genders all the way around. So much for Marcus's "harem." Riva had Wes on one side of her and Brad on the other, and to her surprise, she felt relaxed and at ease. Nothing like the last time they'd gathered out here. Perhaps she really was making progress, one baby step at a time.

Chapter 21

As the eight of them dined, Riva sensed Fiona's interest in Brad was more personal than professional. So Riva focused her attention back on Wes. He was a likable fellow and a good conversationalist. In some ways, he reminded her of Paul. Not in looks since he was taller and had more hair, but something about his confidence and easy humor felt familiar.

She glanced across the table, where Laurel was chatting with Marcus about the upcoming challenges in the school year. She could tell that Laurel was in her element, but Marcus seemed unusually quiet. Perhaps he was worried, like she was, that Kitty would show up and toss a giant Kitty-shaped wrench into the works.

Eventually, dinner was over and everyone was too stuffed to enjoy the frozen dessert Windy had prepared for them. "Why don't we wait until later," Riva suggested.

"Yes," Fiona agreed. "We need some music and dancing first. We can work up our appetites." She poked Brad in the shoulder. "Feel like getting out your guitar?"

"I was just waiting to be asked," he told her.

Riva started picking up the dishes. "I'll clear while you musicians set up."

"But I'm on KP tonight," Fiona pointed out.

"Not if you're providing music," Riva told her. "It's more than a fair exchange."

"I'll help." Wes picked up a large salad bowl and a pitcher of iced tea, then followed Riva into the kitchen. As Riva prepared leftovers for the fridge, Wes carried dishes in, then began to rinse and load the dishwasher.

"You're good help," Riva told him when they finished up.

"My ex used to accuse me of being obsessive about the kitchen." He gave the countertop one final swipe. "But after a big dinner, I never liked seeing a dirty kitchen the next morning."

"I'm the same way." She was curious about his story, but she didn't want to ask. "I got very particular after we remodeled this kitchen. I loved it so much that I couldn't bear to see it all messed up. It got so that I could keep it fairly straight even while cooking."

"Clean up as you go. I do that too. Makes short work later."

"I tried to teach my kids to do it." Riva put the plastic wrap back in the drawer. "But I don't think they appreciated the concept." She shrugged.

"How many kids do you have?"

"Just two." She told him about Brent and Kenzie. "Do you have children?"

"Two daughters. They're in their midthirties and live down in California, near their mom."

"Do you see them much?"

"They visit sometimes. Holidays or vacation time. They grew up in Greenwood, so they have ties besides me up here. They're good girls. But neither are in any hurry to get married or have children. I don't know why so many young people are waiting so long to settle down, but I suppose I could blame myself."

"Why's that?" She rinsed her hands in the sink.

"Because they watched their parents' marriage fail." He pulled out an island stool and sat.

"And you blame yourself for that?" She rubbed some lotion on her hands, studying him.

"Not entirely. It takes two." He toyed with a mason jar of daisies that Riva had picked that morning. "But I think Livvie, that's my ex, had a midlife crisis of sorts. We were empty nesters, and she was restless and unhappy and determined to reinvent herself. And then her mother had health problems and Livvie went down to the Bay Area to help her. Her mom died and Livvie got the house and enticed our girls to come down there with her." He sighed.

"How long ago was that?"

"It's been about five years now."

"Any chance you'll get back together?"

He shook his head. "She's remarried to a guy ten years younger than her. According to my girls, he just wanted a 'sugar mama,' but Livvie actually seems happy so maybe it's working." He smiled crooked. "At least it got me out of paying alimony. One thing to be grateful for."

"Aren't you done in here yet?" Marcus asked as he came inside.

Riva waved a hand toward the clean kitchen. "We were just chatting."

"Oh?" Marcus looked from Wes back to her. "About anything interesting?"

"Just getting acquainted," Wes told him. "We discovered we have the same compulsion for tidying up kitchens."

"Well, they're getting the music started out there." Marcus paused at the sound of someone walking into the kitchen.

Riva turned to see Kitty, dressed in her usual flamboyant style. She looked all lit up and happy. Perhaps a bit too much.

"Well, hello there, peeps," she chirped in a slurry voice. "Am I just in time for din-din? Windy said it was gonna be good tonight."

"We just finished up," Riva answered abruptly. She suspected Kitty had been drinking and hoped to avoid another scene. She exchanged glances with Marcus, but he remained quiet, his face blank. Maybe he was still troubled over last night's fiasco.

"You didn't wait for me?" Kitty's lower lip jutted out as she tugged on a stool, pulling it right next to Wes before she sat down, nearly toppling off in the process. "I haven't had a single thing to eat all day," she told Riva. "Well, besides stale coffee and Diet Coke." She kicked off her platform shoes, then snickered. "Okay, okay, I did have two or maybe it was three martinis with my girls after an exhausting day at my salon. The clientele was a nightmare of cranky old ladies and snarky teen girls. Did you know it's prom night?"

"I didn't know." Riva exchanged glances with Wes, wondering what he thought of her strange housemate.

"But seriously, I'm starving, Riva."

"Well, you definitely need to eat something." Riva wondered if Kitty's current state had anything to do with her day of fasting but didn't care to inquire. "You'll find some great leftovers in the fridge."

"Dinner was delicious," Wes told her. "Be thankful we didn't polish it all off."

"Please, help yourself," Riva encouraged. Hopefully, Kitty didn't expect to be waited on.

But Kitty just sat there like a stone. With her chin balanced on a cupped hand, she stared at her shiny lime-green fingernails, then looked up at Wes as if just noticing him sitting there. "Hey, good-lookin', whatcha got cookin'?" She leaned in closer now, her face just inches from his, and grinned. "*Who* may I ask are *you*?"

"Sorry, Kitty. This is Wes Walker. I forgot you haven't met yet." Riva glanced at Marcus. "Wes and Marcus are buddies."

Kitty stuck out a hand. "Pleased to meet ya, Wes. I guess we're trying to balance out the numbers, eh?"

"Balance out what numbers?" Wes's expression was impossible to read as he studied Kitty. He could've been intrigued or repulsed or amused, Riva had no idea.

"You know, the boy-girl ratio." Kitty jerked a thumb toward Marcus. "Stop the ladies from fighting over that one." She grinned at Wes. "Marcus needed some competition. Bring it! *Right*?"

Wes barely nodded, then slowly stood. "I hear the music playing outside. Sounds pretty good. I think I'll go check it out."

"Me too," Riva chimed in as she opened the patio door. "Go ahead and fix yourself a plate of leftovers," she called to Kitty. "After your tiring day, you might want to take it to your room where you can relax and put your feet up." Not waiting for a response, she slipped outside, silently praying that their so-far peaceful evening wouldn't be derailed by Kitty's unpredictable antics. Three martinis on an empty stomach, really? How was Kitty even walking a straight line right now? Maybe she wasn't.

"Glad you could rejoin us," Laurel said as Riva sat beside her. "Anyone else coming?"

Riva knew Laurel probably meant Marcus, but instead of answering, she just nodded toward the door. "Kitty came home," she said quietly. "In the kitchen."

Laurel let out a groan and now Windy looked worried.

"Do you think she'll come out here?" Windy asked.

"Who knows? But she sounds tired from work . . . and maybe other things." Riva grimaced.

"Like a hangover," Laurel suggested.

Riva shrugged. "Anyway, she hadn't eaten yet, so I encouraged her to fix herself a plate to take to her room." Riva paused as Wes sat down by Windy.

Laurel scowled darkly. "If Kitty comes out I'll just make myself scarce."

Riva didn't know what to say so she segued. "Their music sure sounds good tonight." She tried to sound cheery. "It's fun hearing a trio. Not so loud, and their harmonies are amazing."

Eager to curtail this conversation, Riva leaned back to listen to a pleasant Irish folk tune. It could be such a perfect evening, great food, good company, nice yard, warm weather . . . except for the spoiler lurking in the kitchen. She wondered why Marcus had remained in there. Was he a glutton for punishment or was he simply trying to do damage control with Kitty? Perhaps he was giving her the attention she seemed to insatiably crave. But if he could manage to keep Kitty from coming out here and crashing the party, well, did she really care? Okay, maybe just a little . . . for Marcus's sake. She didn't like to think of a guest martyring himself for the sake of the party.

The music got cheerier and Windy grabbed Riva and Laurel's hands, tugging them to their feet. "Come on, ladies."

The three of them danced to the upbeat music and then Windy called out to Wes, who was watching with interest from his Adirondack chair. "Don't you wanna dance off your dinner, Wes? Make room for the yummy dessert I've got waiting in the freezer?" Windy went over to pull him up. "Come on, shake a leg, old man. It's time for some boot-scooting boogie."

Wes laughed as he joined the women, but after a few more songs, Riva could feel her concern for Marcus growing. Or maybe it was guilt. Had she abandoned him? What if Kitty was in there making him miserable right now? Holding him hostage with her bad manners and nonstop mouth? Was the poor guy too polite to walk away? Did he need rescuing? Since this was her house, which suggested she was the hostess, was she responsible for the welfare of her guests? Maybe . . . And so, sneaking away from the happy dance party, she went back inside.

The kitchen was void of people. Other than the muted sound of music outside, it was quiet. The countertops were a cluttered mess of opened leftovers containers, strewn about and slopped over with random serving spoons and utensils scattered. How could one person possibly create so much havoc? And to do it so quickly? Riva was about to tidy the kitchen again, then questioned herself. Why should she clean up after Kitty? And where was Kitty, anyway? And where was Marcus?

She went out of the kitchen, listening for the sound of voices, but the house remained silent. She went past the library, then caught a bit of movement from the corner of her eye, but the glass doors were shut and, with no lights on in there and only dusky light from the outside, it was hard to see clearly. She cracked open a glass door and peered in to find Marcus in one of the old leather club chairs, head bent down as if asleep.

"Marcus?" she whispered, not wanting to disturb him.

His head snapped up. "Oh?" He blinked as she turned on a reading lamp. "I thought you were Kitty."

"Sorry to disappoint you. I thought you were, uh, napping." She sat down in the chair across from him.

"Just enjoying a moment of peace." He rubbed his temples. "Trying to lose a headache."

"Do you need something for it?"

"No. It's better now. Just needed a quiet hideout."

"Hideout? From what?"

"That wild Kitty in the kitchen. She wouldn't stop talking and complaining and rattling dishes and making messes. I just couldn't take it. I'm sure I made her mad when I abandoned her. I told her I wanted to be alone to think and then I heard her stomp up the stairs. Man, that girl can make some noise. But I'm sure she's inebriated." He frowned. "What are you going to do about her, Riva?"

Riva leaned back and closed her eyes. "I have no idea."

"She's a real piece of work."

"I know," she said. "She's making Laurel crazy."

"I suppose we should be grateful she didn't go out there and go after Laurel again. That's another reason I didn't want to go back out. I didn't want to get her riled up enough to stir things up with Laurel. I would've just gone home, but I brought Wes tonight."

"Sounds like you did the right thing with Kitty. And I do think Wes's enjoying himself. He was even dancing."

Marcus sat up straighter, causing a book in his lap to slide to the floor. "I sneaked one of your books." He leaned down to pick it up.

"Which one?"

His smile looked slightly cheesy as he held up an old Louis L'Amour paperback. "Good ole comfort read."

"Hey, sometimes we need those."

"I'll say. I've read this one before, but it's been ages."

"Did you get very far?"

"Just the first chapter. But then the light faded, and I wanted to rest my eyes."

"I read some of those after Paul and I first got married. He had a small collection. I think they were his comfort reads too. Especially after law school. He needed an escape."

"I guess we all do at times." Marcus almost smiled. "I always liked how L'Amour's characters were so heroic and yet so human."

"That's a good way to describe it. Heroic yet human."

"Something to aspire to." His mouth twisted to one side. "You should be out there with your guests and the music. Don't feel you need to keep me company."

"I just wanted to make sure that Kitty hadn't gagged and shackled you and dragged you off to her lair." Riva laughed. "Sorry, I shouldn't have said that."

He laughed too. "I don't know why not. It's not that far from the truth. She did get mad at me for rejecting her advances just now."

"I'm sorry about that. I have to figure a way to get her to move out." She waved a hand. "But I don't need to trouble you with that."

For a long moment, they both just sat there. The gentle glow of the reading light illuminating the spines of the books made the room feel cozy. And above, the ceiling fan was slowly rotating, so despite the overly warm day, the temperature was comfortable.

"So tell me, Riva, what do you think of Wes? He really seemed to like you. And, believe me, I know the guy, I'm not exaggerating. I never saw him warm up to a woman that quickly before.

To be honest, I was hoping he'd be interested in Windy. I could imagine those two together. Wes seems the kind of man who could use some kind nurturing. Windy would be good for that."

"Yeah, he told me a bit about his ex and his daughters. Sounds like he might've gotten the short end of the stick."

"That's how he and I became friends. We met at church and became golf buddies. Then we discovered we'd been through similar experiences with our wives. Oh, Livvie didn't die like Anne did, but she left Wes high and dry in a similar way."

Riva just nodded. "Both sound hard."

"Yeah. A bad marriage leaves some wounds, for sure."

"I appreciate how Wes takes his share of responsibility for his failed marriage. Not all guys would do that."

Marcus glanced at the book in his lap, fiddling with the bent corner of the cover and then looked up. "I realize I'm partly to blame for Anne's discrepancies too," he said quietly. "I wasn't the most attentive husband."

"I think you told me that before," she said. "I don't know if there's anyone who's been married or is still married who hasn't made mistakes. Even if you're heroic, you're still human, right?" She smiled.

He barely nodded. "I guess you're right."

"I think we all need to move on. We need to remember to forgive ourselves and to forgive others . . . like Jesus taught. I don't think we need to keep dragging ourselves through it or carry that old baggage with us." She told him about drumming with Windy and how freeing and invigorating it had been when she finally allowed herself to move forward. "I had kind of an aha moment . . . when I realized that my inability to participate and enjoy myself socially was related to my last two years of caring for Paul, watching him, well, dying, I felt like a giant light bulb went on."

"How's that?" he asked.

"Well, like I said, Paul was dying. There was no getting around it. Every day I could see him getting weaker, having more pain, steadily fading away . . . I knew he was leaving me." She took in a steadying breath. "I think in a way, I sort of began to go with him. Does that even make sense?"

Marcus leaned forward with interest. "I think it's beginning to, but can you elaborate a little?"

She shrugged. She actually wanted to minimize the experience. But at the same time, it was a very big deal to her. She wanted to be open about it. "While I was drumming with all those women, I began to feel like I was waking up. Like it was time to return to the land of the living. But I had to make a choice. I needed to be willing to do more than just exist. I needed to fully live life again. For some reason, beating on a drum helped. Sure, it was only one small step, but it took me out of my comfort zone, and I really wanted it. As strange as it sounds to hear myself say this, I'm ready to embrace life now." She considered this. "Okay, *embrace* might be too strong a verb at the moment. I know myself too well. But I do want to participate . . . to learn to embrace. I don't want to be shut down or partially dead. I really do want to live now."

Was it her imagination or were his eyes glistening? They both just sat for a bit and then he spoke. "Thank you for sharing that. I needed to hear those words."

"I guess I needed to say them," she confessed.

He nodded with a thoughtful expression. Perhaps he was just soaking it in. But realizing neither of them were speaking now, she got uncomfortable. Was it wrong to be sitting in the same room that she and Paul had so happily occupied together—with another man? Apparently old habits, and thought patterns, really did die hard. But she reminded herself that she was living a new life now, and the awkwardness evaporated. She sighed in relief. Baby steps, she told herself. Just keep moving forward . . . one small step at a time.

Chapter 22

It wasn't until the guests had departed, and Riva's housemates, other than Windy, had shuffled off to bed, that Riva got to hear details about what had transpired out on the patio while she and Marcus were talking. All she knew was that as soon as they emerged from the library, a mass exodus appeared to be taking place. She and Windy politely thanked their guests for coming and told them goodbye. Then, seeing they were alone in the foyer, she turned to Windy. "What happened?"

"Privately?" Windy asked.

"Come to my room," Riva told her. Then with Windy in the chair and Riva perched on the end of her bed, she listened as Windy gave her the report.

"So we were having a really nice time. We missed you and Marcus, but we figured you guys were talking. And that's cool. Anyway, the six of us were enjoying ourselves . . . until Kitty decided to make an appearance." Windy frowned. "I don't like to say it, but we all felt pretty sure she was snookered. Drunk as a skunk."

"Oh, dear. I know she'd been drinking with girlfriends earlier, but I hoped having some food in her stomach would help."

"Laurel is certain that Kitty hides alcohol in her room and that she's been up there imbibing."

Riva wasn't too surprised but didn't know what to do about it.

"Laurel and I took turns dancing with Wes until the band got tired of playing and Fiona put some music on her speaker. Her plan was to teach us an Irish folk dance. Anyway, we were learning some new moves, just laughing and having fun, and then Kitty showed up."

Riva imagined the scene from *The Wizard of Oz* when the Wicked Witch of the West crashed a Munchkin celebration. "What'd she do?"

"Oh, you know, it was typical bad Kitty behavior. She was loud and obnoxious, attention seeking, and flirting with every male out there. First, she wanted to know Marcus's whereabouts, but no one seemed to know, so she set her sights on Wes. Fiona had just been teaching us a tricky spin, and Wes and Laurel were trying it." Windy's eyes widened. "Kitty told us she wanted to dance too and pretty much shoved Laurel aside to claim Wes as her partner." Windy shook her head. "Well, Laurel was not having it."

Riva cringed. "That must've been interesting."

"Honestly, it looked like it would turn into a big hot mess."

"A real Kitty fight?" Riva attempted a weak smile.

"For sure. Laurel was so enraged, I thought she might flatten Kitty."

"But she didn't, did she?"

"No, no . . . thank goodness. Laurel was frothing, but she didn't say anything. Just stormed out. I checked on her a little bit later. That might be when the party started to dissipate. Laurel was getting ready for bed, but she's still furious. She told me in no uncertain terms that if Kitty doesn't go, she will."

"I don't want Laurel to leave."

"None of us do. Well, aside from Kitty. I suspect she wants Laurel to move out. I don't even know why. I mean, it seems like it's about the men and jealousy. But, really, I don't think Kitty sees Laurel as real competition." Windy's brow creased. "So I sort of took the bull by the horns. The musicians were already packing up to go so I pulled Kitty aside to talk. I didn't get angry. I just explained how she'd really hurt Laurel's feelings and that it wasn't the first time she'd stepped on Laurel's toes. Then I told her that Laurel was threatening to move out."

"What did Kitty say?"

"She said 'dibs on Laurel's room.'" Windy shook her head. "She honestly thinks she deserves the ensuite. She even used the word *deserve*."

"How in the world did she draw that conclusion?"

"She claimed it's because of her work. To keep up her image, she needs a better space to fix up. She says Laurel doesn't work so she doesn't need it."

"But Kitty has the hall bath pretty much to herself."

"She doesn't like that Fiona and I take showers there. Not that we enjoy it much. The bathroom is a pigsty." Windy frowned. "I hate saying this, and I hope I'm wrong, but sometimes it feels like Kitty is trying to drive us all out."

"Wow." Riva pursed her lips, trying to think. "Well, I'll read the rental contract tomorrow and try to find a way to gently evict her."

Windy looked amused. "A gentle eviction? Sounds like an oxymoron."

"And until we figure out the Kitty problem, I'd like to boycott male guests. It just seems like it always stirs up trouble where Kitty is concerned."

"It's been fun having dinner parties, but I get what you're saying. I think that's a good idea, Riva."

"It's just not worth the stress. And I don't know about you, but I don't need to have guys around. It's like some women think they're not enough without a man in the picture. But I don't feel like that. And I don't want to."

"I don't either."

"We're enough, right?" Riva looked into Windy's eyes. "Comfortable in our single-woman skin?"

"I am." Windy nodded firmly. "And I think Laurel and Fiona are too. At least, Fiona is. I don't need a guy upsetting my applecart. Especially since I've been really enjoying my new home here with you . . . and with the others. Well, most of the others."

"I'll try to get Kitty to understand what's up tomorrow. In the meantime, if you see Laurel, please, assure her that I'm on it. I don't want to lose her as a housemate or as a friend."

"What if she still gets jealous over you and Marcus?"

Riva blinked. "I don't see why that should make her jealous. Your brother and I are only friends. We were just talking about some of the grief stages we're still working our way through. That was all. Friends. *Just friends*."

Windy held up her hands in a defensive gesture. "I know, I know. Trust me, I'm not the one who was worried." She smiled. "Not about you, anyway."

"Sorry. I suppose I was talking to myself too. Being friends with the opposite sex is still new for me."

"It sounds like a healthy step." Windy stood, placing a hand on Riva's shoulder. "And it's the best way to start any kind of relationship. As friends." She stifled a yawn. "I'm exhausted, but thanks for listening."

"Thanks for putting me on the same page. I promise to talk to Kitty first chance I get. Hopefully by tomorrow."

But Riva didn't get the opportunity to talk to Kitty the next day, or the next. In fact, no one in the house seemed to have spoken to her for several days. They'd heard her coming and going, but no words were exchanged.

"I texted her to let her know I wanted to talk," Riva said, "but she hasn't responded."

"I think she's embarrassed," Windy said. "She's deliberately keeping a low profile."

"Works for me." Laurel opened the door to the patio. "The less I see of that woman, the happier I'll be."

The three of them had adopted the habit of sitting outside with their coffee. After Fiona and Kitty went to work, they'd regroup to catch up and get their daily vitamin D out in the morning sunshine.

"I feel sorry for Kitty," Riva confessed. "She's like her own worst enemy."

"Then she's well matched." Laurel adjusted her sun hat. "And just for the record, if Kitty pulls any more of her drunken stunts, I will be giving my notice, Riva."

"So you've mentioned." Riva wanted to add "at least a dozen times," but she held her tongue. "And in case you choose to go, I've already offered the ensuite to Fiona."

Laurel scowled. "Not even going to wait until the body gets cold, eh?"

"Oh, it's not like you're dying, silly. You know I don't want you to go, but just in case things unravel, I want to ensure that Kitty doesn't sneak in there."

"Then you might want a better lock on that door." Laurel sniffed.

"Speaking of locks, did you notice Kitty has a new lock on her door?" Windy asked Riva. "I knocked this morning to remind her to get her dirty laundry out of the bathroom, but I was surprised to see she's got a deadbolt."

"Seriously?" Riva blinked.

"Did she get permission from you?" Laurel pointed at Riva.

Riva grimaced. "No."

"That should be grounds for eviction." Laurel's tone sharpened.

"Possibly . . ." Riva sipped her coffee, wishing Paul were here to give a legal opinion. Of course, if he was here, she wouldn't be in this situation. "I wonder how she put the lock on."

"She doesn't seem like a real DIY gal to me." Laurel chuckled. "Not with those long nails of hers. Did you see that lime-green nail polish she had on?"

"More than who installed the lock, I'm curious why she installed it," Windy said. "Is she trying to keep someone out? Or something in?"

"Or both?" Laurel added.

Windy pushed a strand of red hair behind an ear. "I didn't want to say anything to anyone, but the other afternoon, I was alone in the house and when I went down to the bathroom, I overheard voices . . . Kitty had a guest in her room . . . a male guest. I didn't want to mention this, but, uh, it smelled like weed."

"Oh my." Riva leaned back, staring up at the cloud-dappled sky. "That's just great."

"More reason to evict her," Laurel proclaimed. "The contract states no smoking or burning of candles or incense. And what about the smoke alarm? Why didn't it go off?"

"I don't know." Riva cringed to think of the fire hazards in an old house like this.

"Seriously, that's like three strikes right there, Riva." Laurel held up three fingers. "And no alcohol in the room makes four. Surely there must be a line about not making modifications without owner permission."

"I remember that one," Windy said. "That's why I got permission to install my AC in the loft."

Riva knew they were right about Kitty breaking the contract, but at the moment she was fixated on the new deadbolt lock and the sudden urge to inspect Kitty's room for safety. "I wonder how she got that lock put on without anyone knowing."

"Come to think of it, I remember hearing some power tool noises when I was upstairs in my loft. I think it was that same day. I thought it was at your neighbor's house since I'd noticed his lawn guy there using a weed eater." Windy bit her lip. "But now I'm sure it was her male visitor installing the lock. Sorry, I should've paid more attention."

"You don't need to be sorry. It's not your responsibility to keep tabs on Kitty. I know I should do better at handling this, but to be honest, it's a bit overwhelming." Riva's voice cracked with emotion. "I really don't know what to do about her."

"Oh, Riva." Laurel groaned. "I wish I'd never connected you to her in the first place. Maybe I should be the one to chuck her out."

"Thanks. But no one is going to chuck her out." Riva took a deep breath. "I have to do it myself. And I need to do it ethically and legally. I don't want any negative recourse on her part."

"She seems the type to do something nefarious." Laurel grimly shook her head. "Maybe that was her plan all along. Become such an obnoxious tenant that you want to kick her out, but you find out she's got a sleazy lawyer on speed dial. You wind up in court with some trumped-up charges and expensive court costs, and she winds up getting your house and you are out on your ear."

"Oh, Laurel," Windy scolded. "That's awful."

"Just ignore me." Laurel's laugh sounded nervous. "I always enjoyed a good conspiracy theory."

"Well, you better stop terrorizing our landlady," Windy warned. "Or she'll want to kick us all out."

The idea of having her home all to herself again did have some appeal. Except that Riva really did like her housemates. For the most part, anyway. "You guys don't need to worry about this . . . or me. I'll get it figured out somehow. When the time is right and I can get her to talk to me. Hopefully sooner than later."

"That's fine, but I think you should get that lock off her door ASAP," Laurel said. "It feels unsafe to me. Like she could be harboring a fugitive in there. Or hard drugs. I remember an old Lifetime movie about a beauty salon that was really a cover for drug trafficking. Maybe that's what Kitty is doing, selling dope instead of doing hair."

"Oh, Laurel, if that were true, Kitty would probably be loaded," Windy said. "She'd be living in a mansion, not renting a cheap room."

"I agree," Riva said. "But the deadbolt is still concerning."

"It's like a flag, warning us that something is off," Windy added.

"I'll speak to Kitty."

"It's your door, Riva." Laurel's tone grew firmer. "You have the right to remove that lock if you want. You don't need her permission."

"I wouldn't have a clue how to get it off." Riva tried to look unconcerned as she sipped her now-cool coffee. "I mean, I do have tools, but aren't those locks specially made to be difficult to remove?"

"I bet Marcus could get it off for us," Laurel declared.

"Of course." Windy held up her phone. "Want me to ask him?"

"No," Riva said. "Not yet. I'd appreciate his help later, but I do want to talk to Kitty first. I'd like to ask her why she felt the need and why she didn't get permission. And if she's willing to let me have a key, I might overlook it."

"I bet she won't give you a key." Laurel folded her arms in front of her.

"Then I'll inform her that I'll deal with it and Windy can ask Marcus to help."

"That should be interesting." Windy looked at her phone. "Maybe we should have Marcus here when you talk to Kitty. Kinda like a safety net. He can be the backup so that if you ask for a key and she refuses, then Marcus can just remove the lock."

"Maybe." Riva did like the idea of Marcus helping and yet . . . "That brings up another topic I've been noodling on lately. Well, since our last dinner party"—she glanced at Laurel—"Windy and I already kicked this around a little that night, but I've decided that we need a moratorium on male guests here at the house. I think it's just too stressful."

"Because of Kitty?" Laurel's brow creased. "That seems unfair."

"It's just a temporary moratorium," Windy explained. "And I agree with Riva. It gets too messy with a mixed group when, you know, some feelings get hurt. It's just not worth it. I'm supportive of boycotting the boys, for the time being anyway."

"I suppose you think I'm part of the problem," Laurel snapped.

"I never said that." Windy held up her hands defensively.

"But that's what you meant, wasn't it?" Laurel stood and dumped the last of her coffee in a potted fern. "You think I'm jealous of anyone who shows interest in your brother."

"Or anyone he shows interest in," Windy countered in a strong voice. "Okay, maybe I do think you're jealous, Laurel, but you have to admit you've been a little unreasonable."

Laurel planted her hands on her hips. "It's only because I thought Marcus liked me."

"He *does* like you," Windy argued. Now she stood and Riva suddenly wondered if this was going to turn into another kind of fight. Instead of staring, Riva decided to step aside and check on the raised veggie bed near the fence. Her friends' raised voices only seemed to prove that it really was time to close the door on male visitors of any kind. Even brothers.

"I mean, I thought he *really* liked me," Laurel said. "I've been alone all these years, Windy. I survived a trainwreck of a marriage and a miserable divorce. And I just never had a nice guy like Marcus pay attention to me. Not once in all these years. In fact, I've been told that I scare men off. So can you blame me for getting my nose out of joint when Riva stole his attention from me?"

"She didn't steal his attention." Windy came over to stand protectively by Riva. "The fact you just said that proves our point. You're not being yourself, Laurel. Not when it comes to men, anyway."

"Okay, stealing was a strong word," Laurel admitted. "But Riva knew I was hoping for something to develop with Marcus yet she kept stepping in and interfering."

Riva bent down to pull a weed, determined to calm her tone before answering her aggravating friend. Then she stood up straight and looked directly at her. "My only interest in Marcus is plain ordinary friendship. And Marcus is well aware of it. In fact, we agreed that's what we both want. To be friends. That's all. So if you and Marcus fall in love and get married, I'll be pleased as punch, Laurel. Good grief, I'll even dance at your wedding." She attempted a lighthearted laugh.

Laurel's brows arched. "Fine. I'll hold you to it. Just as long as you're not dancing with the groom." Her smile looked a little fake. "Excuse me, girls. Fred is waiting for his breakfast." She went inside.

"Speaking of the groom." Windy nudged Riva with her elbow, pointing over the side fence. "Look who's pulling into the driveway. And guess who's with him?"

Riva peered over the fence and her jaw dropped. "It's Kitty," she whispered, moving away from the fence. "Let's not get caught spying on them."

"Why is *she* with Marcus?" Windy stayed put, blatantly staring over the fence. "Or maybe I should ask why is *he* with her?"

"Come away from there. You remind me of Gladys Kravitz." Riva tugged Windy by the hand. "I'm going inside."

Windy followed. "So maybe this is good timing." She paused in the kitchen. "You can confront Kitty and then we'll ask Marcus to help you get that lock off."

Riva held up her hands, palms forward. "Okay, let's put the brakes on that. I want it handled carefully. I need to speak to Kitty first. Privately."

"I know, I know," Windy said quickly. "You talk to Kitty, and I'll keep Marcus occupied until you need him to get that lock off."

"I don't know if you should talk to Marcus about—"

"No, it's a good plan," Windy interrupted. "Come now, dear sweet landlady, time to put on your big-girl pants and just get 'er done." She slapped Riva on the back. "You'll be glad you did. I'll go catch Marcus before he has a chance to leave."

Riva went out to the foyer, bracing herself to meet Kitty as she entered the house. She had never been good at confrontations, but she felt this one was necessary. And Windy was probably right. It did seem an opportune moment to resolve this lock mess. So as Windy went out to talk to her brother, Riva waited by the stairway and silently prayed for wisdom . . . and for God's divine direction.

Chapter 23

Riva stared in confusion and shock as Marcus carried Kitty in his arms like a baby. Or maybe it was like they were newlyweds coming home for the first time. Whatever it was, it was weird. Riva felt somewhat voyeuristic simply witnessing the spectacle.

"She sprained her ankle," Marcus quickly explained, rushing past Riva and Windy and heading toward the stairs. "She needs an ice pack and to keep it elevated."

"I'm on it," Windy called out.

"And I'll take her to her room," he told Riva. "Can you get the door for me?"

"Yes, of course." Riva raced on up ahead of them, but as she got to the landing, she remembered the deadbolt on Kitty's door. She stopped. "Except that I can't open the door," she called out as she tried the knob. "I forgot Kitty installed a deadbolt."

"I have the key right here," Kitty said.

Marcus carried Kitty down the hallway toward Riva. Then, taking the key from Kitty, Riva unlocked the deadbolt.

"Please, ignore the mess, Marcus," Kitty chirped. "The salon has been so busy this week, I haven't gotten around to it."

Riva pocketed the key, swung the door open, and gasped. It

looked like a garage sale gone amok. Clothing, shoes, towels, dirty dishes, and other unrelated miscellaneous items were strewn across the floor, bed, and chair. "It's a minefield," Riva warned Marcus. "Be careful or you might need to be carried back downstairs."

Kitty giggled. "Working girls are not known for good housekeeping."

Riva moved ahead of them, clearing a heap of clothes to make room for Kitty. "Look, I found the bed."

"No small feat." Marcus set Kitty down gently.

Riva looked at Kitty's feet. "Which ankle is sprained?"

"The right one." Kitty frowned. "Can't you see how swollen it is?"

"Oh, yeah." Riva nodded. "It does look a little puffy."

"Here comes the ice," Windy called from the stairs.

"How did it happen?" Riva asked.

Marcus set Kitty's oversized bag on the bed, then removed a pair of very high platform sandals from it. "These dangerous stilts are the culprits." He dangled a sandal by its strap with one finger. "I can't believe women of a certain age still choose to wear these things."

"Not all of us do," Riva corrected him as Windy walked in. Like Riva, she looked a bit taken aback by the jumbled mess.

"Not all of us are *of a certain age*," Kitty told Marcus. "And when I'm too old for cute feminine shoes and expected to wear the kinds of clodhoppers that Riva and her friends wear, well, just shoot me."

Windy flopped a bag of frozen peas onto Kitty's foot, smiling as the patient let out a yowl of pain. "You're welcome," Windy said sharply, then turned and left.

Riva retrieved the deadbolt key from her pocket and held it in front of Kitty. "I'll be keeping this," she said, "until we have a chance to talk about the deadbolt you installed without my consent."

"Why did you need a deadbolt?" Marcus asked Kitty. "Do you feel unsafe here?"

Kitty nodded with a dramatic expression. "I am unsafe."

"Why is that?" Riva asked.

"It's my ex. I think he found out I'm living here. I'm sure he's been stalking me. In fact, that's why I tripped and sprained my ankle. I was trying to avoid him."

Riva fought against her skepticism. "Why's he stalking you?"

"Because he wants me back." Kitty sighed. "Thanks to my fatal charm."

Riva wanted to laugh but wondered if Kitty was serious. She turned to Marcus. "How did you manage to find Kitty after her sprain?"

"We'd both been getting coffees at The Bean." He began a story about seeing Kitty trip outside the coffeeshop and how he helped her into his pickup. But instead of listening closely, Riva's attention was on the bedroom. She was trying to determine if there was any contraband or any illegal activities going on in here, but nothing seemed to stand out. Until she noticed the disconnected smoke alarm with batteries sitting nearby.

She picked it up and turned to Kitty. "Why did you take this down?"

"It kept beeping."

"I changed the batteries in the alarms right before all the tenants moved in." Riva glanced at Marcus, wondering how long he planned to remain up here. "Is it possible the beeping was due to smoke?" she directed to Kitty.

"I guess I should go," he said as if getting the hint.

"Thanks for your help," Riva told him, then wondered if she really felt grateful for having Kitty returned to them like this. Not that it was his fault.

"No problem."

"My knight in shining armor." Kitty extended her hand to him as if she were Lady Guinevere. "I will have to properly thank you for your chivalry later."

"Uh, yeah." He ignored her hand, nodding nervously. "See you all later."

Relieved to have Kitty's undivided attention, Riva asked if she'd been smoking. "In case you didn't read your rental contract, that's not allowed." Riva picked up the alarm and reinserted the batteries.

"I was really stressing over my ex," Kitty said. "I left the salon early. I was on the verge of a panic attack. My buddy Marty brought me a joint to help me relax. The alarm went off and Marty took it down. I guess we forgot to put it back up."

"Is Marty the one who installed the deadbolt?"

"Yeah. That was his idea. Sorry I forgot to mention it, but I didn't think you'd mind. I just wanted to be safe."

"Is your ex dangerous?"

"He might be." Kitty's gaze moved downward. She was fidgeting with her jangly bracelet, turning it round and round.

Riva cleared off the chair and sat, carefully studying Kitty. "Please explain."

"Well, my ex, my first husband, Danny claims he still loves me. I've managed to avoid him, because if he's been drinking, he says scary stuff like if he can't have me, no one can."

"Some people act out of character when they've over-imbibed." Riva nodded at Kitty. "Even you."

Kitty's expression grew cloudy. "Are ya gonna kick me while I'm down?"

"I didn't think I was kicking you. Just calling it like I see it." Riva was determined not to cave to Kitty's manipulation.

Kitty's eyes grew moist. "What am I going to do, Riva?"

"About what?"

"Everything." Kitty let out a sob. "I'm such a god-awful mess of a girl."

Riva studied her. Was this sincere or just more manipulation? If Laurel was right, if Kitty really was a narcissist, it was most likely manipulation. But what if it wasn't? "For starters, Kitty, you're not a god-awful mess. You're more of a Kitty-awful mess. And for the record, you're not exactly a girl anymore. According to my calculations, you're only a few years younger than me. And I haven't been a girl in years."

Kitty pouted. "That's your problem, Riva."

"I don't see it as a problem."

"Fine. But just because you're content to grow old doesn't mean I have to be."

Riva rolled her eyes. "You know the only problem I'm having right now is directly related to you. You've broken so many rules of the rental contract that I'm pretty sure I could evict you this moment. Your housemates would be glad if I did. But I'd prefer to give you a couple weeks' notice. Long enough for your ankle to heal and for you to find another place to live."

Kitty blinked her big blue eyes and then began to cry. "Women always end up hating me. I should've known it would happen here too."

"No one hates you, Kitty, but we're tired of all the drama you bring to the house. We're tired of your excessive drinking, weed smoking, deadbolt installing, and smoke alarm disabling. Not to mention leaving the bathroom filthy." She kicked a shoe out of the way. "And your less than tidy bedroom."

Kitty had tears streaming down her face now. But they seemed like crocodile tears to Riva. She wasn't buying it. "What am I going to do?" Kitty sobbed. "I can't live at the salon. I can't afford an apartment . . . You're throwing me out on the streets?"

"Don't be silly." Riva could feel herself softening. "You must have friends? Women who work for you? Someone with a spare room you can use?"

Kitty shook her head and wiped her nose with the edge of a rumpled sheet. "No one wants me. It's the story of my life. I overwhelm everyone, Riva. I scare people away."

Riva considered this. "That's kind of true, Kitty. You do frighten people."

"Women are intimidated by me and the only men I seem to attract are the wrong ones. I don't know what to do."

Riva took a deep breath. "Have you ever tried to change?"

"Change?" Kitty looked like Riva had just suggested she shave her head.

"I'm not talking about outward changes." Riva frowned. She thought less flamboyant clothes, makeup, and hair might help, but she wasn't going there. "I'm talking about inside changes."

"I'm not following you."

"Well, in my case, the inward changes are associated with God. Knowing he loves me, has a plan for my life, wants to lead me . . . all of that changes my interior. And that makes me see my world and the people in it differently."

"Which explains why you're such a Pollyanna Goody Two-Shoes."

Riva shrugged. "I suppose it might look like that to you. Although I don't think I've been very Pollyanna-like. Not since Paul died. But I'm trying to make a comeback."

Kitty seemed to soften a little. "You really loved your husband, didn't you?"

"Yes. He was my soulmate, my best friend. I still miss him and he's been gone a year and a half."

"Lucky you." Kitty let out an exasperated sigh.

Riva pursed her lips. Kitty's lack of sensitivity was a bit disturbing.

"Sorry. I didn't mean you're lucky that your husband died." Kitty wiped away some tears. "It's just that you're telling me about something I've never experienced. And in all likelihood, I never will, so it's kinda like rubbing my nose in it."

"Then maybe you should let me finish what I was trying to say. Yes, Paul was a wonderful husband. None better as far as I'm concerned. But having God's help has made all the difference. I wouldn't have survived losing Paul if God hadn't been there for me. And anything good inside of me is a direct result of God's influence. I guess I'm suggesting that you consider asking him for help. Because you do seem to need some help."

"Thanks a lot." Kitty scowled.

"You're the one who just told me you're a god-awful mess, Kitty. If you don't want my advice, just say so."

"Are you going to kick me out?"

Riva thought hard, silently begging God to lead her. "Not today. But I am giving you notice. If some things don't change, you will have to find other arrangements."

"There's that word again. Change. I don't know how to change."

"Are you asking for suggestions?"

Kitty stuck out her bottom lip. "I'm not sure."

Thinking this might be her best chance to have Kitty as a "captive audience," Riva decided to go for it. "For starters, I don't think you should be drinking at all. Give the party girl act a break."

"Seeing that I'm confined to my bed at the moment, I suppose I don't have a choice."

Riva glanced around the messy room. "You don't have alcohol hidden in here, do you?"

Kitty just shrugged, but her eyes darted to the closet, which appeared to have regurgitated its contents, with clothing and purses and shoes pouring out. But what caught Riva's eyes was a pair of tall black boots, standing up straight. And this was definitely not boot season. She got up to take a closer look. One boot contained a partially full bottle of vodka. The other held a nearly empty Jack Daniels.

"Classy," Riva said as she pulled out the bottles.

"Excuse me. I was stressing over Danny."

"And this helps?"

"It dulls things." Kitty fidgeted with the frozen peas on her foot. "Do you think I need to see a doctor? I don't really want to, and I'm sort of between insurance providers right now."

Riva took a peek at the ankle and shrugged. "I guess that's up to you. Doesn't look too serious to me. Do you have any elastic bandages to wrap it with?"

"No."

"Well, I have some in my first aid cabinet."

"You have a first aid cabinet?"

"Of course. I had a wild, sports-obsessed son who was good at injuring himself." Still holding the two bottles, Riva opened the door. "Any more booze hidden in here?"

"I'm not an alcoholic."

Riva frowned at the bottles in her hands. "Sure could've fooled me."

"Ha ha." Kitty growled. "Thanks. Now I'm craving a Manhattan."

"I'll get that elastic wrap."

As Riva closed the door behind her, Laurel poked her head out of her room. "Windy told me about Kitty's ankle. Do you think she's faking it to get you to feel sorry for her so you'll let her stay?"

"Being that she injured it before I had a chance to tell her about our concerns, I have to assume it's legitimate."

Laurel's brows arched. She nodded toward the liquor bottles in Riva's hands. "Wow, you hittin' the hard stuff now?" She laughed as Riva headed down the stairs.

"I hope this is all she had in her room, but the place is such a disaster area, who knows?"

"Did Kitty get an X-ray?" she asked, following Riva.

"No, she doesn't seem to want to see a doctor."

"Right. Easier to fake it and milk it for all its worth." Laurel followed Riva through the kitchen.

"Maybe . . . but I have to admit the ankle is a bit swollen." Riva dumped the contents of the bottles down the sink drain. "And Brent had his fair share of twisted ankles. This looks similar. Brent's sprains usually healed fairly quick though. He'd often be off his crutches after just a week. But then he was young. At our age, well, it probably takes longer."

Laurel snorted. "Like Kitty will ever confess she's our age, or even close."

Riva dropped the glass bottles into the recycling bin, then rinsed her hands.

"Does Kitty have crutches to get around or will Marcus be stopping by to transport her as needed?"

Riva ignored Laurel's jab. "No crutches yet, but I think Brent's spare set is in the garage."

Laurel continued to shadow Riva as she perused the first aid cabinet, eventually unearthing the storage container with elastic bandages. She held the plastic box out to Laurel. "How're you at wrapping an ankle?"

"Seriously? You want me to help that little witch?"

"Oh, Laurel." Riva frowned and shook her head. "What would Jesus do?"

"Tell her to get up, pick up her bed, and walk?" Laurel smirked. "Maybe have her fix us something to eat, then go and sin no more?"

"Funny." Riva handed Laurel a rolled bandage. "I happen to remember heroic tales of you playing school nurse when no one else was there to step in, and I also happen to know you're first aid certified. Why don't you handle this while I hunt down the crutches? That could take me a while."

"Fine. But if she gets gangrene because I wrap her foot too tightly, don't sue me."

"As long as you don't put a tourniquet around her neck, I won't report you." Riva reached for a bottle of Advil. "Offer her a couple of these for the pain, Nurse Ratched."

"Or just give her the whole bottle with a stiff drink?"

"Laurel!" Riva scowled. "I never knew you were so wicked."

Laurel looked genuinely contrite. "I'm sorry. I don't know what gets into me sometimes. I never used to think of myself as hardhearted. But that woman—she just pushes all my buttons."

"Maybe God is giving you an opportunity . . . a lesson in turning the other cheek, loving your enemy." She held out the Advil. "Being a good Samaritan."

"Yeah, yeah." Laurel waved a dismissive hand, then grabbed the pills. "Save your preaching for Sundays, Riva."

As they parted ways, Riva thought about her little sermonette. Truth was, she wasn't much fonder of Kitty than Laurel was. But she felt sorry for the confused and complicated woman. It went against the grain to help someone so self-centered, cynical, and irresponsible.

Except that, unless Riva was being gullible, it seemed Kitty had experienced a true aha moment just now. After all, she'd just admitted she was a mess and recognized her need for help. What if this really was a turning point? What if God's plan for Kitty was to keep her right here and to use Riva and the other women to guide the poor lost lamb toward a better path? Okay, that might be a long shot at best, but maybe it was better to try and be wrong than to be wrong and not try.

Chapter 24

"That woman is a real piece of work." Laurel slammed the bag of peas on the kitchen counter. "Now she's demanding a real ice pack for her ankle, which, in my opinion, hardly needs it. That is, if it's even sprained at all. It's barely swollen."

"Well, that might be from keeping it chilled and elevated. And I had meant to get a real ice pack to Kitty by now." Riva picked up the soggy bag of peas. "Windy only used these as a temporary measure."

"Speaking of Windy, do you have any idea what she's doing right now?" Laurel filled a glass with water.

"No." Riva put the peas in the freezer, then dug out the ice pack that she used to keep handy for her kids.

"Well, kindhearted Windy is cleaning Kitty's room."

"No small task." Riva cut the tuna fish sandwich she'd just made for Kitty in half, then set it on the plate, along with some apple slices and carrot sticks.

"And she had the gall to ask me to clean the bathroom that Kitty has pretty much trashed."

"Oh?" Riva studied Laurel. "And?"

Laurel shrugged as she snitched a carrot stick from Kitty's lunch plate. "I told her I'd think about it, but only because I peeked in there and, no kidding, it looked like a death trap. Especially with crutches. And whether or not Kitty's ankle is actually sprained, she could fall down and break her neck and sue the socks right off you, Riva. Have you seen it?"

Riva shook her head.

"Well, I came down to get a garbage bag. My plan is to temporarily clear all Kitty's excess clothes and shoes and any other crud that I think she could live without and eliminate the tripping hazard." Laurel rooted around in the under-sink cabinet. First, she pulled out a pair of rubber gloves and then a carton of big black yard bags. She tugged one out and shook it open. "Then I'll put her mess in this."

"And then what?" Riva imagined the hissy fit Kitty would pitch. "You wouldn't dare throw it away, would you?"

"No, of course not. But she obviously doesn't need all this junk while she's off her feet. I'll just stick it in the garage for now. I'll label the bag with her name so it's not mistaken for trash. Although," she added, "it all looked pretty trashy to me."

"Well, I think it's kind of you to clean that bathroom, Laurel. I think Kitty will too. She seems to want to start making some changes in her life." Riva set a damp sponge by the sink. "Maybe we can help her."

"Seriously?" Laurel tugged on a rubber glove. "I'd like to help her—by packing her bags and calling her a taxi."

Riva considered asking Laurel to take the lunch up to Kitty but didn't want to push her luck. Instead, she followed her, listening as Laurel continued to grumble about Kitty all the way up to the second floor.

Parting ways in the hall, Riva entered Kitty's room to see Windy holding up a hot pink garment that was either a cocktail dress or a sparkly swimsuit. "How about if we put this away for now too," Windy was saying. "It doesn't seem like the type of dress you'd wear very much. Especially with a sprained ankle."

Kitty waved a hand. "Whatever. I don't care right now. Just as long as I can get to the box if I need it."

"Like I said, I'm just going to put this in the linen closet." Windy smiled at Riva. "We're trying to make Kitty's room more livable."

"We as in Windy." Kitty pushed herself up to a sitting position. "Is that for me?" she asked Riva, nodding toward the food. "I don't have much appetite."

"I thought you could use a little nourishment. It's only tuna fish." Riva handed her the plate. "Do your best."

Kitty wrinkled her nose but didn't reject it.

"And I found those crutches in the garage, but they were so dusty I took them outside to hose them off. They're drying in the sunshine."

"Thanks," Kitty said with a full mouth. "Not that I can get around with them. Even if I can manage, how will I get down the stairs?"

"You probably don't need to worry about that right now." Riva picked up a pair of silver sandals with tall spiky heels, then handed them to Windy. "I'm guessing she won't need these for a while either."

Windy dropped them in a box with shoes and boots and purses. As Kitty ate, Windy and Riva continued to clean and organize the bedroom. Windy focused on gleaning frivolous items as well as trash, while Riva collected the more practical clothes and shoes and placed them in the closet. After about an hour, they were done. Windy was taking the last box out, and Riva collected the empty lunch plate.

"Can I get you anything else?" Riva noticed her copy of *Pride and Prejudice* mostly hidden under the bed. "Do you remember our agreement when you moved in, Kitty?" she asked, stooping to pick up the book.

"About reading that?"

"Yes. That was part of the deal. And you did promise to read it."

"Or to watch the movie."

"The book group might've agreed to that, but I never did." Riva handed her the book. "Since you have nothing better to do and since I'm still not sure about you remaining here, I suggest you keep your end of the deal and get reading."

Kitty scowled as she opened the book. "Fine, but don't blame me if it puts me to sleep."

Riva glanced around the transformed room. "Does it feel good to see order in here?"

"Yeah, whatever."

Riva didn't expect a personal thank-you, but a little appreciation would be welcome. Couldn't she see how much better this room looked? "Happy reading." Riva carried the plate out, quietly closing the door. As she went downstairs, she wondered just how far she and the other housemates should go to help the mess of a woman who didn't seem to want their assistance or even think she needed it.

After several days of catering to Kitty, Riva and the others were getting fed up. It wasn't that it was that much work when shared by four women, but it was irritating to witness Kitty's ingratitude and complaints.

"It's understandable that she'd be edgy from being cooped up and in pain like that," Riva said to the others while she finished loading a dinner plate for Kitty. "And she's probably lonely too. I mean, none of us have been overly friendly to her, and she doesn't have her salon gals around. I'm surprised none have come to visit."

"Maybe they feel the same about her as we do," Windy said glumly. "Safer to keep a distance."

"But she needs friends," Riva argued. With that thought in mind, she decided to take her own dinner plate upstairs.

"I'd rather befriend Cruella de Vil," Laurel declared. "And I happen to adore sweet little puppies,"

"Well, I'm going to make an attempt." She picked up both plates. "If you ladies will excuse me, I'll be eating with Kitty tonight."

"Don't be too sure. She might just toss you out," Fiona said. "I brought her a pastry from work and she just yelled at me."

"Hurt people hurt people," Riva said. "But I'm prepared for her rejection. I might be right back."

"Good luck," Fiona told her.

"You'll need it," Windy added.

"Watch your head," Laurel warned.

By now they were all questioning how serious Kitty's "sprained" ankle really was. Laurel was certain she was faking it, but Riva wasn't so sure. Kitty seemed the kind of person who would be up and running if her foot was okay. Well, unless she was depressed . . . or hiding out . . . or both. Riva knew that Kitty was concerned about her ex showing up. At least, she claimed to be. Although Laurel claimed that was a hoax as well.

Riva knocked quietly on the door, then poked her head in. "Dinnertime."

Kitty looked up from the book she was reading, squinting as if to focus. "Oh, it's just you."

"Who were you expecting?" Riva asked a bit hotly.

"Guess I should've said, *oh, good, it's you*." Kitty smirked. "Dinner already?"

"It's past seven." Riva handed her a plate. "I thought I could join you, if you want company. I don't want to intrude."

"Well, your company is better than others in this house." Kitty picked up her fork.

Riva sat down, biting her tongue. She wasn't going to allow Kitty to bait her into a silly argument like Laurel kept falling for. "Looks like you've made good progress in that book."

"Yeah, once I got past the seriously boring factor, it got kinda interesting. Plus, I remembered how Marcus said he liked Jane Austen books."

"Right." Riva wasn't surprised that Kitty would be more inclined to read Austen because of Marcus, just aggravated. "So can you relate to any of the characters?"

Kitty nodded as she forked into potato salad. "I think I'm like Jane."

"Jane?" Riva blinked. "Why Jane?" She held back from pointing out how Jane was a shy, kindhearted, sensitive person.

"Jane was the beauty of the house and the whole neighborhood."

Riva sighed. "That's true."

"But I think Jane should go for Mr. Darcy instead of Mr. Bingley."

"Why's that?"

"Mr. Darcy is a better catch. He comes across as a smug know-it-all, but he's handsome and rich. More exciting than Bingley."

"Right . . ." Riva considered informing her that Jane does end up with Bingley and Elizabeth gets Mr. Darcy, but she didn't want to spoil the ending. "What do you think of Lydia?"

Kitty chuckled. "What a little airhead."

"A pretty airhead," Riva said. "Remember how I told you she was a jerk magnet."

"But she hooked George Wickham, and he seems like a pretty good catch too. He's not rich like the other guys, but he's fun. I could go for him."

"And you probably have too."

"Huh?" Kitty paused her fork in midair.

"I guess you'll find out as you continue to read." Riva decided to change the subject and asked about Kitty's ankle. "Is it still hurting a lot?"

Kitty shrugged. "It's okay until I bump it trying to get around on those things." She nodded to the crutches leaning against her bed. "Just getting back and forth to the bathroom is a real pain. I told Laurel she should switch rooms with me so I could have a bathroom nearby."

"How'd that go for you?"

Kitty rolled her eyes. "How do ya think it went?"

"Pretty sure she declined."

"I know I'm not popular here." Kitty bit into a roll. "But I'm used to it."

"Used to it?"

"Oh, you know. Women always resent beautiful women. I've seen it all my life. No big deal."

"Do you have any women friends, Kitty?"

Kitty looked down at her plate. "I have friends."

"We haven't noticed you getting any visitors." Riva cut off a piece of chicken.

"My friends aren't like that." Kitty made what looked like a forced smile. "They're more into having fun than visiting someone stuck in bed, but that's okay."

"I guess it's okay if you don't mind." Riva bit her lip. "But I've discovered, especially as I get older, I like having friends I can count on. Although I'll admit I didn't really figure this out until Paul got sick. He'd always been my best friend, but losing him showed me how much I needed good dependable friends."

"Good for you."

Riva pointed to the book lying open on the bed. "One thing I like about that story is how the sisters, especially Jane and Elizabeth, are also such good friends. Loyal and devoted."

"Not to Lydia. They treat her like the black sheep of the family."

"I think it's because they can't relate to her. When they try to help her or advise her, Lydia doesn't listen. She just wants to go her own way and have fun."

"You can't blame a girl for that."

"I guess not. But her actions remind me of a saying my grandmother liked to use. If you dance to the music, you have to pay the fiddler."

"Unless it's Fiona." Kitty chuckled. "She fiddles for free. At least for us."

"Right." Riva knew she wasn't getting through and, although her dinner was only partially eaten, she no longer felt hungry. She was about to excuse herself when Kitty spoke up.

"I know, I know. You think I'm just a hopeless hot mess. You're right for the most part. I am a mess."

"Are you okay with that? Being a mess, I mean?"

Kitty shrugged. "Sometimes . . . and sometimes not."

"Do you think you'll do anything about it?"

"You mean, will I change?" Kitty asked.

Riva nodded.

"Because if I don't change, you'll kick me out?"

"I wasn't going to say that, but yes, if you keep breaking the rules and living like you're in your twenties, I'll ask you to leave."

"What if I can't change?" Kitty slumped back.

Riva wasn't sure if that was a question or a challenge.

"What if I don't know how to change?" Kitty tried again.

"I think if you want to change, you will need to be open to help. And I think the women living in this house could all be of help. In fact, they already have been." She waved a hand to the still-tidy room. "But I'm not even sure you thanked them."

"Thanked them for feeling sorry for me? Thanked them for their pity?" She scowled. "That doesn't work for me."

"Hurts your pride?"

"Yeah, it does. And sometimes that's all a girl has left. Her pride." Kitty nodded firmly. "Gotta protect it, right?"

"I understand, but I don't agree. I've personally found pride to be problematic. I'd rather work on my humility than protect my pride."

"Yeah, but you're different than me."

"Everyone is different."

As they continued to eat, bantering conflicting ideals over strength and pride and whether a person could change, Riva realized that, short of a miracle, teaching an old dog new tricks would be challenging at best, even one who imagined she was a young pup.

Chapter 25

Satisfied that Kitty was keeping her word by reading *Pride and Prejudice*, Riva tried to reassure her other tenants that Kitty was opening up to change.

Of course, Laurel doubted this. "She's just manipulating you, Riva," she said over coffee the next morning. "She knows how to work people. It's all in that book I told you about."

"Maybe you should be reading a different book," Riva suggested.

"Or maybe you need to read it for yourself. It's a real eye-opener."

"Well, I'm glad it's been helpful to you, Laurel. Books can be wonderful tools." Riva stood and excused herself into the house, then went straight to the library. She wanted to find just the right book to give Laurel another perspective. But what was it?

Suddenly one spine seemed to shine out among the others. Riva reached for *Redeeming Love* by Francine Rivers. She knew this story well, but she skimmed the copy on the back anyway. A western retelling of an ancient story with a gripping theme of grace and forgiveness . . . Would Laurel be willing to read it? She put the book under her arm as another spine caught her eye. A title she'd enjoyed years ago, and read twice, one of her favorite novels. In the book the protagonist, a dear older woman named Penelope, reflected on her life, had a love of gardening and cooking, and in some ways reminded Riva of Windy.

As she pulled out *The Shell Seekers*, a light bulb went on in her head! She would give all her tenants a reading assignment—just like she'd done with Kitty! And since they'd all agreed their book group wouldn't start until autumn, they should have plenty of time to read something else. Plus, during their hiatus from entertaining males, the women could focus on reading instead. Why not? Now she needed one more book.

Fiona was the busiest of the bunch so she wanted to pick a quick read for her. Spotting *Small Things Like These* by Claire Keegan, she knew she'd found it. Well, unless Fiona had already read it. Fiona had just mentioned feeling a bit homesick so she hoped the familiarity of the Irish setting might be uplifting. Tonight at dinner, she'd make her recommendations. She'd use Kitty's enforced reading as her inspiration. What was good for Kitty was probably good for all of them. Kind of a restart perhaps. Hopefully they wouldn't balk at the idea. But if Kitty could stretch herself to read Jane Austen, the others should be willing to step up too. It would be like book group therapy. Maybe she could claim it was a prerequisite for housing. She could even change the rental agreement to include a book clause, requiring them to read more. Or would that be going too far?

Riva removed the orange-glazed salmon from the grill, then set it on the oversized platter alongside the grilled veggies and ears of corn.

"It's ready," she called out to her friends seated at the patio table.

"Looks lovely," Fiona said as Riva set the platter in the center of the table.

"I'm so glad you could join us tonight," Riva told her.

Laurel reached for the bowl of fruit salad. "Yeah, it's not often you have the night off."

Fiona nodded. "We've gotten some brilliant gigs since playing The Brewery."

"That's not surprising." Windy reached for an ear of corn.

When their plates were all full, Riva suggested she say a blessing. They didn't always pray before a meal, but with all the ups and downs in the house lately, Riva had decided it was time to switch things up or maybe to calm things down.

After the blessing, Laurel snickered.

"Was that funny?" Riva asked as she dished out some veggies.

"It's not you," Laurel said quickly. "I was just thinking it's good that Kitty is stuck in her room or she might protest the prayer."

"She's not a complete heathen," Riva said.

Laurel took a piece of salmon. "If she's not, I'd like to know who is."

"Fortunately, God loves us all, heathens included." Riva gave Laurel the same stern look that she used to reserve for her children when they were acting out.

"Speaking of Kitty, I saw that she was more than half finished with *Pride and Prejudice*," Windy said. "I was impressed."

"I talked with her about it for a bit yesterday," Riva told her. "I was surprised at how well she seemed to be following the story, especially for a nonreader."

"That's only because she's afraid you'll kick her out if she doesn't," Laurel added.

"Riva wouldn't do that," Fiona told Laurel.

"Don't be too sure," Riva said. "Although, to be fair, I was about to ask her to leave for other infractions of household rules."

"And the list is long," Laurel said.

"No one could blame you for giving Kitty notice," Windy told Riva.

"And if Kitty moved on, we could probably put the brakes on our male moratorium," Laurel added. "I miss those little shindigs we were having." She pointed her fork at Fiona. "Your music was so lively, and those dancing lessons—so fun. That is, until Kitty would blow in and ruin everything. I sure don't miss that."

"I have to agree," Windy said cautiously. "Even now, it's nice with just the four of us here peacefully dining together. To be honest, I don't miss Kitty either."

Riva looked nervously toward the house. Fortunately, Kitty still couldn't manage the stairs with crutches. But the thought of her overhearing them was unsettling. Kitty's room faced the front of the house, so there was little chance she'd overhear anything. Still, Riva didn't appreciate conversation that felt mean-spirited and gossipy to her. "Kitty does have problems," she said quietly, "but if she's willing to make some changes, I'm willing to give her a second chance."

Laurel grunted. "And third and fourth and—"

"Come on, Laurel, let's not kick her while she's down." Riva decided it was time to segue this conversation "Okay, ladies, I have a challenge for you."

"I like challenges." Laurel took a sip of her water.

"Good." Riva took a deep breath. "Since I forced Kitty to read a book, I've decided it's only fair to impose some mandatory reading on you guys too. Okay, mandatory is a strong word. I obviously didn't include this in your rental agreement like I did with Kitty. But as a goodwill effort, I would appreciate it if you humored me."

"I've already read *Pride and Prejudice*," Windy said. "But I'm willing."

"I've read it too," Fiona added.

"That's not what I had in mind." Riva reached for the small stack of books under her chair, then set them on the table beside her. "I picked out three titles from my library for each of you, just like I did for Kitty with *Pride and Prejudice*. I tried to choose books I thought you might like." She picked up *The Shell Seekers*. "This is one of my favorite novels, Windy. You may have already read it." She handed the thick hardback to her.

"*The Shell Seekers*?" Windy studied the front. "Pretty cover."

"You haven't read it?"

"No. I've read other Rosamunde Pilcher novels, and I adore her writing style, but I've never read this one before."

"The main character is named Penelope," Riva said with enthusiasm. "She's about our age. She loves gardening and cooking, and she is looking back on her, well, somewhat dysfunctional life and family. But she's a good, kind, and strong woman."

"Sounds like my kind of book. Thanks, Riva."

Riva had expected Windy to be an easy sale. Now she handed the small hardback novella to Fiona, but before she could explain it, Fiona lit up.

"I wanted to get this when it came out, Riva. It's set in the same era as when I was growing up. I've heard it's absolutely brilliant."

"You won't mind a little Christmas in July?" Riva asked.

"Not at all. I hope it snows in the book. That'll cool me down on my lunch breaks at the bistro. It gets miserable hot in the kitchen." Fiona hugged the book to her chest. "Thank you, Riva. I can't wait to start it."

"I suppose that one's for me." Laurel reached for the last book on the table. "*Redeeming Love*?" She snorted. "Looks like a romance novel."

"There is a romantic thread," Riva conceded.

"Well, I suppose I could get into that." She tapped a knuckle on the cover. "It's pretty thick though."

"I read it years ago but want to read it again." Riva held back from describing the premise about grace, forgiveness, and second chances. She'd let Laurel discover it for herself.

"I've read it too," Windy told Laurel. "It's a beautiful story."

"I'm so glad you're all on board." Riva beamed at them. "I hope we can all finish our books and meet before long. Then we can share what we thought about our books. I think I might even have some questions. It'll be kind of a premiere to our book group in the fall. And to sweeten the deal, I'll provide some special treats. Something cool involving chocolate."

"Count me in," Windy said.

"I hope we can work around my schedule." Fiona refilled her iced tea. "I don't want to miss it."

"Just let me know what day's good for you." Riva smiled with satisfaction. Her book project was off to a solid start. Well, other than Laurel who was still scowling down at her book. "So when is your next music gig?" she asked Fiona.

"We're booked for Saturday night," Fiona explained. "A friend of my brother's is having a barn wedding. It'll be craic."

"Crack?" Laurel looked worried. "As in drugs?"

"It's an Irish word that means great fun," Riva told Laurel.

"So when's your next gig that's open to the public?" Windy asked Fiona.

"Not for nearly a fortnight. I think we're booked at The Brewery again."

"Be sure and let us know." Riva helped herself to more fruit salad. She missed Fiona's cheerful music and looked forward to hearing them perform again, but that could wait for another day. For the time being, her priority was restoring peace and order to her home. Like the four of them were enjoying tonight. There was no denying that Kitty's absence from their table, albeit temporary, improved the general atmosphere dramatically.

Chapter 26

Riva was just bringing Kitty's breakfast tray downstairs, trying to block out her complaints about "soggy toast and cold coffee," when she heard the doorbell. It'd been ten long days since Kitty's injury, and her ankle was no longer swollen. Riva was certain her contrary tenant should be mobile by now. Laurel claimed she'd seen her getting around without crutches, but Kitty still claimed to be in pain. Each of Riva's attempts to bring up the topic of moving on were met with hostility and resistance. The doorbell rang again, and Riva set down the tray to answer her persistent guest. But she didn't recognize the man standing on her doorstep. He wore a faded Dodger's cap, a deep tan, and a nervous-looking smile. She opened the door, and he asked if Kitty was home.

Riva studied him closely. "May I ask who wants to know?"

"I'm Danny, Kitty's ex, and I, uh, I know she rents a room here. Mazy at the salon told me."

"Oh?" Riva realized that other than Kitty, she was home alone right now. Windy and Laurel were on a grocery run and Fiona was at work. And based on what Kitty had said about Danny, she didn't know what to do. Was this man truly dangerous? "Well, Kitty is laid up with a sprained ankle at the moment, and she's

. . . um, not taking visitors. Sorry." She started to close the door, but he blocked it with his heavy work boot.

"Please, wait," he insisted. "Can I talk to you?"

"Me?" She peeked through the opening, gripping the door handle.

"Just a few minutes. *Please*?"

His expression and tone didn't sound aggressive or threatening, just insistent, so she stepped onto the porch and closed the door behind her before folding her arms in front of her. "Yes?"

"I apologize for showing up like this," Danny started, "but I'm concerned about Kitty."

Riva waved to her neighbor, who was edging his lawn, then went over to the porch rockers. "Care to sit?"

"Thank you." He sat, removing his cap.

"So what can I do for you?"

Leaning forward with his elbows on his knees and a forlorn expression, he shook his head. "I know I made loads of mistakes with Kitty, and we were both drinking way too much when we were married, but I never quit loving her."

Riva didn't know what to say. Why was he telling her this?

"I really want to talk to her. I think she needs me . . . but she's too proud to admit it. I want her to know I've changed my ways." He twisted his cap in his hands. "I've been on the wagon. Regularly attending AA. Sober for more'n a year." He looked at her with clear blue eyes.

"That's great. I'm sure Kitty will be glad to hear it." Riva was confused. Hadn't Kitty claimed her ex was a threat? Wasn't she hiding out from him? And yet he seemed polite and decent, even rather nice. "Can you clarify something for me, Danny?"

"What's that?"

"You were Kitty's first husband, right?"

"Yes." His eyes darkened. "Her second husband was a real piece of work."

"Kitty mentioned that." She scrutinized this guy. Was he playing her?

"When Kitty and me first got married, things were great, but we both got into partying a little too much and, well, things unraveled. But Kitty got a good divorce settlement from me. Unfortunately, from what I hear, she's blown right through it and is about to lose the salon too. I've been trying to connect with her for weeks, but she just keeps slipping through my fingers."

"Why do you want to connect with her?"

"I guess I feel kinda guilty."

This surprised Riva. "Guilty for what?"

"I'm the one who got her into partying and drinking in the first place. According to what I've learned in AA, I need to take responsibility for that. I need to apologize."

"Why not just write her a letter?" She studied him closely as he continued to crumble his cap with his hands.

"I guess, in a way, I still love her. At least, who she used to be. And I feel sorry for her. I mean, her life is a real mess. Besides being on the brink of losing the salon, she lost her apartment and can't even drive."

Riva raised her eyebrows. "She can't drive?"

"She didn't tell you about all her DUIs? That her license is revoked?"

"So that's why she walks." Riva sighed.

Danny nodded. "Mazy thinks her car was repossessed too. It's a real mess."

"So, is she totally broke?" Riva shook her head.

"Worse than broke. She's underwater on her bills. Mazy says the salon might not even have water and electricity by next month. Not that it should matter since they've lost so many clients. They can't make enough to keep the doors open."

"And Kitty's missed work for over a week now. That can't help." Riva sighed as she imagined being stuck with Kitty indefinitely. "You say you want to help her. May I ask how?"

"I'd like to talk to her. I know it's a long shot, but I've wondered about us getting back together. I inherited a place out of town. My parents' old farm. It's a little rundown, but it's quiet and peaceful. I think she could be happy there. It's a good place to get sober. That is, if she's willing to stop drinking. That's my one condition."

"That sounds like a good condition. I do think Kitty could have a drinking problem."

"Yeah, Mazy said the same thing. Kitty was drinking at work and after work and just getting out of control."

Riva nodded.

Danny looked up at her. "So if you could help me, I'd really appreciate it."

"Help you *how*?"

"Just talk to her, tell her I was here, ask her to see me."

Riva stood. "Okay. I guess I can do that. But don't expect a miracle. Kitty is a pretty stubborn woman."

Danny smiled. "You're not telling me anything I don't know." He put his cap on and stood. "I might be crazy, but I still love her."

They exchanged phone numbers and Riva promised to let him know how it turned out before heading back inside. She picked up the breakfast tray, then remembered Kitty's bad attitude about the lousy food and service here. She set it back down. It was high time to give Kitty a serious wake-up call.

As Riva knocked on Kitty's door, she silently prayed, asking for help with what would be a dicey conversation. When Kitty answered, Riva braced herself and went into the room in time to see Kitty scrambling back into bed.

"Looks like you were up," Riva said. "Good for you."

"Had to put the shade down. Too much sun in my eyes," Kitty grumbled.

"Right." Riva sat on the chair by the bed and explained about their unexpected visitor and some of their conversation. "He wants to help you."

"Sure, he wants to help me. Right into the poorhouse, he wants to help me."

"What makes you say that?"

"Just the fact that he's stopped my alimony."

"Because you remarried?" Riva waited.

"Yeah, that's true. But after the divorce, well, Danny kinda stepped up again. I guess he was worried about me. Or maybe he thought we'd get back together. I don't know. But that all came to an end a few months ago." Kitty's eyes grew moist. "I need that money, Riva."

Riva just nodded. "I'm sure you do."

"My bills are piling up." Kitty reached for a Kleenex and dabbed her eyes. "I might even lose my salon."

"Danny mentioned that too."

"How does *he* know?" Kitty growled.

Riva shrugged. "I don't know. All I know is he wants to help you."

Kitty rolled her eyes. "Yeah, right. Danny hates me. He's been stalking me. I know he wants to ruin me. He's told me enough times. He'd love nothing more than to see me go down."

"You told me he was dangerous when you moved in here, but he seemed genuinely nice to me. And sober."

"It's all an act, Riva. I can't believe you fell for it. But you're so gullible, you probably have the deed to the Golden Gate Bridge tucked away somewhere." She laughed grimly.

Riva decided to ramp up this conversation. "Well, I suppose I was gullible to believe *you*, Kitty. To trust you and allow you to have a room in my home."

She pouted. "So are you kicking me out now?"

"No, I'm just trying to talk to you, to help you figure things out. Whether you can admit it or not, you're in a predicament."

"Maybe I am. But it's my predicament."

"Not completely. It's my house so that makes it partly mine too."

"Then throw me out." Kitty pointed to her foot. "Just toss the poor little injured girl out on the streets. That'll solve all your problems."

Riva laughed. "You need a blizzard, a hungry babe in arms, and Fiona playing a tragic tune on her fiddle to make your pathetic image really work."

Kitty picked up her book, then opened it toward the back. "If Danny comes back again, you have my permission to call the cops."

"Why would I do that?"

"Because he can make a big stinking mess. Especially if he's drinking."

"I told you. He's been sober for a year. He goes to AA."

"Good for him." Kitty pursed her lips.

"And he's inherited some property out of town. His parents' farm."

"Lucky Danny. That place is a dump, but I suppose he could sell it."

"He wants to keep it and fix it up, and he really wants to talk to you."

"So you've said."

"Look, Kitty, I realize you're in a tough spot. And I actually care about you. I'd like to see you get your life on track. I can tell you're unhappy, and you admitted you were a mess. But if you're not willing to let others help, and I don't mean by bringing you food and cleaning up after you, well, I'm not sure there's much more we can do. Your foot should be healed enough to move out so you can get on with your life. I suppose I should give you notice."

"Is this supposed to be tough love?" Kitty pouted.

"Yeah, I think so." Riva stood. "So, what do you want me to tell Danny? I promised him I'd call."

"Seriously?" Kitty shook the book in the air. "You remind me of Elizabeth Bennett. If you ask me, that woman's a royal pain, always butting into other people's business and messing things up. She should fix her own life."

"I happen to like Elizabeth Bennett." Riva moved toward the door.

"Big surprise there." Kitty laid the still-open book in her lap. "Look, if you're determined to play bossy Elizabeth and you wanna force me to talk to Danny, why don't you go check him out for me. See if his story is really true. I bet you'll find him living in squalor and drunk as a skunk on his parents' stinky old farm." She laughed. "Bring back pictures. I need some amusement."

Riva wondered how much she really cared to get involved in their domestic differences, and yet, if it could help Kitty—and get her to move on—it might be worthwhile. But what if Kitty was right? What if Danny was playing her? After all, Kitty was a pro at playing her housemates. She and Danny might be cut from the same cloth. He could very well hide whiskey bottles in his boots too!

"I don't know why I'm so nervous about this," Riva said to Marcus as he drove through the countryside later that day. "I feel like a baby for asking for your help, but Windy insisted I needed a man along. Still, it feels kind of silly now. I'm sure I could've done this myself."

"Based on what Kitty has said about her ex, I don't think you're being overly cautious."

"But Danny seemed just fine this morning. He was very nice to me."

"Didn't you say Kitty seemed nice when you first met her? And she took Laurel in as well. But now that you've gotten better acquainted—"

"Don't remind me. You know what they say about like attracting like. Danny and Kitty could be two of a kind."

"That's what worries me." Marcus stopped at a crossroads to

check his phone's GPS. "According to Wes, Danny's place is just a mile down this road. Wes has known Danny since they were kids. He admitted that Danny has had some troubles, but they've been out of touch for a few years."

"So how is Wes?" Riva gazed out over a lush green field bordered by tall fir trees. Not a bad place to live if you didn't mind being off the beaten path.

"He's doing okay. He asked me about you too. I think he's hoping for another invite to your house. He really enjoyed that last little shindig, but I told him about your ban on men." He chuckled. "Windy explained the reason for the new rule to me. Not a bad idea, really. At least while Miss Kitty is part of the mix." He turned down another country road and checked the address on his GPS. "That woman can throw a real wrench in the works."

"You're telling me."

"Looks like that's it." Marcus pointed to the address on a rural mailbox. "Ready for this?"

Riva nodded, but her nerves spiked. "Do we need an escape plan? I mean, what if he's been drinking or he gets out of hand like Kitty warned me could happen."

"Then we'll just quietly leave."

"Kitty told me to take pictures. She expects the place to be quite a dive."

"Doesn't look half bad to me." He pointed toward a freshly painted barn. "Someone's been busy."

Riva took in the red structure, the fenced pasture with several cows contentedly grazing, the white farmhouse that looked pretty worn around the edges, and the beat-up black pickup parked out front. "That's the truck Danny had this morning, so it looks like he's here."

"And he doesn't know you're coming?" Marcus parked behind the pickup.

"I wanted to catch him off guard, you know, see his true colors.

Just in case Kitty was right." She removed her phone from her purse and opened her camera.

"And if he's a mess, will you still take photos?"

"No way." She shook her head. "If he's a mess, we'll just vamoose."

"Good plan."

As it turned out, Danny was a mess. A smelly mess. But only because he'd been cleaning out barn stalls that had clearly been neglected for years. "I just finished," he said as he welcomed them in. "After I painted the barn, it seemed a shame to leave this smelly old mess in here. My parents used to keep horses back when I was a kid. It got to be too much for them eventually, but I got to thinking I might want a horse or two . . . in time."

"This is a handsome barn." Marcus patted a solid-looking post.

"It's old but holding up pretty good."

"Mind if I take some photos?" Riva held up her phone. "I told Kitty I would."

"She wants pictures?" He brightened. "Sure, go for it." He picked up a pitchfork and struck a pose. "Wanna get Farmer Dan too?"

"If you don't mind."

"I don't mind, but Kitty might not like it. I'm pretty filthy right now."

After Riva took several photos, Danny led them over to the house. "It's not much to look at, but feel free to take some pics while I clean up a little."

"I love this big front porch." Riva paused to photograph a pair of old chairs and a pot of geraniums before they went inside.

"Help yourself to a cool drink," Danny called as he bounded up the stairs. "Make yourselves at home."

"So, far so good," Marcus whispered, following Riva to the kitchen, where she went straight to the fridge, which was mostly loaded with sodas and bottled water.

"Not a single drop of alcohol here." She helped herself to a bottle of water, then turned to see Marcus exploring the kitchen by opening cupboards. "Want a soda or water?"

He came over to look, then chose a root beer. "I get the impression Danny's on the up and up."

"Me too." She closed the fridge, then took some photos of the kitchen and then of the sparsely furnished living room. "This place could use some paint and elbow grease, but it has good potential." She filled Marcus in on some of the ways Danny said he wanted to help Kitty. "He wants to take responsibility for how some of his bad choices affected her."

Marcus took a swig of root beer. "I've heard that's part of AA. Owning up to old things. Cleaning the slate. But to want to take Kitty in . . . well, that's a lot to ask of anyone."

"Unless he still loves her," she whispered.

Marcus nodded as he gazed out the front window. Maybe he was remembering how he took Anne back after she'd broken his heart. He turned to face Riva. "Well, I've heard through a friend that Danny's been working at the tire store in town, but he hopes to get this farm going well enough to be self-sustaining."

"Seems like a nice goal." Riva sat down on the sagging sofa, taking a sip of water.

Marcus turned back to the window. "I wonder how much land he has."

"*He* has eighty-five acres, give or take," Danny said as he came down the stairs. "And he's got a dozen steers." He grinned. "And he's hoping to get chickens and pigs in a few weeks." Danny sat in a worn recliner and laughed. "I don't usually refer to myself in third person."

"You have a lovely farm," Riva told him. "I think Kitty would be lucky to come live here . . . well, if you two were compatible. I guess you've got to figure that one out. But I think I can give her a good report."

"Get enough photos?" he asked.

"How about if I get a shot of you cleaned up?" She stood with her phone ready.

"Go for it." He sat up straighter, smiling. "And you can take shots of bedrooms and baths if you want. I try to keep 'em kinda cleaned up, but it's pretty sparse. I got rid of so much furniture and junk after my dad died. Probably went overboard. But it might've been therapeutic, you know, to get past the grief. Plus, working so hard on this place helped me to kick alcohol. I could almost feel my dad patting me on the back each day I stayed sober."

"Well, I'm impressed," Riva said.

"Think Kitty will be?" He sounded hopeful.

"That's anyone's guess," Riva answered glumly.

"Kitty seems a little, you know, unpredictable," Marcus told him.

"Believe me, I know." Danny let out a loud sigh. "I just thought it was worth a try. If I could get her to listen, see how I've changed . . . I thought maybe there's a chance to help her, possibly reunite someday."

"It's a wonderful goal." Riva smiled. "I'll do what I can to get her to at least talk to you."

Danny turned to Marcus. "Got any tips for me? Suggestions for how I can win her back?"

Marcus rubbed his chin. "Well, I'm no expert . . . and Kitty is not exactly easy." He glanced at Riva. "If I wanted to win over a woman, I'd probably just go the traditional route."

"What's that?" Danny asked.

"Oh, you know, flowers and candy and best foot forward . . . probably the sort of things no one really does anymore. I haven't played the dating game in literally decades so I'm not one to give advice."

"Thanks." Danny stood. "I just remembered I haven't filled the watering trough and it's been a pretty hot day. I should probably get to it before my steers start protesting. Do you mind?"

"Not at all." Riva stood too. "Thanks for showing us around." She crossed her fingers. "Here's to hoping Kitty will be ready to talk."

Danny pointed upward. "I've been asking the Big Guy up there to help me get her back. After all, he helped me get sober, I'm sure he could help with this."

"I'll be praying too," Riva promised.

"Me too," Marcus said as they went outside. He looked out toward the barn and pasture. "It's really a great farm, Danny. You're a lucky guy."

Danny nodded glumly. "Yeah, I guess so." He shook both their hands, thanking them for their help and advice. "Even if Kitty refuses to give me a second chance, you guys are welcome out here any time."

They thanked him and got into Marcus's pickup. It was anyone's guess how Kitty would respond, but Riva planned to plead with the "Big Guy up there" on behalf of Danny. Not just because she hoped to shake free from her tenacious tenant either. She could almost imagine Kitty being happy out here. And why not? In fact, if Riva felt any attraction to Danny—and she didn't—she could live out here in the country. Well, except that she'd miss her home . . . and her library . . . and even her housemates.

Chapter 27

Laurel was sitting on the porch when Marcus drove Riva up to the house. Worried this could turn awkward, Riva quickly thanked him and started to get out of the pickup.

"Do you need any help talking to Kitty?" he asked.

She looked at him. "I, uh, I don't know."

"I was thinking that maybe she could use a friendly intervention."

"An intervention?" She pondered this. "You know, that's not a bad idea."

"And knowing Kitty, not that I really do, I wonder if it'd help to have a man involved. I hate to say it, but she seems to respect men more than women."

Riva smiled. "Well, I'm not sure if it's respect or attraction that she has for the male species, but I suppose you could be right. You might be more persuasive."

"What about your moratorium on men?" His grin looked sly. "Don't wanna be accosted at the door."

"The ban was for social occasions. This is different. If you want to help, I wouldn't mind." She got out and headed up to the porch where Laurel was casually sipping iced tea, watching them with a wary expression.

"What have you two been up to?" she asked.

Marcus sat down on the top porch step while Riva explained about her visit with Danny that morning and what they'd seen on his farm. "So I guess we're striking while the iron is hot," she finally said.

"Striking how?"

"We're staging an intervention," Marcus said. "Wanna join us?"

"An intervention for Kitty's drinking problem?" Laurel frowned. "As far as I know, she's been sober since we removed her alcohol, but she's pretty sneaky."

"This isn't really about alcohol, although that's part of it." Riva explained how Danny wanted to talk to her. "Except Kitty doesn't trust him. Or so she claims. It could just be an excuse to hide out here. Because it seems to me that's what she's doing. Her world seems to be unraveling, and I don't think she wants to face it."

"And you think Danny is the answer?" Laurel sounded skeptical.

"Well, she loved him enough to marry him once."

"Yeah, well, I loved my ex too, but I wouldn't touch that man with a ten-foot pole now."

"Danny seems like a nice guy," Marcus told her. "He's making good choices, trying to get on with his life. He's got a great farm he's been working hard on."

Riva showed Laurel some of the pictures on her phone.

"Wow, if Kitty's not interested, put me on the list." Laurel studied the shot of Danny all cleaned up. "He's not half bad either. In a rustic cowboy sort of way."

"Is my sister around?" Marcus asked.

"I think she's in the garden," Laurel told him.

"I'll go see if she wants to help us with the intervention." Marcus stood. "The more, the merrier."

"So, you want to help us?" Riva asked Laurel.

"I guess I could. But you know Kitty's not a fan of me. I wouldn't want my presence to sour the deal."

"I think numbers may help us to convey the urgency of our concerns. Every time I try to get her to consider doing anything, she gets defensive, acting like she's in pain, and when that doesn't work, she resorts to anger."

"Sounds like the little witch."

"Oh, Laurel. You know she's just hurting inside. That's why she lashes out. But her rejections are our opportunities to show unconditional love."

"Kind of like that book you gave me to read?" Laurel made a face. "I think I'm getting the message, Riva. Kitty is like Angel and we're all supposed to keep forgiving her."

Riva blinked. Laurel was getting it.

"But that's a lot easier said than done, Riva. I have to admit I've never hated anyone like I hate Kitty. She gets under my skin and pushes my buttons and just makes me want to scream and pull my hair out. More honestly, I want to pull *her* hair out—by its dark roots."

Riva patted Laurel's hand. "We all know Kitty's targeted you. I think it's because you're a strong woman. She probably envies you."

Laurel laughed. "She envies me?"

"Kitty's self-esteem and confidence seem to come from male approval, and you're the kind of woman who doesn't need that."

"Maybe I don't need it, but I don't mind . . . if it's the right male." Laurel looked over her shoulder.

"You mean like Marcus?"

Laurel sighed loudly. "I know Marcus isn't interested in me, Riva. He's just been a gentleman, polite and kind. Windy straightened me out on that one. And if it's any consolation to you, I'm done making myself a fool over him." She glumly shook her head. "I can't believe how juvenile I've been . . . and toward you too." She looked into Riva's eyes. "I'm so sorry."

Riva hugged her. "No worries, sweetie. I think we've all been getting used to living in a houseful of females."

"Kind of like a boatful of fools?"

"Maybe a little." Riva waved at Windy and Marcus who were walking around the side yard toward them.

"Windy is willing to join us," Marcus said.

"I'm not too sure how helpful I'll be with an intervention," Windy admitted, "but maybe I can offer some friendly persuasion."

"You be good cop and I'll be bad cop," Laurel teased.

"I think we should all be good cop," Riva said. "At least to start with. And if anyone needs to get tough, I guess it should be me."

"With backup," Marcus told her.

"Okay, team," Riva said. "Ready?"

"We'll beard the lioness in her den," Laurel joked.

"I never understood that saying," Riva admitted as they went inside. "A lion already has a beard."

"I think it just means to face them on their own turf," Marcus said as they stood in the foyer.

"We're the fearsome foursome," Laurel declared. "Let's do this!"

Marcus blocked the stairs. "Would anyone object if I said a brief prayer before we go up?" The women agreed and he quickly asked for God's grace and help and direction. "Most of all, we ask that you make us vessels to pour out your love," he said finally. They all echoed his amen.

As they went up the stairs, Riva saw Marcus in a whole new light. He truly was a good man, and she was grateful for his friendship . . . and maybe even something more. But it was something she couldn't really wrap her head around at the moment or maybe she didn't want to.

Kitty's initial shock over being invaded by the "fearsome foursome" turned into anger. Instead of reacting to it, the four surrounded her bed and took turns encouraging her to take the challenge and reinvent herself.

"Your party-girl lifestyle isn't working for you," Windy said gently.

"And it will work even less as you get older," Marcus added.

Laurel crossed her arms across her chest. "And like it or not, we're all getting older."

"This is your chance to start over," Riva told her. "Doesn't a fresh start sound appealing?"

Kitty shrugged.

"When Marcus and I visited Danny today, I was blown away by how great his farm looked." Riva sat on the edge of the bed and pulled out her phone. "We're not suggesting you get back with him, but we are encouraging you to at least talk to him."

"What did you think of him?" Kitty asked Marcus.

"I like him. And I really like his farm."

Riva showed Kitty photos and watched her expressions as she flipped through the shots.

"I guess it's not as bad as I thought," Kitty conceded.

"I think you'll find Danny is changed too," Marcus told her. "He seems to be taking his sobriety very seriously."

"In fact, that's the one condition Danny mentioned," Riva said. "He won't get back with you if you're still drinking."

Kitty rolled her eyes. "Well, thanks to the temperance society here, I haven't had a drink in ten days."

"That's a great start," Marcus told her. "Congratulations."

"How's your ankle?" Laurel asked her. "Can you walk on it yet?"

"I don't know."

"Why don't you give it a try," Windy suggested.

"It'd probably feel good to get out of this stuffy room." Laurel picked up her crutches. "You must be getting cabin fever up here."

"And it's a beautiful day outside," Windy said. "The garden is looking better than ever."

"You'll feel better if you get out, Kitty. It'll improve your entire outlook." Riva smiled. "And you'll get some vitamin D from the sunshine. That'll help heal your ankle."

"Come on, Kitty, take my hand," Marcus offered. "I won't let you fall."

The women all stepped back as Marcus helped her up. They watched as Kitty sat up, then swung her legs over the side of the bed. Laurel offered her the crutches, but Kitty waved a dismissive hand. "I don't need those stupid sticks. They just trip me up." And just like that, she walked across the room and out the door. They cheered and followed her as she slowly went down the stairs. A small victory perhaps, but it was progress.

By the time they were all sitting outside in back, Kitty seemed almost happy. "I guess I should thank you guys for pushing me like this."

"We're just glad you were willing to try," Riva assured her as she pulled out her phone again, opening up photos to have another look at Danny's farm. "And I'm hoping you'll be open to giving Danny a try too. At least, talk to him. He really is concerned for your welfare, Kitty." She showed her the picture of the red barn surrounded by the green pasture. "His place has some great potential."

Laurel poked Kitty in the shoulder. "And I decided that if you give him the heave-ho, I might have to check him out. He's not hard to look at, and his farm might need some work, but it could be fun."

"Yeah," Windy agreed. "Especially if you're interested in gardening like I am." She winked. "Maybe I'll go after him if Kitty declines."

"Yeah, yeah," Kitty said. "I don't think you gals are even his type."

"His type might've changed," Riva told her. "Now that he's committed to sobriety."

"And again, that's something you should carefully consider before you talk to him," Marcus said somberly. "It's pretty much a make-or-break for Danny."

Kitty was still studying the pictures on Riva's phone. "Danny looks pretty good. He used to be a sweetheart . . . but there's been a lot of water under the bridge."

"Alcohol-tainted water," Laurel said glibly.

Riva tossed her a look.

"Anyway, things might be different, you know, if you were both committed to sobriety." Laurel's tone turned surprisingly gentle. "To be honest, if my ex cleaned up his act as much as Danny, and if he wasn't already with someone else, I'd probably give him a second chance."

Kitty looked dubious but nodded. "Well, I'll think about it. And I should thank you guys for getting me out of my room. You're right, it does feel better to be out here. But where does a girl get a drink?" She winked at Riva. "A *soft* drink."

As Riva went inside to get Kitty a soda, she felt a small welcome rush of relief. Okay, maybe the Kitty dilemma was not fully resolved yet, but at least she was walking again. They definitely seemed to be on the right track.

Chapter 28

Over the next several weeks, it seemed Kitty's intervention was working. As far as Riva and the others knew, Kitty was maintaining her sobriety. And she was even doing her part with household chores and yard work. Kitty had cautiously allowed Danny back into her life and was now regularly attending AA meetings with him. No one was surprised when she lost her salon, and in some ways, she didn't seem to care since her hairdresser's license was still good and she could get work anywhere.

Riva suspected, despite Kitty's complaints, she was relieved to be free of her business responsibilities, but whether she would be able to pay her next month's rent was anyone's guess. Riva decided not to obsess over it yet. It seemed more important to do what she could to get Kitty on a better path. And the housemates were doing all they could to encourage her too. Even Laurel had gotten better at holding her tongue when Kitty mouthed off.

Riva felt pleasantly surprised at their first "ladies only" book group. Not only had everyone, including Kitty, read their "assigned" novel, they seemed to have gotten something out of them. More importantly, the women seemed to have developed a new appreciation for each other. There was a new camaraderie in the house. Even Kitty was treating her housemates with a bit more respect. Albeit a bit savory.

"What was the single most important thing you learned from your book? The big takeaway," Riva asked as they lounged in the library. I'll go first. As you know, I went ahead and read *A Gentleman in Moscow.*"

"I thought that was the pick for our first official book group," Laurel said. "Or have we scrapped that plan completely?"

"I guess time will tell. But since I was already reading it, I decided to use it for tonight. So anyway, without giving away too much plot, the thing that hit me was how the protagonist, that's the main character, was in a prison of sorts. Partly enforced and partly of his own making. He was trapped, not just physically in the hotel but emotionally too. It made me realize I had sort of trapped myself right here in my lovely but lonely home, stuck in reliving old memories, trying to hold on to remnants of my previous life, refusing to embrace the larger life that was still out there waiting. But this guy's world opened up through relationships. You ladies forced me out of my comfort zone and helped me to create a new life with friends and activities and community." She smiled. "Thank you!"

Next came Fiona. "I absolutely loved reading *Small Things Like These*. It took me back to Ireland . . . and to my childhood. Bittersweet." Her voice cracked with emotion. "It's hard to explain how it moved me, but it made me want to be a better person, even in something as small as a kind word or a friendly smile. Things that could go unnoticed but turn out to be important. Especially at work."

"That's wonderful," Windy told her. "I'd like to read that book."

Fiona handed it to her. "It's a quick read."

"Thanks." Now Windy held up *The Shell Seekers*. "This was not a quick read, but it was really good and I hated for it to end. The best thing I got out of it was how we can create family from the people around us. After losing my husband, I missed that family feel." She beamed at them. "But I feel I've found it here. Thank you, girls, for becoming my family."

"Even if we're somewhat dysfunctional?" Laurel teased.

"Aren't all families dysfunctional?" Kitty asked wryly.

"Hey, we're the kind of family that puts the 'fun' into dysfunctional," Windy said, making them laugh.

"Okay, I guess I'm next." Laurel held up her book. "I'll admit I've never particularly cared for fiction, and my first impression of this book was that it would be a romance novel. But as I got into it, I could see it was more. Much, much more." Laurel looked close to tears. "But the most important thing I discovered was that real love, unconditional love, is relentless. It never gives up. It's like God's love for us and the way we need to love others. But it's not easy to do. It's a lesson I'm still learning for myself." She blinked back tears and smiled at Riva. "Thanks for making me read it."

As Riva poured tea and shared scones, muffins, and éclairs she'd picked up at the bakery earlier, the women continued to chat about their various books, exchanging them with each other. When they were done, they all asked Riva to continue recommending books. She gladly agreed.

As the summer rolled on, Riva was pleased to see that Kitty was maintaining her sobriety. Besides regularly attending AA meetings with Danny, she'd started spending time out on his farm. While he was working at the tire store, she was doing farm chores and housecleaning. She seemed to have given up on finding hairdressing work and had recently expressed interest in doing some home improvements at Danny's place. She began by asking Windy for some decor ideas and then, to everyone's surprise, Laurel actually offered to go out there with her every day to help with some simple repairs and interior painting. Would wonders ever cease!

"It's really kind of you to help fix up Danny's place," Fiona told Kitty one evening as they cleaned up after dinner. "Most generous."

"It's not as generous as it looks," Kitty admitted. "Danny's paid me some, which is the only reason I could afford rent this month."

"Oh, I think there's more than that going on," Laurel teased her. "Unless I'm mistaken, you and Danny have been getting along pretty well." She chuckled and turned to Fiona and Riva. "I caught the two of them sneaking a kiss out in the barn."

"Oh, Laurel!" Kitty laughed. "We didn't sneak anything. Don't be such a prude."

"I'm not a prude," Laurel claimed. "I'm just not a floozy like some people I won't name." Just like that, the two of them were arguing. But it was a good-natured disagreement, one that left all five of them laughing hard.

Kitty seemed to be enjoying the quiet farm life—and her own sobriety—more than anyone had dreamed possible. It was obvious to Riva that Kitty and Danny were getting along just fine. By mid-August, Kitty came home from Danny's place sporting a modest engagement ring. Soon she was happily informing her housemates that they'd set a wedding date!

"We thought about eloping, but we've made so many friends at AA, and there are you girls . . . so we decided to have a small ceremony out on the farm," Kitty told her housemates as they sat down to dinner on the patio one evening in August. "And no worries, no alcohol will be served."

"How exciting," Windy told her. "When's the big day?"

"The last Saturday of the month. Danny wants to have it in the barn and then we'll have music and dancing afterward." She grinned at Fiona. "We already booked a local band."

"So wear your dancing shoes," Fiona told them.

"Miss Kitty getting married in a barn," Laurel said. "Now I've heard everything."

"As you know, it's a very nice barn," Kitty reminded her. "Doesn't even smell too bad anymore. We'll have a real hoedown wedding.

I'm planning on wearing my red cowboy boots with my wedding dress."

"I love it," Windy said.

"What can we do to help?" Riva asked.

"I don't know where to start. Danny and I are determined to keep costs down and make it a DIY wedding."

Laurel pulled out a writing pad and pen. "Let's make a to-do list and assign responsibilities. Let's see, you'll need food, flowers, decorations . . . people to set up and clean up . . ."

Just like four mama hens, they were suddenly talking and planning with Laurel furiously taking notes. And by the end of the evening, they all had tasks to complete before the wedding, which was only two weeks out.

Riva thought Kitty and Danny's wedding was one of the sweetest she'd ever seen. As they repeated their vows, there wasn't a dry eye in the barn. And with strings of golden lights glowing on old wooden posts and beams, combined with the fragrant scent of hay, it was magical. Windy's floral arrangements of humble field flowers and ferns in mason jars were the perfect touch, and the simple barbecue foods prepared by Riva and the housemates were just right. And, of course, the music was cheery.

"I guess it takes a village to raise a wedding," Laurel whispered to Riva as they watched Danny and Kitty opening the dance floor.

"Kitty looks sweet in her lacy dress and cowboy boots," Windy said wistfully. "They make such a cute couple."

"God bless them," Riva said quietly.

Soon everyone was dancing. Marcus and Wes were taking turns with the roommates, and everyone seemed to be having a merry time. But the barn was getting warm and Riva decided to step outside for some fresh cool air. She was just admiring the colorful sunset over a golden field of grass when she heard footsteps behind her.

"Mind if I join you?" Marcus asked. He had two mason jars of cider in hand. "Thought you might need some refreshment. You looked a little flushed."

"Thanks." She smiled, reaching for one. "You read me like a book."

He nodded. "Speaking of books, I'm curious if you'll ever start up that book group we dreamed up earlier in the summer."

"Interesting you should mention that." She took a cool sweet sip. "My housemates and I were just discussing our moratorium on men and we're ready to lift it. I think it's time to schedule our book group meeting."

"Good to hear. I've been wanting to revisit your amazing library."

"You're welcome anytime."

He nodded, looking out over the field with a smile on his face. "Can you feel autumn in the air?" he asked. "Perfect timing to start up a book group. Give us something to look forward to when the winter closes in on us."

She lifted her glass. "Here's to our book group."

He clinked his against hers. "And here's to our friendship, Riva." He smiled.

She nodded. "Yes, to friendship. I've been wanting to tell you how grateful I am for the way you helped me with Kitty and Danny . . . and the way you helped those two work out their differences."

"My pleasure. Danny is a good man. I've enjoyed getting better acquainted with him."

As the sun set, they continued to visit amiably. And although the air was cool, Riva felt an unexpected warm rush going through her that had nothing to do with overheating in the barn. It had to do with Marcus. He wasn't only a good man. He was a good friend. A very good friend.

Epilogue

LATE SEPTEMBER

Riva's house settled into a happy hum of four women "of a certain age" taking turns with chores, according to Laurel's charts, sharing clothes and beauty tips and recipes, and just enjoying a refreshed sense of sisterhood. Perhaps it was partly due to Kitty's chaotic time spent there, and her quiet absence now, that it seemed all four housemates had a healthy respect for personal space and individual differences. But the house felt peaceful.

The book group was officially formed with the four housemates, Kitty and Danny, plus Marcus and Wes, as well as one of Fiona's bandmates. Ten altogether, which made things rather cozy . . . but nice. Thanks to Windy, they started with an informal buffet dinner before settling into the library with coffee and tea and dessert.

"Welcome to our first book group," Riva told everyone. "Our efficient secretary Laurel has suggested we start our meeting by compiling a list of books for our upcoming year, and as you know, everyone is going to suggest one title."

Laurel held up her notebook. "I'll list them all here and then email everyone a copy."

They went around sharing their book choices, and thanks to their varied interests and expertise, the list was quite diverse. "Great," Riva said after the last title was down. "Looks like we're all booked up."

Everyone clapped. And now Marcus lifted his coffee mug toward Riva. "Before we start, I'd like to make a toast. Here's to Riva, a woman who has lived up to the meaning of her name."

"What does her name mean?" Laurel asked with a creased brow.

"Her name is related to the word *river.*" Marcus turned to Riva with a happy sparkle in his eyes. "And I must agree that our host is like a cool, clean, refreshing river." He turned back to the group. "Her name also means to *join things together.*" He waved his coffee mug toward everyone. "And if you ask me, that's exactly what Riva's done here. She's joined us all together, uniting us with her books. But even more than that, she's united us with her kind and gracious love. Here's to Riva."

"To Riva!" they echoed.

Riva looked around her library, filled with the same books she used to call friends, as well as her real living, breathing friends. She smiled at Marcus. "Thank you, but I don't think I deserve the credit for bringing us together. I'll give that credit to God." Then she addressed the whole group, "And what God has joined together, let no man—or woman—split apart."

They all laughed, and Kitty and Danny both said a hearty amen!

Marcus clicked his mug against Riva's with a knowing nod. "And amen."

Read on for an excerpt from Melody Carlson's

Available now wherever books are sold.

Chapter 1

Honey

Honey McKerry suppressed the urge to firmly lower the cast-iron skillet directly onto her husband's slightly balding noggin. Instead she blew out the breath she'd been holding during her attempt to count to ten, then slowly turned away, reminding herself for the hundredth time, *CT can't help it.* She set the heavy pan back on the stove and opened the upper cabinet, removing the overly familiar jars of peanut butter and honey. Jif Extra Crunchy and McKerry's homegrown honey—CT's favorite go-to sandwich, well, unless he changed his mind midstream, like he'd done just now.

"You're sure you don't want eggs, then?" She carefully placed the pair of freshly laid brown eggs back into the recycled egg carton. Her Plymouth Rock hens had really started producing when spring warmed up, but like so many things in her life since CT's illness had progressed, caring for chickens had become too much, so she'd given them to Marta and Anna next door. She repeated herself. "Sure you don't want eggs, CT?"

"No, no. My legs are okay," he replied confidently.

"I said *eggs*." She peered into his face to make sure he understood her. "Not legs." Although it wasn't a leap to speak of legs since his bothered him some. When he ignored her, she put her last carton of homegrown eggs back in the fridge. Maybe she'd fry up a couple for herself later, if she got hungry. She should've known when CT demanded scrambled eggs for breakfast, he would forget or change his mind. And by the time he'd dressed and made his way to the kitchen, a task that took nearly an hour, their morning egg conversation had floated off to the twilight zone.

"Oh, yeah." He nodded as he picked up the newspaper. "Eggs *are* good."

Sometimes she felt as confused as him. Maybe it was catching. She studied him before speaking. "So you don't want the peanut butter sandwich after all?"

"Yeah. Eggs and a sandwich. Like I said." He slid his chair toward the kitchen table, then opened the paper and pretended to read. She knew he was just looking at photos, maybe trying to make out a few headlines. But it had been almost a year since reading for retention became too much for him. For some reason she liked that he kept up the pretense. Maybe it made them both feel better . . . or at least gave her a moment of peace, knowing he was occupied.

She got the eggs back out. "You must be pretty hungry, CT."

He patted his flat stomach. "Oh, yeah. Ravished."

"Okay then." She smiled at his misused word. It just went with the territory. Eighteen months had passed since his diagnosis. She still remembered CT's response when the neurologist explained that he had FTD.

"Am I going to deliver flowers?" he'd asked with a twinkle in his dark brown eyes. They'd all laughed at his wit, but underneath Honey's cheery veneer, a cold chill had swept through her. She'd heard of FTD, and it wasn't good.

Oh, she wasn't blindsided by the diagnosis. Clearly, something had been going on for some time. But at the beginning of the testing, she'd never expected anything this life-altering and serious. At first the professionals blamed CT's forgetfulness on his hearing loss, then perhaps sleep apnea, and finally, after dealing with both issues, the doctors had suggested hydrocephalus, which was treatable. But after six months of acquiring new hearing aids, a frustrating month trying a CPAP machine, and various doctors and specialists and tests, CT's brain scans revealed frontotemporal dementia—or *disorder*, her preferred substitute for the *D* word. "Just like Bruce Willis," she would sometimes say to lighten things up. After all, CT had been a big *Die Hard* fan. But unfortunately, most of the time, the poor guy didn't really get it.

"Did you feed the cat?" she asked absently as she cracked an egg into the pan.

"No. Don't need a hat."

She rolled her eyes and picked up another egg. "Got your hearing aids in, CT?"

He reached up to check an ear, then sheepishly shook his head before returning to his faux reading. She knew she should nag him to go fetch them instead of simply getting them herself. While it was good for him to do what he could while he could, it was just so much quicker to do things for him. She put the last of the eggs in the pan, gave them a quick stir, then jogged up to the bedroom, where his hearing aid charger was supposed to be plugged in on his bedside table.

To her dismay, though not her surprise, the charger was AWOL again. Now it was off to the various other locales where he liked to *relocate* miscellaneous items. Never mind that she'd told him time and again that the bedroom was handiest. "The Lone Rearranger strikes again," she muttered as she checked his bathroom, which looked like it had been hit by a small tornado and smelled like a middle school boy's locker room. Next she looked in the den, where CT kept an odd assortment of unrelated bits and pieces and piles of books he'd once read and liked to imagine he would read again someday. She quickly sifted through a basket of charger cords, dead batteries, and a dysfunctional wristwatch and was about to hit the storage room under the stairs when she heard the smoke alarm going off.

The eggs!

She dashed back to the kitchen and turned off the flame beneath the now-blackened eggs, which were solidly adhered to the pan. She opened a window, then flipped on the exhaust fan, attempting to ignore her frantic husband as he hopped around, yowling and flapping his arms like a crazed chicken. "Make it stop!" he cried, covering his ears and wearing the anguished expression of a frightened four-year-old.

"Go outside." She took him by the arm and directed him toward the back porch. "Check on your bees." She nodded toward the stacked boxes of hives and led him outside. She wasn't a big fan of bees, but for some reason CT adored the buzzy little beings. He used to call his hives his *peaceful place*.

He nodded, clutching her hand and groaning with each step as he ambled down the porch stairs. On solid ground, he began to mumble. "My bees . . . yeah, bees don't burn down your house. Coming, bees, coming."

"Right." She watched him weaving slightly as he made his way to his beloved hives. Reassured he was okay, she went back inside. The kitchen was still smoky and the alarm still blaring. She got out her stepladder and, stretching high, reached for the smoke alarm, balancing precariously as she pressed the red button and waited for it to stop screaming at her. As she climbed down, she felt a bit shaky. This was something her big, strong husband used to do for her. A lump swelled in her throat, but she reminded herself this little event was not tear-worthy. Better to laugh . . . when she could.

Still, it was hard to let go of some things. Her can-do, capable husband used to handle so much for her. CT, at six foot six, was a man's man who could build almost anything, repair almost anything, hunt wild game. Like a country boy, he could survive. The man could plant and grow and dance a pretty good two-step. He even managed the bills and knew how to file tax returns, something she was still grappling over. But after their checking accounts got seriously messed up a few years back due to CT's disease, she'd taken over the business end of things and let him take over the simple things that hadn't overwhelmed him at first, like replacing light bulbs or smoke alarm batteries or taking out the trash.

But those days were gone now too. CT always forgot which day the garbage truck came. Sometimes she'd go racing out in her bathrobe, running the can down their driveway, waving to the truck driver to stop. Ladders messed with his balance. Tools were dangerous. And unexpected noises like a smoke alarm were unnerving. Even if he could've handled the noise and scaled the ladder, he'd probably forgotten how to make the smoke alarm stop blasting by now.

Honey sighed and scraped the burned eggs into her clean white sink, staring for a moment at the blackened ugliness as she washed it down the garbage disposal. Then realizing the skillet would require more attention, she decided CT would have to settle for a peanut butter sandwich after all. Along with a big glass of milk and a banana. He'd have forgotten about the eggs by now anyway. One benefit of FTD.

She carried his breakfast into the clean outside air and found him investigating something by the barn. Feeding the barn cat? She doubted it as she whistled for him, waving him over to the picnic table. She watched as he attempted to insert more spring in his step, but he still walked like a man two decades older than his years.

"That's what I want." He pointed to the sandwich. "Peanut butter 'n honey. Honey from my Honey." He grinned at her. "And from my bees too."

"How are your bees?" She watched him ease himself onto a bench.

"Happy. Happy bees . . . happy honey." He looked up with adoring eyes. "Bee honey is sweet. Not as sweet as my Honey."

She patted his shoulder. How many times had she heard that line? And yet she never really tired of it. "CT is sweet too."

"Is the house burned up?" His creased frown revealed he was dead serious.

"No, dear, the house is fine. The kitchen is fine."

"You be careful. Stove is hot. Dangerous."

She remembered when she used to tell him that very thing, back when he still thought he could cook. Now she just removed the knobs when she was done cooking. She was tempted to point out that she'd been on his errand, off looking for his missing hearing aid charger, when the stove got dangerous, but why bother?

"Where's your sandwich?" he asked as she turned away.

"I'm going back for it," she said, even though she had no intention of having peanut butter and honey. It was easier to play along than explain. By the time she brought back her coffee to sit with him, he wouldn't remember. Then as she went up the porch steps, her phone rang from her pocket. Planning to ignore it, she peeked at the caller ID to see it was Jewel. And since her daughter rarely called, she answered.

"Hey, Jewel," she said pleasantly. "How's my favorite girl?"

"I'm your *only* girl, Mom. But I guess I'm okay."

Honey heard the terseness in her daughter's tone. "So, what's up?"

"It's Cooper. I'm getting worried."

"Well, Cooper is almost fourteen. It's natural to be a little concerned. But she's always been a good girl." Honey poured herself a cup of coffee and sat down at the kitchen table, tracing a finger over the wood grain. This old oak table once belonged to her grandmother, right here on this very same farm.

"I'm worried about the new friends Cooper's been making."

"Oh, new friends?" Honey felt a spark of concern. She'd worked in a middle school for twenty years, long enough to know that new friends could be good . . . or bad.

"You know how kids are, Mom. How influential peers can be at this age."

"Yeah." Honey sipped her coffee.

"Especially to a girl with low self-esteem."

"Since when has Cooper had low self-esteem?"

"Since her best friend Molly dumped her and started talking smack about her."

"Oh, that's too bad." Middle school girls could be so cruel.

"So Coop started hanging with these *new* friends, and I don't like to judge anyone, but they seem pretty rough. I think their parents totally ignore them."

"That's not good."

"And school lets out on Thursday." Jewel's tone was desperate.

"And you're worried about her being unsupervised for the summer?" Honey brightened. "Why don't you send her up here to visit? I could actually use a hand."

"With Dad?"

"Well, him . . . and farm work and lots of things." Honey looked out the window to where the lavender field was just starting to green up, but the weeds were greening up too. And then there were the pumpkins that hadn't been planted yet . . . She doubted CT would be up to it this year. "I'm positive we could keep her busy."

"And out of trouble." Jewel let out a relieved sigh.

"And your dad would love having her around."

"Tell me the truth, Mom. How is Dad?"

Honey stood, phone in one hand and coffee mug in the other, and went to look out the back window. CT was still sitting peacefully at the picnic table, peeling his banana. "He's okay. Well, for him, anyway."

"But the illness. How is he handling it?"

"Oh . . . the same as before. He forgets things. Overreacts to things. Tires out pretty easily. Not much has changed since the last time we talked. Only perhaps . . ." She bit her lip. "A little worse." Okay, that was an understatement. But why worry Jewel? She had her hands full single parenting a teenager and running a struggling business in a less than stellar economy. "How's the art gallery doing?"

"About the same as the last time we talked," Jewel parroted her. "Not so great."

"Maybe with summer coming it'll pick up?"

"Look, Mom, I have an idea." Jewel's tone was suddenly lighter. "What if Cooper and I *both* come back to Oregon? We can help with the farm and spend some time with Dad while he can still remember our names."

Honey felt slightly defensive, as well as uncertain. She'd welcome help but knew Jewel could be a handful at times. And while the farmhouse had enough bedrooms, the shared spaces would be a challenge. How would it feel to share her kitchen with a stubborn young woman with strong opinions on almost everything? Who knew where that might lead? Add to that mix a teenage girl recently uprooted from her friends—it sounded like a recipe for disaster.

"Oh, I don't know, sweetheart." Honey tried to think of a tactful rejection. "That's a big change for you and Cooper. It's too much to ask of—"

"It's not too much. In fact, it's settled. My friend Jess has been begging to buy my gallery since Christmas, and I'd almost made up my mind to sell to him. It was a fun project, but I'm done now."

"Really?" Honey wasn't so sure. "You love that gallery."

"That was then. This is now. Honestly, Mom, I think we've come up with the perfect plan. Cooper and I will help you with Dad. And I'll have more time for my art, something I've missed lately. Plus, it'll get Coop away from her new friends. It's decided. I'm going to call Jess right now and—"

"You need to give this careful consideration, Jewel," Honey interrupted. "That's a huge life decision. Don't be too hasty and—"

"I'm not being hasty. It's been silently percolating in me for a while now. I just didn't have time to really wrap my head around it. But we're coming, Mom. You can count on us. I gotta go. I need to work out a deal with Jess and a dozen other things. Talk to you later. Love you." And before Honey could protest, Jewel hung up.

Honey just shook her head as she went to finish cleaning up her eggs. Frowning at the messy skillet, she pulled out a Brillo pad and began to scrub. Jewel was too impulsive. Dropping out of college just one semester before graduating. Then her hasty marriage to wealthy Rodney Benedict, a man with four failed marriages behind him. What a mismatch that turned out to be. Then her ill-timed pregnancy, hoping it would save her unraveling marriage. Even if marrying Rodney had been a mistake, Cooper was a treasure.

Then without thinking it through carefully, Jewel had invested her entire divorce settlement into that art gallery—just a few months before the COVID pandemic hit. Although, in Jewel's defense, Honey thought that had turned out all right. So why did she want to abandon it now?

Honey ground the steel wool into the cast iron with a vengeance. Sure, not all Jewel's impulsive choices had foreseeable results, but leave it to that girl to jump out of the frying pan and straight into the fire. Honey just hoped her impetuously headstrong daughter would come to her senses before letting history repeat itself . . . again.

Melody Carlson is the award-winning author of more than 250 books with sales of more than 7.5 million, including many bestselling Christmas novellas, young adult titles, and contemporary romances. She received a *Romantic Times* Career Achievement Award, her novel *All Summer Long* has been made into a Hallmark movie, and the movie based on her novel *The Happy Camper* premiered on UPtv in 2023. She and her family live in central Oregon. Learn more at MelodyCarlson.com.

MEET
Melody

MelodyCarlsonAuthor

AuthorMelodyCarlson

A Note from the Publisher

Dear Reader,

Thank you for selecting a Revell novel! We're so happy to be part of your reading life through this work. Our mission here at Revell is to publish stories that reach the heart. Through friendship, romance, suspense, or a travel back in time, we bring stories that will entertain, inspire, and encourage you. We believe in the power of stories to change our lives and are grateful for the privilege of sharing these stories with you.

We believe in building lasting relationships with readers, and we'd love to get to know you better. If you have any feedback, questions, or just want to chat about your experience reading this book, please email us directly at publisher@revellbooks.com. Your insights are incredibly important to us, and it would be our pleasure to hear how we can better serve you.

We look forward to hearing from you and having the chance to enhance your experience with Revell Books.

The Publishing Team at Revell Books
A Division of Baker Publishing Group
publisher@revellbooks.com